TruthSeer

THE TRUTHSEER ARCHIVES
BOOK 3

MIKE SHELTON

TruthSeer
Copyright © 2018 by Michael Shelton
2nd edition © 2020

ISBN: 0-9987935-8-2
ISBN-13: 978-0-9987935-8-0
Library of Congress Control Number: 2018905114
Salem, Oregon

Cover Illustration by Christian Bentulan
https://coversbychristian.com/

Map by Robert Altbauer
www.fantasy-map.net

For More information about Mike Shelton and his books
www.MichaelSheltonBooks.com

mikesheltonbooks@gmail.com
www.MichaelSheltonBooks.com
https://www.facebook.com/groups/MikeSheltonAuthor/
https://www.facebook.com/mikesheltonbooks/
http://www.Twitter.com/msheltonbooks
http://www.Instagram.com/mikesheltonbooks
https://www.pinterest.com/mikesheltonbooks/

ACKNOWLEDGEMENTS

This was a fun series to write and there were many that made it happen. My wife is always my biggest support. I love the covers in this second edition that were created by Christian Bentulan.

The editors at Precision Editing (Heather, Crystal, Jennie, Lisa) continue to help me be a better author. Their input really helps to tighten up my writing and polish the story.

My daughter Danielle (Danny) helped in providing some research for the stones used in this series.

TruthSeer is a work of fiction. Names, characters, places and incidents are the products of my imagination and are used fictitiously. Any resemblance to actual events, locales, or persons, living or dead, is entirely coincidental. I alone take full responsibility for any errors or omissions in this book.

-Mike-

BOOKS BY MIKE SHELTON

WESTERN CONTINENT BOOKS:

The Cremelino Prophecy:
The Path Of Destiny
The Path Of Decisions
The Path Of Peace
The Blade and the Bow (A prequel novella to The Cremelino Prophecy)

The Alaris Chronicles:
The Dragon Orb
The Dragon Rider
The Dragon King
Prophecy Of The Dragon (A prequel novella to The Alaris Chronicles)

The Dragon Artifacts:
The Golden Dragon
The Golden Scepter
The Golden Empire

The Wizard Academies:
Mark of the Medallion
Search for the Medallion
Power of the Medallion

GEMSTONES OF WAYLAND BOOKS:

The TruthSeer Archives:
TruthStone
TruthSpell
TruthSeer
The Stones of Power (A prequel novella to The TruthSeer Archives)

MAP

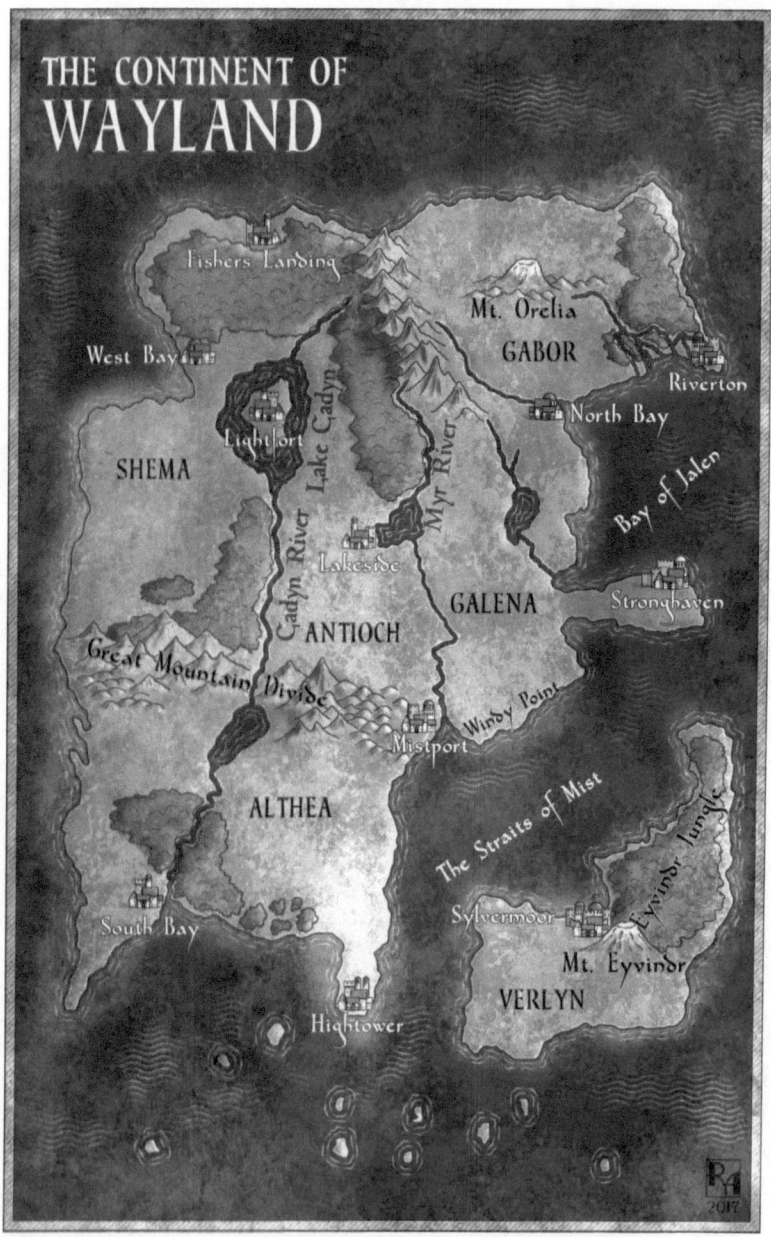

See Color map at www.MichaelSheltonBooks.com

STONES OF POWER ON WAYLAND

TruthStone—Moldavite—Green—All Kingdoms

IntelligenceStone—Labradorite—Blue—Kingdom of Galena

StrengthStone—Red Jasper—Red—Kingdom of Gabor

SpeedStone—Garnet—Orange—Kingdom of Antioch

HearingStone—Celestite—White—Kingdom of Althea

HealingStone—Azeztulite—Pink—Kingdom of Shema

KINGDOMS OF WAYLAND LEADERSHIP
(as of the beginning of this book)

Galena: Regent Warin, Heirs: Calix and Basil, TruthSeer: Erlinda,
    Wizard: Faegon

Gabor: Queen Victoria, Heir: Diamonique, TruthSeer: Justyn,
    Wizard: Tessalaine

Antioch: King Eadric, Heir: Marcus, TruthSeer: Lana, Wizard: Jarom

Althea: Queen Emmony, Heirs: Noelle and Raimund, TruthSeer:
    Wain, Wizard: Cara

Shema: King Haelen, TruthSeer: Julianna, Wizard: Martin

Verlyn: Empress Veronia, Heir: Brevin, Master Keepers: Lorelei and
    Melindra

CHAPTER ONE

Shaeleen squinted in the morning summer sun and tried to make out what she was seeing ahead of them. Her brother, Cole, moved up on one side while Basil, Prince of Galena, moved next to her on the other. The last two remaining members of her party, the younger Orin and his father—the crown prince of Antioch, Marcus—spread out to her right. It had been three days since they'd left the coronation ceremony in Stronghaven.

Her thoughts went back to the events that had brought them to this point. After revealing to Prince Basil that he was not actually the oldest twin and heir to the throne, she expected Basil to fight back. He'd lost his kingdom and his fiancée to his twin brother, Calix. But, as she should have expected, his honor made him agree to his brother's rule. That didn't mean he agreed with Calix, only that he would not directly fight him for the throne. Basil loved his people, and the ceremony of Calix accepting the throne of Galena had been hard on him.

Using the power of the SpeedStone, Shaeleen had whisked away the small group that now stood next to her. They were running west and away from King Calix in order for Shaeleen to retrieve the last two stones—the pink Azeztulite HealingStone and the white Celestite HearingStone. Then along with the SpeedStone, IntelligenceStone, and StrengthStone—all imbedded now in the TruthStone—she would be ready and armed to meet the shadow keepers and restore the stones of power to the kingdoms of Wayland.

Coming upon a small village a few days west of Stronghaven, Shaeleen and her group now stood facing a group of angry villagers.

"What do you think this means?" Shaeleen asked out loud, pushing her long, brown hair out of her light blue eyes. She held a hand up to her forehead to shade the sun.

"We were received well in the last two villages," Prince Basil said.

Shaeleen turned her head to look at him and bit her lower lip when he brought his eyes down to her. There was still haunting pain hidden there—pain that Shaeleen had caused. As a TruthSeer, she had been forced with the decision to keep a lie—with all the physical pain that brought her—or tell the truth and watch Basil's world be destroyed. Deep inside, however, she'd realized that the truth would come out eventually.

Basil, who was kind, considerate, and loved his people, had been preparing to be king since his birth. Shaeleen had discovered mere weeks before that his twin brother Calix was actually the oldest—a secret held by their mother for years.

"It's not your fault." Basil leaned over and spoke with a quiet voice. "Let the pain go, Shae."

Shaeleen pulled on the power of the TruthStone that was held securely in a pouch in a pocket that hung under her lightweight cloak. She felt some measure of peace for a moment. Her mind flashed back to the moment less than a week before—a moment that continued to haunt her—when she had told Basil he would not be the next king. The look in his eyes at that time almost killed her. Even now, after Calix had taken over, Basil was fiercely loyal to his people and wanted to help them. *How can I ever be as good as him?*

The sound of a sword being unsheathed pulled her attention back to the problem at hand. A slight sizzle ran down the length of the sword, and Cole took a step out in front of the rest of the group. Cole's dark, shaggy hair, tall stature, and broad shoulders went well with his new responsibility and powers. He was her wizard guardian protector and, although he was as new to his powers as she was to hers, he was determined to protect Shaeleen from any more harm.

"There's at least thirty of them," Cole spoke from up front.

"Not the greeting I would have expected from such a small village," Basil said.

"Maybe they have sided with your brother," said Marcus. He was himself a crowned prince, since the shadow keepers had killed his two older brothers. He and his son, Orin, would travel with the rest of the group only as far west as the Myr River, then he planned to depart south and return to his own kingdom of Antioch. He needed to help his father establish peace—peace that was being destroyed by those who wanted to outlaw magic on the continent of Wayland.

"Calix holds the peninsula, Stronghaven, and the throne," Basil said. "But I have been told by my generals that the rest of the kingdom is still loyal to me—though I don't know how much good that will do."

Shaeleen turned to Basil and put a hand on his arm. "We'll find a way, Basil."

"*Prince* Basil, Shae!" Cole turned around and faced the group. "If we are going to help him and accomplish anything on our journey, you must show respect for him by using his rightful title."

Killjoy! She wanted to stick out her tongue at her older brother.

"I must agree with Wizard Cole," said Marcus. "If Basil is to take back the throne, it will be because he is still a prince of the kingdom—not just a commoner."

Basil put up his hand, and his face grew serious. "As a TruthSeer, Shaeleen doesn't hold any deference to anyone here—or in the rest of Wayland, for that matter—and I currently have no right to the throne. It is lawfully my brother's. I will respect that right."

"As long as he is still alive, but . . ." Orin spoke for the first time since they had stopped. He wiped drops of sweat away from his forehead and pushed his unruly blond hair out of his eyes. Shaeleen smiled at him. They had reformed their friendship lately, but it was still fragile. He had lost his powers of the SpeedStone, and Shaeleen had invaded his mind and forced the truth from him. Oh, she justified that it wasn't really him, but a shadow keeper who had infused Orin's blood with some of the power of the ShadowStone, but all the same it had torn their friendship apart for a while.

"Orin," Basil said forcefully. "We are not killing my brother."

"I'm just saying, if an accident happened..." Orin smiled and ran his finger across his throat.

"Basil," Shaeleen called the prince's attention back to her, earning a glare from both her brother and Marcus. "Why don't you take the lead here? These people in the countryside should still honor you as a prince of their kingdom, even if your brother does not."

The day after Calix took the throne, they'd heard that Calix had put a bounty on the head of his brother. He was to be returned to Stronghaven, alive if possible. Shaeleen didn't know what Calix would do to Basil, but as long as his brother still lived, he was a threat to the throne.

As the group approached the town, they saw more clearly that indeed about thirty armed men stood in front of the town entrance. They did not appear happy to see the prince. One man walked out in front of them and approached the group.

Basil called Shaeleen over to him, then said to the others, "Shaeleen and I will talk to him. She will know if he is telling the truth or not. The rest of you stay alert. This may or may not end well."

Shaeleen walked next to Basil, his presence distracting her from the people in front of them. Two years older than her fifteen years, he stood at least ten inches taller than her height of five-two. His hair was dark, like her brother's, but shorter— cut above his ears. His eyes were a dark blue that held both intelligence and compassion.

As if sensing her thinking about him, he turned and smiled at her. The dimple in his right cheek drew her attention. Shaeleen blushed and turned back. One man came forward. Shaeleen and Basil stopped in front of him.

The man, slightly taller and wider than the prince, bowed slightly. "Prince Basil, we don't want any trouble here. I am

Mayor Dallin of Greenville."

Shaeleen glanced around her. The town lived up to its name. Sitting in the middle of Galena's lush middle valley, summer vegetable crops and abundant green fields spread around them.

"Neither do we, my good man," Basil said with a smile. "We are only looking for a place to lodge for the night."

No lies yet, Shaeleen thought, but she had a bad feeling about this. Drawing upon the power of the TruthStone—and its embedded IntelligenceStone, StrengthStone, and SpeedStone—she stood next to Basil, ready for anything to happen.

"We must turn you away from our village," said the man. "There is no room here for your party."

Pain! So much for telling the truth. Shaeleen bent over with the pain of the lie from the mayor. There indeed was room for them. With a hand on her stomach, she leaned back up to find Cole at her side, Marcus and Orin only a few steps behind them.

Cole's sword was out and held at the man's throat, the blade sizzling with yellow and orange power.

Basil put his hand on Cole's arm and brought the sword down. "We are not here to cause any harm."

"But the mayor lied." Cole didn't look very happy.

"Indeed, he has," Basil said. "I would like to understand why."

By this time, the mayor had stepped back a few feet and was looking at Shaeleen. She knew that her age and height belied the strength she held. She stood in front of him with black riding pants, white shirt, and a light blue cloak, her hair blowing around her face in the morning breeze.

"Why have you lied?" she asked bluntly.

"The TruthSeer," came a whisper from behind, and the words were picked up through the group. The men moved tighter together, and Shaeleen could almost feel their fear. But they held their ground in front of the small town gate.

The mayor looked from Shaeleen, then back to Basil, spending a frightened instant on Cole, who had stepped back next to the prince. The mayor clearly didn't know who to speak to. Shaeleen almost laughed at the thought. Who would think that two months ago, when Keeper Melindra had given her the TruthStone, she would be in the company of such an imposing group of men?

"I will know if you lie." Shaeleen took a step toward the man.

The mayor took a deep breath and let it out. "I am sorry, my prince, my lady, but we just can't let you into our village."

The lie hit Shaeleen again, but she stayed upright—if only barely. The TruthStone gave her the ability to sense lies spoken by herself or others, but that information came in the form of intense physical pain.

"Am I not still a prince of Galena, my dear sir?" Basil said politely, but Shaeleen could tell that even he was getting frustrated.

The man nodded.

"Tell him, Mayor," shouted a younger man, drawing a sword and walking up behind the mayor. The group with him started walking closer. "Tell them what happened to the others.

It's time for these people to leave—before *they* come for us."

"Leave now!" shouted a man from the back.

"Leave!" The men took up the chant.

CHAPTER TWO

Shaeleen heard a sound behind her. Without warning, Marcus drew upon his weak powers of the SpeedStone and before anyone knew it, the man behind the mayor was pushed in one direction, while his sword flew to the other side. Panting, Marcus returned to stand next to Shaeleen, with Orin coming up on her other side and drawing a sword of his own. She remembered the powers of the SpeedStone that Orin once held. That was before she knew who he was—the grandson of King Eadric of Antioch.

The group of townsmen surged forward, swords and thick sticks in their hands. From the back, Shaeleen saw a lone arrow fly through the air. She drew upon her own powers of the StrengthStone and felt her legs swell with muscles. Adding in the power of the SpeedStone, she leaped into the air and grabbed the arrow before it could do any damage. Coming back down on the ground, she brought her hand up in front of her and gathered a ball of green fire from her TruthStone, ready to blast it forward, but Cole beat her to it.

Blue fire flew from her brother's outstretched hand and raced with precision through the crowd and into the man who had shot the arrow. Shaeleen was impressed by his accuracy and didn't know if she could have done that.

"Protect the prince," Cole yelled. Shaeleen prepared to

move over to Basil, but in doing so, she missed another arrow coming toward her.

"Shae!" Orin pushed her to the side, the arrow narrowly missing her.

Shaeleen stood up and turned to thank Orin, but gasped instead. "Orin!"

Her young friend was on the ground, an arrow protruding from his gut. His father was instantly there and pulled Orin back farther behind the battle line.

That arrow was meant for me!

Shaeleen turned around. Cole and Basil were surrounded by the thirty angry men. Both were two of the best swordsmen in the kingdom, but the odds were not good. They fought side by side in a similar manner, though Cole was more on the offensive, while Basil seemed to be trying to only block and defend. Shaeleen knew he didn't really want to hurt his own people.

Pulling on the combined powers she now held—all those given to Wayland's five kingdoms except for the HealingStone and HearingStone—Shaeleen brought a ball of fire up and blasted it on the ground in front of the attackers. She tried not to kill anyone, but it would be hard to avoid that if they continued their attack.

Using the SpeedStone again, she raced through the crowd. Everything slowed around her. She moved in between each man and pushed them to the ground until she came to the mayor, who was now contending with Basil. Both of their expressions showed hesitancy and fear.

Shaeleen grabbed the mayor and pulled him away from the

crowd, then came out of the speed. "Stop now!" she yelled at the group, half of which were on the ground from Shaeleen's speedy attack. "Basil and Cole." She called the men over, and they obeyed the voice of the TruthSeer. "It's time we found out the truth." She grabbed hold of the mayor's arm and began to dig deep into his mind. She readied a TruthSpell to use on him.

"Why have you attacked us?" Shaeleen asked the man. "Why won't you let us into your town?"

The mayor's eyes bulged wide, and he stuttered for a moment, catching his breath.

"Shae!" shouted Basil. "No!"

Shaeleen pushed Basil's concern to the side. A sound behind her made her look over her shoulder. It was Orin, groaning on the ground. His father stood over him, trying to deal with the arrow in his stomach. Orin turned his head to the side and stared hard at Shaeleen. His eyes pleaded with her not to force the man to tell the truth. He opened his mouth to say something, but his father pulled out the arrow and Orin fainted.

But the look on Orin's face pierced her heart. As much as she wanted to force the mayor to tell the truth, she knew it wasn't good to take someone's will away. She pulled back her hand, and the power of the TruthStone receded, but she still held on to the mayor with her other hand.

"Tell me why." She lowered her voice to a menacing whisper, but she held back from forcing him.

The mayor slumped to the ground, and Shaeleen let him fall. Basil and Cole gathered around.

"Orin needs help," Marcus yelled.

Shaeleen nodded her head at Cole to go and help. She and Basil needed to hear the mayor's words. The rest of the men moved up behind the mayor. Their recent attack seemed to shame them.

After taking a few sips of a waterskin, the mayor turned his head up to Shaeleen and Basil. Tears filled his eyes. "I am sorry, Prince Basil. I never wanted to hurt you, but . . ." He stumbled for words. "They killed the others. I had to protect my town. You must understand."

"Understand what?" Basil asked. "Who killed whom?"

The younger man that had yelled out earlier took a step forward. Shaeleen glared at him, but he was not deterred. "King Calix's men. They've been following you. And each town that has given you lodging, soldiers have gone in and hurt them— killed those who tried to fight back."

Prince Basil fell to the ground next to the mayor and put his hands over his face. Shaeleen joined him more slowly and put a hand on his shoulder.

"We didn't know," Basil said, looking at the mayor and the rest of the men. "How did you find out?"

"A carrier pigeon was sent this morning warning us, my lord," the mayor said. "I really meant you no harm. I serve the kingdom, but . . ."

"But you must protect your people." Basil smiled. "I commend you for that."

The mayor appeared skeptical. "You're not going to kill us?"

"Why would he kill you?" Shaeleen asked, shaking her head. "He loves his people." She glanced over at Basil and smiled. His true love for the people of Galena—poor, rich, noble, farmer, or fisherman—was the strength that drove him, even after losing the kingdom.

The men all seemed to breathe a sigh of relief and lowered their weapons. All but one—the young man that had spoken earlier. "You must leave now, please," he said. "I have a wife and children."

"Yes. Yes, of course." Basil stood up. "I truly do not want to bring you any harm." He reached down and pulled Shaeleen up with him. After using her powers, she was tired and hungry.

Marcus walked up next to them, and Shaeleen looked behind her. Cole sat on his knees next to Orin. The two had never gotten along well. Orin had been a thief of a kind— stealing from the rich and giving to those in need, and Cole had once caught him. Her brother didn't have any leeway for those who broke the rules. But right now, Cole looked up at Shaeleen with compassion—he knew Orin was her friend. He shrugged his shoulders as if saying he didn't know if he would live or not. *Oh, Orin!*

"Could we bother you for some bandages?" Marcus pleaded with the mayor and his men. "I am a prince of Antioch, and this is my only son, the only grandson of the king. I can't lose him."

The mayor looked at the men. One of them stepped out in front. "I will get some bandages and ointment for you. I only have one living son also."

Marcus nodded his thanks.

"And some food?" Shaeleen asked.

The young man who stood out front shook his head. "No,

you need to go now. As soon as you get the bandages."

The mayor turned to Basil. "You will find the farms to the north of here ready with an early harvest of asparagus and broccoli. There might be some radishes, also."

"Thank you, sir," Basil said. "I hope one day that things are different here. My brother's newly betrothed, Princess Diamonique from Gabor, might temper my brother's anger."

With the mention of the queen's name, Cole gave Shaeleen an empty, haunted look.

Shaeleen and Cole had been sent to retrieve Diamonique so she could be betrothed to the king on the day of the coronation. Of course, most people thought that meant to Prince Basil, but his cruel brother had announced his betrothal to her instead—his right as the new king. Cole and Diamonique had developed an instant friendship, and it hurt Shaeleen to think about what he had lost. But they both understood duty, and Princess Diamonique's duty had always been set for her: to marry a king of a nearby kingdom to strengthen their ties.

"There are a line of rabbit traps by the creek also," the mayor added.

The man returned with the bandages, and Marcus and Cole took a moment to wrap them around Orin's stomach.

Prince Basil turned back to the mayor. "I hope you stay safe, Mayor. Was there anything else in the note from the other village that could be of help to us?"

The mayor put a hand to his chin as if thinking, then said, "The words more or less were, 'Do not let Prince Basil and any with him lodge in your town. The red army are hurting and killing all those who protect or house them.'" The mayor paused. "The rest of the note was about a few specific individuals who were known here."

Prince Basil nodded, a frown forming on his face. Shaeleen opened her mouth to say something, but Basil shook his head at her. Marcus joined them, with Orin in his arms, and Cole's gaze took in the group of townsmen once more before walking away.

Shaeleen's group turned north and walked through a copse of trees and into the farmlands of Galena. They stopped and gathered a few vegetables that the mayor had mentioned, but couldn't take any extra time to find the rabbit traps.

At one stop to pull a few bunches of radishes, Basil walked up to Shaeleen. "Why the scowl?"

Shaeleen hadn't realized she was scowling. "I don't know. Just thinking about something better to eat, I guess. I was looking forward to a nice meal in an inn tonight."

"And some sweets, I would guess." The prince laughed.

Shaeleen laughed too. *I really do need a sweet roll!* "Yes, that would have been nice." She paused a moment, then grew serious. "You heard what the mayor said about the red army?"

Prince Basil nodded his head.

"Galena's army is blue—the color of the Labradorite IntelligenceStone," Shaeleen said.

"But red—" Basil started.

Cole came up behind them and finished his words. "Red is the red army of Gabor—the kingdom of the Red Jasper StrengthStone," Cole said through thin lips. "The kingdom that Commander Kerr is trying to take from Queen Victoria and her daughter, Princess Diamonique."

"So it is Commander Kerr's army that is chasing us, not my brother's," Basil said.

They stood quiet for a moment. After gathering the vegetables they had time for, they set out once again.

"I have a plan," Basil said as they walked.

"A plan to do what?" Shaeleen asked. "We need to get to Lightfort."

"And get help for my son," Marcus added.

"Just hear me out." Basil looked each of them in the eye. "We must go back to Stronghaven."

CHAPTER THREE

Shaeleen shook her head. "No, No. No. You can't go back to Stronghaven, Basil. It's too dangerous."

"I agree, Prince Basil." Cole's eyes surveyed the flat land around them. "We need to get as far away from here as possible."

Before Basil could say anything more, Orin groaned and opened his eyes. His father had set him on the ground when they'd begun discussing Basil's plan.

"What happened?" Orin asked.

"You got shot in the stomach," Shaeleen said. She bent down and moved to put a hand on him.

Orin pulled away and shook his head. "I don't think I can live through your touch right now, Shae." His eyes held a mixture of fear and compassion.

What have I done? Shaeleen's heart burst with shame, and she lowered her eyes. The power of her touch seemed to bring Orin pain—a side effect of having been poisoned with a portion of the ShadowStone. Georrod, one of the powerful shadow keepers working under the direction of Prince Brevin of Verlyn, had taken Orin's power of speed while attempting to take all the stones of power and their magic from the continent of Wayland.

"Shaeleen and I will go back to Stronghaven," Basil repeated. Shaeleen was sure the glares of the others in the group were a mirror of her own face. "My brother must listen to reason. Gabor's army can't go traipsing around our kingdom, killing and harming our people." He took a breath, then pushed on. "Maybe at least Princess Diamonique will listen to reason."

Cole perked up at the mention of the queen and cast a quick glance Shaeleen's way.

Shaeleen's head pounded at the thought of Calix listening to reason—that would never happen, she was sure—but the idea of appealing to Diamonique didn't seem to cause her any pain. Once again, Shaeleen felt that Diamonique still had an important part to play in the events that were unfolding.

"Monique might listen to us—" Shaeleen began but was interrupted.

"Shae!" Cole blurted out. "She is the queen-to-be."

Shaeleen rolled her eyes. Why did people get so caught up with titles and names? "I am sorry, Sir Guardian Protector Wizard Cole, I will refer to her as Princess Diamonique if that would be more pleasing to your disciplined mind."

"Shae!" Basil censured her. "Don't tease him so. He is correct."

Orin let out a small chuckle from the ground. Shaeleen shared a smile with him. *At least Orin can be reasonable in these things.* Shaeleen breathed in deep, then took back control of the conversation and pushed forward. "All right. Basil . . ." She stopped and began again. "Prince Basil and I will return to Stronghaven under the cover of night."

Cole opened his mouth. Shaeleen was sure he was going to contest them going alone. Before he could say anything, she answered his concern. "I can protect us both with the power of the stones, and Basil is an excellent swordsman. The two of us can get in and out quicker than all of us could. We will contact Diamonique"—she cleared her voice—"the princess, then if it is deemed safe or necessary, we will meet with the king."

Basil nodded his head as she continued, but Cole glared at her, obviously not wanting to let her go away without his protection.

Shaeleen pointed at her brother. "You, Cole, will continue to travel with Marcus and Orin to the Myr River and find passage to Mistport. With your powers and Marcus's limited ability to speed, you should be all right. "

"What about my son?" asked Marcus. "He won't make it to Mistport in his condition."

Shaeleen nodded her head. "Without Basil and I with you, you will be able to travel in disguise much better. No one will know who you are. Stop at the next village and get a healer to look at him. If you're lucky, once you get to the Myr River, you may find someone from Althea with the powers of the HealingStone."

Marcus looked down at Orin.

"I can do it, Father." Orin smiled and stood up on his feet. He grimaced with pain, but stayed standing. "See, already feeling better."

"Orin's a tough one," Shaeleen said, though his rapid recovery concerned her. She drew upon the power of the TruthStone and looked at him through truth's eyes. When he pulled his hand away from his stomach, she saw the familiar tendrils of the ShadowStone swirling around him. *Well, at least it seems to be helping in his recovery.* Though she didn't understand what that meant for him long-term. *One more thing to deal with later.* She sighed and turned back to the others.

"We must stop Commander Kerr's army from hurting my people," Basil closed up the argument.

"Then it's settled." Shaeleen moved over toward Basil, passing Cole on the way.

"This isn't settled, Shae." Cole's eyes flashed angrily at her. "I must stay with you. That is what I pledged to do, and yet you keep finding ways to go places without me."

Shaeleen pulled her brother away from the rest of the group. "I'll be fine, Cole."

"It's not whether you'll be fine or not. I should be there with you. I wasn't there in Riverton or Mistport or even part of the time you were on Verlyn. I am your protector."

Shaeleen smiled at his concern. She really did love her brother for his capacity to help others. "This is the best way, Cole. Marcus and Orin need someone with them. You are helping me by protecting our friends. After you get Orin and Marcus to Mistport, see what you can do to help them with maintaining peace, then meet me in South Bay."

"South Bay?" Cole's eyes opened wide. "If I escort Marcus and Orin to the river, then I am coming back for you in Stronghaven."

Shaeleen stomped her foot. "You can be so stubborn, Cole. All right. Meet us back near Stronghaven, then I need to go to Lightfort. The pink Azeztulite HealingStone calls to me already. The power to heal is one of the strongest stones." Shaeleen spoke as she thought through it all. "Then we can take the Cadyn River down to South Bay. The last stone will be there."

A short distance away, they heard a horn blow.

"The army," Shaeleen whispered. "We must all leave now."

Cole glared one last time at Shaeleen, opened his mouth to say something, but then turned back to Marcus and Orin instead, and the three of them began running west, trying to find the cover of trees as soon as possible.

Shaeleen stood for a moment, then called out. "Orin!"

He stopped and turned around. Cole took a few steps back and grabbed hold of him and started to pull him back along.

"Orin," Shaeleen said again, a bad portent arising inside her. "Be careful of the shadow."

The three turned behind some trees and were gone from her view.

"What did that mean?" asked Basil.

Shaeleen didn't know for sure and shrugged her shoulders. "The TruthStone," was all she could say. As a TruthSeer, she was beginning to see things in the future—not clearly, and with only a small premonition, but they were coming more frequently now. Thoughts of Orin and the shadow brought back thoughts of Taegen, a young keeper of the stones on Verlyn who had befriended her and helped her—but was also tainted by the ShadowStone.

I need to stop the shadow before anyone else gets hurt.

Basil motioned for her to follow him then crossed over a small creek and headed back west. As they moved silently along the bank of the creek, Shaeleen mentally went down the list of troubles she needed to fix: contention in Galena, treachery in

Gabor, the compound in Antioch trying to destroy magic, the shadow keepers on Verlyn taking control, and she hadn't even traveled to Shema and Althea yet.

All the stones were failing, and it was her task to gather them in and restore their power again. A task she had no idea how to accomplish yet. She let out another deep sigh—something she found herself doing more often lately.

CHAPTER FOUR

After a short time of heading back west, Basil abruptly stopped in front of Shaeleen. A shout was heard in the distance. He turned around and looked back toward Greenville. A pained longing filled his eyes.

Shaeleen knew instantly what he was thinking. "We can't help everyone, Basil. We have to keep moving."

"But I can't just let the people of Greenville suffer on my behalf," Basil said. "I can't do anything about the other towns, but I can help out here—or at least make sure they are safe."

Shaeleen nodded her head and smiled. It wasn't her natural tendency to help people like Basil did, but it was the biggest thing that defined who he was and would have made him a great king. "I'm not going to be able to talk you out of this, am I?"

He shook his head, and his dimple highlighted his grinning face. "Not a chance."

"All right." Shaeleen sighed. "But"—she poked a finger at his chest—"if you are in danger, I have the right to pull you out. Right now, you can do more good alive for all your people than dying in a brave attempt to save a few villagers."

"Agreed." Basil grabbed Shaeleen's hand and pulled her toward the town they had just left. Shaeleen almost jumped at the feel of her hand in his. *Silly girl! Stay focused.*

Backing around the town, they came up on the far side of it. A small hill stood between the town and fields of vegetables—many of which were raised to support the growing population of Stronghaven. Laying down on their bellies, Shaeleen and Basil scooted to the top of the hill and peered over.

A small company of about fifty men rode up on horseback. The soldiers were dressed in leather armor with red capes flying in the air behind them. Stopping about two hundred feet in front of the village, a large man in front dismounted. The same villagers from before came out to meet them. The mayor of Greenville and the captain of the company walked toward each other.

"I wish I could hear them," Basil mumbled. "I need to know if the villagers are threatened or not."

With the hot sun warming her back through her cloak and shirt, Shaeleen pulled on the power of her stones. She turned her head to Basil, smiled, and spoke. "I can do that."

Basil gave her a questioning look.

"Just stay here next to me," Shaeleen said, closing her eyes. She pulled on the power of the TruthStone and felt her magical spirit rise up into the light of the day. In short order, her spirit flew over the space between her and Basil and the two groups of men. She came down close to the ground and silently approached the two leaders.

"Captain." The mayor bowed his head. "We don't want any trouble here. We are good citizens of Galena."

"Do you think I care about that?" the captain said. He was a tall, broad man with short, dark hair. He and his men definitely had the power of the Red Jasper StrengthStone flowing through their blood. "Have you seen Prince Basil?"

The mayor shook his head. "No, we have not."

Shaeleen felt the pain of the lie, though not as strong as if she would have been in her body. The captain wasn't convinced. In two large steps, the captain was in the mayor's face, looking down at him.

"I am sure you have heard about what happens to those who hide the prince and his fellow traitors," the captain said to him.

Out of the crowd came the townsman that had caused Shaeleen and her group trouble before. "Sir, the prince and his people were here."

The captain grabbed the mayor's arm and squeezed hard. "You lie to me." With that statement, the ring of swords filled the air as each of the soldiers brought their weapons up in front of them. The townsmen took a few steps back.

The mayor stumbled on his words. "Y-yes. Yes. We did see them, but we turned them away. Look." The mayor pointed to some of his men whose arms and legs were bandaged. "They fought us when we told them they couldn't stay here, but they left."

"Is that the truth of it?" The captain stared hard at both the mayor and the other man, defying them to lie again.

A new voice came from the back of the line of soldiers. It was high-pitched and familiar to Shaeleen. "He is telling the truth."

Shaeleen whipped her head around and groaned. It was the TruthSeer Erwin, apprentice to the aged TruthSeer Justyn of

Gabor—and from what she had learned on Verlyn, he was also a holder of a ShadowStone.

The man rode forward on his horse, a creature bowed down by the man's weight. Erwin dismounted and strutted forward, jowls shaking with each step, red robes billowing out around him.

The mayor seemed to understand the new threat and went down on his knees. "Please, sirs, our village is small. We have caused no trouble."

Erwin appeared quite small next to the captain, but it was plain the TruthSeer was in charge. He walked to the mayor and, with a hand full of golden rings, touched him on top of the head. "Tell me!" he ordered. "Tell me where they went."

The mayor's back went straight, and his face looked up at Erwin. He was under a TruthSpell—one very familiar to Shaeleen. One that shouldn't be used on people—but one she had used on occasion. She wasn't proud of it.

"The prince and his party went north from here," the mayor said. "They were going to the Myr River. One of their own was hurt—a boy no older than fourteen."

"Captain!" Erwin ordered. "We ride north!"

Both the captain and Erwin went back to their horses, and Shaeleen flew back through the air and inside her body. She blinked her eyes and looked at Basil.

"Shae?" he said with concern. "Where did you go? Your face went blank and your body went stiff. I didn't know what to do."

"I was listening to them." Shaeleen pointed back at the men.

The captain was waving his hand forward for the men to follow. As the troops rode past the mayor and the townspeople, Erwin pointed his hand and a black tendril of fog jumped out from his hand and raced toward the mayor.

Shaeleen pulled upon the power of the SpeedStone and raced down the hill to where the mayor was standing back up. She watched as the shadow power of Erwin moved toward the mayor. She used the power of the StrengthStone to pick the mayor up and move him two feet to the left. She then sped back to Basil.

The ShadowSpell from Erwin flew past the mayor and landed on dry ground with a puff of dust and shadow. Erwin appeared perplexed, and the mayor himself gazed down at his own body as if wondering how he got there.

Shaeleen giggled, and Basil asked, "Did you do that?"

Shaeleen nodded her head.

"Your powers have grown," Basil said without judgment.

Erwin moved his horse closer to the mayor and the townspeople. Shaeleen watched carefully, preparing to help again.

"TruthSeer!" the captain shouted loudly from farther out. "Hurry up."

Erwin glanced at the soldiers, then back at the townspeople. He turned his horse to move away, and Shaeleen blew out a breath of relief. She turned to Basil, and in that moment, Erwin decided to act again.

A scream filled the air. Shaeleen whisked her head back around again. The mayor lay on the ground clutching his arm, and Erwin sat up on his horse with a triumphant smile on his fleshy face.

Stupid me! I should have kept paying attention. Shaeleen stood up and took a step forward. Basil grabbed her legs, pulling her back to the ground.

"We can't be seen or people will be hurt," Basil said.

"The mayor was hurt."

"I know." Basil held his lips tight. "But at least he wasn't killed, and no one else was hurt."

"That weasel TruthSeer deserves to be hurt." Shaeleen slapped Basil's hands away from her legs. "He uses the power of the ShadowStone."

Basil's eyes blazed with fury. "We need to get to Stronghaven and tell my brother about this. This can't keep going on."

"No." Shaeleen shook her head. "We have to go after the soldiers."

They heard the whinny of a horse, and Erwin took off to join with the rest of the soldiers from Gabor.

"What do you mean, 'no'?" Basil asked.

"They are going after my brother, Marcus, and Orin," Shaeleen said. "They can't hold out against that many soldiers—though Cole will sure try."

The two stood up and moved back down the hill away from the town. "Can't anything be easy?"

Shaeleen laughed. "No, Your Highness. Things for us commoners are not that easy."

Basil glared at her.

She realized she had hit a sore spot. Basil had never acted superior to others.

"Sorry," Shaeleen said and put her hand on Basil's arm. "Sometimes my tongue runs faster than my brain."

Basil nodded but still didn't smile. "I told your brother the first time we met that you had a sharp tongue. Just be careful who you cut with it. Some of us are your friends."

Shaeleen felt her face redden. "Basil, I really didn't mean it. You have always treated me—well, everyone for that matter— with goodness and respect." She was rambling but couldn't quite stop. "I'm the one who is rude and selfish, but just so you know, life is hard sometimes and things never go my way."

Basil did smile at that, if only for a bit. His dark blue eyes twinkled at her. "I'm sure that kind of apology was hard for you, TruthSeer."

Shaeleen furrowed her eyes at him but couldn't help a small grin forming at the edge of her lips. "Look who's got the sharp tongue now, Prince of Galena."

"How about the others?" Basil asked, getting back down to business.

"Grab my hand," Shaeleen said.

Basil complied, and soon she was pulling him with the power of speed back toward where they had left the others. Trying to concentrate on their task, she instead found her mind wandering to the warmth of Basil's hand. Shaking her head to clear her thoughts again, she maneuvered them between the captain and his men. Out of spite, she swatted a few of their horses—Erwin's included—with such force that the horses reared up and threw their riders off. That would slow them down for a bit.

Shaeleen and Basil raced over fields of summer vegetables,

around trees, and over creeks and fences, looking for the others. Shaeleen reached inside and felt for the impression of her brother—a connection they shared ever since she had made him her wizard guardian.

There he is.

Adjusting her course slightly, they caught up with the group. Coming out of the speed, they appeared in front of Cole without any warning. Marcus, Orin, and Cole yelled out at once, and in an instant, Cole had pulled his sword and held it at Basil's throat.

"Whoa, Cole. It's me, Basil." Basil held his hands up in the air.

Cole lowered his sword with a deep breath. "Sorry, Prince Basil. You caught us by surprise." He turned to Shaeleen with a grim look. "What's wrong?"

Shaeleen took a moment to catch her breath. "A company of soldiers is coming your way on horseback, led by a TruthSeer apprentice who has been tainted by the shadow."

Cole grunted in frustration.

"What do you have in mind?" Marcus asked. "There are no places to hide around these fields. I must say, I am out of sorts here—having been on the sea for most of my life."

"And if a storm is chasing you on the sea, Captain Marcus, what do you do?" Shaeleen asked.

"You go as fast as you can in another direction," Marcus said.

Shaeleen raised her brows and smiled. "That's right. We double back, head south past Greenville, then you can turn west again toward the Myr River."

Off in the distance, the horses of the soldiers could already be heard. There was only one thing that Shaeleen could do. She glanced at Orin.

"Oh no you don't." Marcus walked closer to Shaeleen. "I know what you are thinking. It will kill him."

"It's our only hope," Shaeleen said. "We only have a few minutes."

As if in answer to her concern, the sound of hoofbeats began to shake the ground, and they could see a puff of dust behind them.

"Orin?" Shaeleen asked him. He was looking much better than when she had left them before. *The ShadowStone is healing him. What does that mean?*

Orin grimaced. "You're never going to stop trying to kill me, are you, Shae?"

Shaeleen noticed Orin's use of her nickname—his way of letting her know he still cared for her.

Marcus pushed Orin toward Shaeleen. "Take the rest of them, TruthSeer. I will draw them away, then catch up with you later."

"There they are!" one of the soldiers yelled.

So as to fool them as much as possible, Shaeleen led the entire group forward, running as fast as they could behind a small group of trees. Once they were briefly out of eyesight from the soldiers, she grabbed Orin's hand and motioned for Basil and Cole to grab onto her shoulders.

"Take care of my son." Marcus waved at Shaeleen, then sped off in front of them using his speed at a level that the soldiers could still follow.

Shaeleen reached for her own power and took Cole, Orin, and Basil racing back the way they had come. Orin roared in pain once, but then stayed quiet. They ran through the oncoming soldiers, only taking a moment to clear through them. Reaching the back of the group, Shaeleen had a quick thought and reached her empty hand out toward Erwin. She grabbed his wrist for a brief moment and pushed in as much power of the TruthStone as she could. She felt a burning when her power met with the ShadowStone—but also a strange balance.

Erwin roared, grabbed his wrist, and fell off his horse. As Shaeleen raced with the others, she heard him faintly yell out for someone to stop and help him. She couldn't help but smile. She remembered Orin and came out of the speed a safe distance away. All four of them stumbled a moment, then steadied themselves. Cole grabbed hold of Orin and held on to him.

"Your sister needs to learn some finesse," Orin said but sent a wink over to Shaeleen.

They all caught their breath, then Shaeleen glanced at Basil and took a few steps toward him. He was walking at the edge of an apple orchard and looking up into the trees. "I wish it was autumn."

"Why's that?" Shaeleen asked.

"I love apples."

Shaeleen laughed. "Boys. All they think about is food."

Cole walked up next to them. "What about your sweets, Shae?"

"That's different. A woman is entitled to some enjoyment

in life, isn't she?"

The three laughed.

"At least we're safe for now," Cole said. He began to pat his hands around his body, and a look of concern crossed his face.

"Cole?" Shaeleen asked.

"Speaking of food, where are my waterskin and the radishes I picked?"

The three looked back at Orin, who sat on a small rock in the spot where they had come out of the speed. He was picking leaves off the radishes and popping them into his mouth.

"Why, that little thief." Cole stomped over toward Orin.

"Orin!" Shaeleen yelled out to help her friend.

Cole reached Orin before the young man knew what was happening. Cole reached a hand out to grab Orin's arm. With a jump, Orin stood up, his eyes filled with black, and pushed Cole backward.

"Ouch," Cole yelled. "Orin!"

"Orin!" Shaeleen raced over to him, most likely the only one who had seen the small tendril of black filling the space between them. "Stop!"

Orin shook his head and looked up at Shaeleen, radishes still dangling in his hand. Cole was on the ground, glaring at him.

"What?" Orin said, all innocence. "What are you doing down there, Cole?" He reached a hand down and helped Cole back up. "Want a radish?"

"Aaargh!" Cole yelled and stomped away. "Shaeleen, you better take care of this!"

CHAPTER FIVE

Shaeleen grabbed Orin's arm and pulled him away from the other two. At that moment, she didn't care if she hurt him or not. When they were about thirty feet away, he pulled his arm from her and started rubbing it.

"You're hurting me, Shae," Orin said. "What's going on? What's Cole's problem?"

"This is serious, Orin. Do you remember taking Cole's things?"

Orin's face lit up in surprise. "His things?"

"The radishes and waterskin."

"No." Orin shook his head. "You told me not to take things anymore, Shae."

"And what about pushing him down?" Shaeleen gazed into Orin's eyes, wanting to force the truth from him—the real truth—but knowing that doing so could kill him.

"What are you talking about, Shae?" Orin waved his hands around. "I couldn't push your brother down. He's too big . . . and fast." The last was apparently hard for Orin to say. His face fell, and he stared at the ground.

Shaeleen took a deep breath and softened her voice. "Orin?"

Orin looked up at Shaeleen, but his face was a mask of differing emotions. Out of the corner of her eye, she saw Basil and Cole talking in low whispers. Shaeleen put her fists on her hips. "Orin, we have a problem."

"What?"

"You."

Orin opened his mouth to protest, Shaeleen was sure, but before he could, Marcus appeared next to them. He fell to the ground, gasping for air. Orin ran over to him and helped him sit up. Cole and Basil walked over more slowly with their eyes questioning Shaeleen. They all came together in a circle around Marcus.

He looked up at them. "They should be confused for a while." He glanced around and saw the somber faces of the group. "Is something wrong?"

Cole looked at Shaeleen with eyes willing her to tell. She sighed and thought about what she should say. "Orin's connection to the ShadowStone is growing. He reacts more strongly to someone with the power around him, he is doing things without remembering, and his strength is growing." Shaeleen plowed forward as the mouths of each person around her dropped open.

Orin was the first to recover. "That's ridiculous," he said but took a few steps away from the group.

"Orin." Shaeleen stretched her hand toward him to beckon him back, but he mistook it as a potential attack.

Orin's eyes grew dark, and he thrust his hand out in front of him. A black shadow flew from his fingers and whizzed toward Shaeleen. With the reactions of a wizard, Cole brought his sword up and blocked the shadow, sending it racing off and dissipating into a nearby tree.

"Stay away from me!" Orin yelled, his voice not entirely his own. He turned around and ran away from the group.

"Orin!" Marcus called. He started to chase after his son. His speed was spent, but he was fit and could still run fast with his own physical strength.

"Marcus," Shaeleen called out to stop him.

He turned back around. "I have to get him, Shaeleen. I have to save him and get him healed. Carry on without us."

Shaeleen nodded her head. She hated to let Orin go this way, but maybe it was for the best. "Be careful, Prince of Antioch. You are needed back home to save your kingdom."

"You're telling me to leave my son?" Marcus roared, his face filling with anger.

Shaeleen squeezed her eyes shut for a brief moment. Her heart hurt for Orin. He was her friend, had saved her many times, and was with her when they were captured by the people of the compound—those trying to take magic out of Antioch. The Shadow Keeper Georrod had taken Orin's power of speed but had replaced it with something else—something evil.

Marcus was awaiting an answer, though it pained him to stay put. She was a TruthSeer, and he had been trained to honor the stones of power and their holders.

"Take care of him, Marcus. Get him to a healer, then back home," Shaeleen said. "I will meet you there as soon as I can."

Marcus nodded his head, turned back around, and started after his son. "Orin! Orin!"

Shaeleen plopped down on the ground and whispered, "And tell him I am sorry."

Shaeleen stayed on the ground by herself for a few

moments. She could hear the whispers of Cole and Basil. She wished she had the power of the HearingStone so she could hear what they were saying. She barely stopped a groan as she realized that soon she would have that power also, and she shook her head.

"Shae?" Cole came up next to her, Basil trailing behind.

Shaeleen looked up at the two, but stayed seated. This time, she did let a small sigh escape. "Why does everything have to be so hard?"

Cole just shrugged. "I told you I needed to stay with you, Shae. And now here I am."

Shaeleen grunted. Everything came easily for Cole. Maybe that's what happened when you grew up obeying all the rules and telling the truth. She turned her attention to Basil. His eyes still held a deep hurt from losing his people, but he was able to show compassion for her.

Basil reached a hand down, and Shaeleen took it in hers. After she stood back up, he lingered before letting go. She realized that things hadn't been easy for him either, and she felt guilty for wallowing in her own pity. Basil had already lost more than she ever had—an entire kingdom and a princess to marry.

"We just keep on going, Shae," Basil said, "and try to do our best."

Shaeleen shook her head and smiled. "You're the most positive person I have ever met, Prince Basil."

Cole smiled at her use of the prince's title, and she had really meant it as a compliment. He really was an incredible person—the dimple didn't hurt either. She blushed and turned around, hoping neither man would notice. Cole chuckled softly and she knew he had, but Basil had the good graces to turn the other way.

"Let's go." Basil motioned. "Stronghaven is two days' walk from here."

"Not if you have a SpeedStone." Shaeleen turned back around and skipped up to Cole and Basil.

"Are you sure?" Basil asked. "You're not too tired?"

"I'm fine. For a while."

CHAPTER SIX

Not more than a quarter of an hour later, Shaeleen pulled them out of the speed, and all three tumbled to the ground. In the back of her mind, she felt a reluctance to let go of Basil's hand, but the scene in front of them drove all thoughts of comfort or love from her heart.

The three slowly stood and faced the opened gate of a town they had stayed in only a few nights before. Words choked Shaeleen's throat, and she leaned over and heaved, but there wasn't enough in her stomach to actually come out.

A dog barking in the distance and a flock of crows scattering off the ground and into the sky were the only sounds around them. The stench of dead bodies had all three of them covering their noses. As Basil moved forward, Shaeleen watched his shoulders from behind. With each step, they dropped lower.

Shaeleen saw the twisted body of a man lying on the front porch of what used to be an inn—now it was a burned-out shell. To the left, a woman sat in a chair on a porch, an arrow protruding from her chest. Basil continued to walk in front while she and Cole followed. Townspeople were scattered on the ground—all dead. Shaeleen tried not to gag again.

The meow of a cat brought their attention to another building—a shop of some kind. Fire had taken a portion of it. The rest had collapsed in on itself, most likely trapping others inside. *How can anyone do this?* It was the most horrible thing she had seen in her life. Never had she supposed that such evil could exist in the world. Was this what she was supposed to be fighting against—this time of evil and malice?

Shaeleen continued to look around, but her mind could barely register the atrocities before her. An entire town decimated. As they walked, she began to hear other sounds in the back of her numb mind. Pushing through the scene in front of her, she became more alert.

The pained cry of a child pierced the air, and all three turned toward the direction of the sound.

"Up ahead and to the right." Basil pointed. His shoulders grew taller as he took control of the dire situation.

The three took off at a run, following the cries. They soon came to a home that appeared intact. Basil pushed open the door. Cole, with hand on the pommel of his sword, entered next. Shaeleen followed.

The once-tidy home had been ransacked. Simple furniture was broken and scattered on the floor. Dishes and other kitchen utensils were tossed on the ground. The crying came from up ahead, behind a closed door, which Shaeleen supposed was a bedroom.

Basil reached the door first and pushed it open slowly. Huddled in a corner behind an upturned bed crouched a young girl—not more than four or five years old. Tears streamed down her dirty face, and her tangled brown hair was full of debris. Upon seeing Basil and Cole, she crouched back farther into the corner.

"We're here to help," Basil said with a kind voice. The girl stayed where she was.

"Put the sword away, Cole," Shaeleen whispered to her brother. "You're frightening her."

Basil turned, and Shaeleen could see the tears in his eyes as she walked forward. She swallowed hard and put her hand out toward the little girl. She thought of her own younger sister, Alva, and pushed back the tears, thinking of how she would feel if anything happened to her family.

"Come on out, sweetie," Shaeleen whispered, coaxing her forward. "What's your name?"

The girl wiped her eyes but stayed where she was. "Madeline," she said in a soft voice. "But my friends call me Maddi."

Shaeleen took a step closer and knelt down, pushing aside a broken piece of a bureau. "Maddi, I will be your friend."

The young girl stood, eyes wide. She glanced over at Basil and Cole before taking any steps.

"These are my friends, my brother, Cole, and Prince Basil." Shaeleen called the girl's attention back to her. "We all want to help you."

Maddi took three steps and fell into Shaeleen's open arms. She hung her arms around Shaeleen's neck and wouldn't let go for an entire minute. Cole and Basil stood quietly behind, though about halfway through the hug, Shaeleen felt Basil's tender hand on her shoulder.

Maddi finally pulled away, and Shaeleen lifted her up in her arms. "Do you know where your family is?"

Maddi shook her head. "The bad men took them away."

Shaeleen's heart was about to break, but deep inside of the raw emotion, another sensation was slowly building—one that she had to push back to keep at bay. With the power she held, her anger could cause unintended consequences.

"There may be others," Cole said.

Basil nodded, and the three of them, with Maddi in tow, walked back out of the home and toward the town square. Shaeleen tried to hide the destruction and gruesome bodies from Maddi, but the devastation was too much to conceal. The young girl grabbed Shaeleen's hand and clenched it tight. A sob caught in Shaeleen's throat.

Basil grabbed a crate from the side of a burned-out building and brought it to the middle of the town square and set it upside down. He stepped on top. He cupped his hands around his mouth and raised his voice. "Citizens of Galena, I am Prince Basil. Come to me, and I will help you. Come out of hiding and fight the evil red army from Gabor. This is Galena, and it is our kingdom!"

Basil's words were short but to the point. Shaeleen was glad he had done something. It wasn't what Shaeleen would've done. She would have yelled threats against Kerr and Calix, letting the anger inside of her grow bigger. But Basil gave a message of hope, and he ruled with love and compassion.

Soon, a lone man came walking toward them from the end of the road. He limped, and his shirt was torn, but he came nevertheless. A woman came out between two buildings, two young children clinging to her dirty dress. Two young teens—a boy and a girl—walked forward from behind the inn. Their faces held anger and sadness, but their eyes showed a hope and determination that Shaeleen suspected hadn't been there moments before. It couldn't have been more than a day or two since Kerr's army had been there.

Shaeleen looked at Cole, and he smiled and shrugged. Neither could comprehend how Basil did it, but with only a few words, he had brought hope to his people—hope that Shaeleen realized would separate them once again. He couldn't leave his people alone in Galena and travel with her to Shema and Althea.

Basil stepped down from the crate and walked forward to meet his people. They approached him with reverence. With a few words of encouragement to the man, and a soft greeting to the woman with two children, he began gathering in his people, one by one. They continued to come for the next hour, and more throughout the afternoon. He asked someone to look for food, others to search for people, and others to inspect the buildings. He gave each person a task—something important to do. Maddi's care was given over to a family that she appeared to know well.

As nighttime settled in, a loud noise was heard outside of town. The people—now almost forty in number—had already gathered in a building that hadn't been destroyed. Basil had them preparing a meal and bandaging the wounded. He motioned for Cole and Shaeleen to follow him, and they walked to the eastern edge of the town.

In the darkness ahead of them rode at least thirty men on horseback. It was too dark to see what colors they wore, but Shaeleen prepared for the worst.

Shaeleen groaned. "Another fight."

Cole and Basil drew their swords, and Shaeleen readied her powers. As the soldiers approached, Basil put his hand up in the air and called out, "Hail, soldiers. Who is your commander?"

An armored man rode out front. "It is I, Lord Gregory, General of Galena. Who are you?"

Basil motioned for Cole and Shaeleen to stand down, then ran forward. "Lord Gregory, it is I, Basil."

"Prince Basil," Lord Gregory said as he removed his metal helmet. "We've been searching for you."

Prince Basil motioned Lord Gregory and his men into town. Passing by Shaeleen and Cole, Lord Gregory's eyes opened wider, and his face broke into a massive grin.

"Miss Shaeleen. You keep popping up in the most unlikely places, don't you?"

Shaeleen smiled back. "Gregory, nice to see you again. It will be nice to have you and your men here."

"Sir Cole, if I remember right." Lord Gregory gave a nod.

"Lord Gregory," Cole said as he too nodded to Galena's general.

"Looks like we have a lot to talk about," the general said to Prince Basil as his men came into town. "You have a lot of supporters, my lord."

"Supporters for what?" asked the prince.

General Gregory dismounted and walked closer to Basil. "To take the throne back from your brother Calix, my lord."

Basil's lips went tight, and Shaeleen knew he was torn. "Lord Gregory, the throne belongs to my brother rightfully. I will not fight to take it back."

Lord Gregory let out a deep sigh, and a grim smile covered his face. "I knew you were too honorable for that. That's what

I said. But we do have a problem, then."

Basil raised his brows in question.

"Galena is going to be split in two. The crown, North Bay, and Stronghaven and its peninsula belong to your brother, but the rest of the land belongs to you." With a sweep of his arm to the west, Lord Gregory had everyone turn. Torches came into view, then a small group of people followed behind the torchbearers. Then more and more. Some were on horseback, some in carts, and some walked or carried others. Thousands of them soon filled the small town.

Turning to Basil, Lord Gregory spread his arms to the side. "Prince Basil, behold your people. We've been searching for you."

CHAPTER SEVEN

All through the night, people from the countryside of Galena flocked toward Prince Basil. Shaeleen recognized a few from the city that had worked in the castle under Prince Basil and Regent Warin. She thought about the remainder of her family—her mother, father, and younger sister—and wondered how they were faring with the changes.

She and Cole got a few hours of sleep early in the morning, but Shaeleen doubted that Basil had taken time for any rest at all. He wanted to personally greet each person and was the focal point of orders to determine where to house everyone. He organized a few of the soldiers to take care of the difficult task of finding and burying the dead.

A substantial camp grew overnight outside the western edge of town. In the morning, Shaeleen awoke to see a new sign erected at each end of the town—Freetown, it was now called. Freedom from the rule of King Calix and the Gaborian army.

Shaeleen walked the town alone for a few moments, taking in the sights and sounds. She shook her head in amazement at what had occurred overnight in this small town. Off to her right, a few soldiers were trying to lift a heavy beam that had fallen down and blocked the entrance to one of the inns. The main structure appeared to be salvageable. She strode over to it.

"Care for some help?" Shaeleen said with a warm smile.

The men smiled back, and one gave a quick chortle, but

they soon returned to their work. Straining as hard as they could, the three of them tried to lift one end of the beam, but they barely got it off the ground. Shaeleen stepped closer and put her hands underneath.

"Miss, please, we have this," said one of the men. "No need to hurt yourself."

Shaeleen laughed. At least the man was polite about it. But she ignored him and took a deep breath, pulling on the power of the Red Jasper StrengthStone. She felt her muscles bulge with increased capacity, and new energy buzzed through her body. With a small grunt, she lifted the end of the beam until it was above her head.

The men let go and stepped back—speechless and surprised.

"Well, don't stand there gawking at me, boys," Shaeleen teased. "I can't hold this thing up forever. Where do you want it?"

One of the men pointed above the doorway where the post ended.

"Shae!" Cole yelled from the street. "What are you doing?"

Her brother rushed over. He and the other soldiers grabbed the other end of the beam. Together, they lifted it to where it needed to be. Shaeleen had a hard time reaching high enough, but with a small jump, she got it. Stepping back, she clapped her hands together to wipe the dirt off. The soldiers rushed around her, expressing their thanks. Shaeleen nodded and walked back out in the street with her brother.

"It's nice to do something good with these powers," Shaeleen mused.

Cole laughed. "The prince has been up all night. I don't know how he does it."

Shaeleen nodded her head in agreement.

Suddenly, she heard a loud scream in the camp. She looked toward where the new camp was being built up and noticed the top of a tall pine tree swaying, beginning to fall. Pulling on the powers of the SpeedStone, Shaeleen raced forward. She felt Cole at her side. Reaching the falling tree just in time, she stood on the ground underneath it and braced for the weight of it. While she did, Cole sped around and moved people out of the way.

"Cole!" Shaeleen screamed as the weight of the tree landed on her. She pulled more of the power of the TruthStone into her, and it buoyed up her strength for a few moments longer.

"Let it go," Cole yelled.

Shaeleen used her last portion of speed—still tired from the previous day—and took a step back. The large tree hit the ground with a sound like thunder, and the ground shook. Shaeleen stood, breathing hard. She peered down; a soft green glow surrounded her. She turned toward Cole and noticed all the people around the camp staring at her in shock. A lone clap sounded in back, then more followed, and soon the entire camp cheered for what she had done. Cole was swarmed with a dozen people thanking him for moving them out of the way.

A man covered in saw dust and holding a long saw walked up. "Thank you miss." He bowed his head to her. "I thought I had it under control, but then it fell the wrong direction."

Shaeleen smiled and was happy that she could help. She turned back to her brother, "We need to move on."

"I know, but Prince Basil needs to stay here."

Shaeleen nodded her head, her heart growing heavy with every step. Soon, they reached the inn that Prince Basil and Lord Gregory had made their headquarters. They entered the room, and a few of the soldiers nodded their heads respectfully. Moving over to a table, Shaeleen and Cole joined Prince Basil and Lord Gregory.

"Basil." Shaeleen cleared her throat. Cole and Lord Gregory gave her firm looks. "Uh, Prince Basil," she started again, and the prince looked up at her.

A large smile spread across his face. His eyes were tired, but they held a firm resolve. He was at his best when helping others. Shaeleen hadn't known until this exact moment how hard it would be for her to leave him. She had grown quite fond of him. Shaeleen took a deep breath in through her nose and steeled her resolve. "I must leave."

Basil's eyes tightened, and his demeanor fell. "You don't have to go," he said with a husky voice.

Shaeleen bent over in pain, and Basil was at her side in a moment. He wrapped his arm around her shoulders. "Shae, Shae," he murmured. "I'm so sorry. Please forgive me. My own selfishness caused you pain."

As the pain in her stomach receded, her heart lifted. She stood back up, pushing the remaining pain away. "So you admit you will miss me." She smiled and raised her brows at him.

He gently brought a hand out and touched her arm. His fingers sent a shock through her body. Replacing the familiar pain in her stomach was instead a fluttering of butterflies, and she felt lighter. The only comparable feeling was when she soared in the light with the power of the TruthStone. And with that power now in her, she locked eyes with Prince Basil and spoke the only thing that she knew with certainty at that moment. "I will return to you."

Shaeleen was aware of every eye in the room on her and Prince Basil. She blushed and stepped away from him. Lord Gregory cleared his throat and winked at Shaeleen. The rest of the men turned and resumed whatever they were working on before Shaeleen and Cole had walked in. Shaeleen looked down at the table Basil and Gregory stood in front of. It was a map of the area and had markings of troops and people. The IntelligenceStone flared inside her.

"Commander Kerr has spread his armies too thin." She pointed at the map. "If you send a small group to North Bay, you can retake the city. They have no love for Calix. That will force Kerr to sail directly to and from Riverton for additional troops and supplies."

Lord Gregory nodded his head.

"But the real threat is the apprentice TruthSeer Erwin," Shaeleen continued. "He is leading a company of men westward, seeking Prince Basil. By now, I assume they've realized they were tricked. He will try to come back. If you get enough men, you can block them from joining with Kerr in Stronghaven. That will weaken him considerably. But you must be careful of Erwin—he serves the shadow and has additional powers."

"What about help from Antioch or Verlyn?" Basil asked.

Shaeleen shook her head. "Not yet. Antioch has their own shadow keeper wreaking havoc there, and Verlyn is falling apart. Until I gather the HearingStone and HealingStone, you will have to keep peace on your own."

"I will go to Calix and talk to him," Prince Basil said, arms held tight against his hips.

Lord Gregory shook his head. "That is not wise, Prince Basil. He will not listen to reason. But . . ." He paused.

"But there are others there who would listen to reason," Shaeleen finished his sentence. "Regent Warin has stayed there, and others, like Diamonique, are loyal to the crown. They might not fight against Calix, but they can guide him away from chaos."

"I can see why you don't want this one to go, Prince Basil." Lord Gregory's oversized body shook with laughter.

Shaeleen blushed and glanced at Cole, nodding her head toward the door. It was time to go.

"Stay for a meal before you go," Basil called Shaeleen's attention back to him. She couldn't deny him.

Soon, a small table was cleared in the corner of the room, and a meal of roasted chicken and fresh vegetables was served to Shaeleen, Cole, Basil, and Gregory. Talk turned away from the troubles of the land, and Shaeleen felt her body relax and the power of the stones strengthen inside of her. *This is good for me.*

One of Lord Gregory's men strode up to them. "Horses and gear are ready for you, sir and lady."

Shaeleen opened her eyes wide in surprise. She hadn't expected that. "Thank you," she said and stood up, motioning Cole to join her. "It is time for us to leave now."

Prince Basil and Lord Gregory stood as well. Basil

swallowed hard but didn't speak. Enough had been said earlier.

"I will return," she repeated again with fierceness.

She and Cole walked to the door and found horses waiting. Bags of gear were tied to the sides. They climbed up on the horses and waved at Prince Basil, Lord Gregory, and their soldiers before heading west through town.

As they rode past, the people stopped moving. All business was forgotten as, one by one, they knelt with a knee on the ground.

"Cole?" Shaeleen whispered to her brother. "What are they doing?"

"Hail the TruthSeer!" cried out a lone voice from the side of the road.

"Hail the TruthSeer," echoed others.

"They love the TruthSeer," Cole said to Shaeleen. "Wave at them. Give them hope."

Shaeleen felt uncomfortable doing so, but she heeded her wizard's words and waved at the people, who stood back up and cheered. Cole joined with her, and chants of "TruthSeer" and "Wizard" filled the air around them as they rode through town. *These people are so good*, Shaeleen thought. Could she really save them all from the weakening of the stones and the advances of the shadow keepers?

"Why so melancholy, sister?" asked Cole.

Shaeleen let out a deep breath. "It's just so much sometimes. Galena, Gabor, Antioch, Verlyn—troubles abound. The shadow keepers have sown chaos everywhere."

"And now onto Shema and Althea," Cole added.

"Where I'm sure we will find more trouble."

Cole laughed. "As long as you're there, I'm sure we will."

"Hey!" Shaeleen joined in the laughter. But it was true. Trouble seemed to follow her, or she followed it.

The cheering of the crowd faded as Shaeleen and Cole got farther away from Freetown. The day was hot, and Shaeleen wiped her brow from the humidity in the air. Birds, without any care, chirped up in the trees above them.

In the still afternoon air, from behind her, she thought she heard the soft words of Basil. "Hail the TruthSeer. Hail Shaeleen."

Stay safe, my prince!

CHAPTER EIGHT

Later that night, Cole found a good place for them to stop for the night. There was a small copse of trees next to a stream, allowing the horses to drink. Shaeleen pulled out a small bag of oats that had been given them and fed the horses by hand for a few minutes. Their big lips tickled her hands, and she let out a small giggle.

"Nice to see you happy, Shae," Cole said as he came up beside her. He took some oats and joined Shaeleen in feeding the horses. "It's been a tough few months for you, I imagine."

Shaeleen nodded. "But we've met some amazing people too, Cole." Her eyes opened wide. "I've met a king, a queen, an empress—"

"And a prince," Cole interrupted with a laugh.

Shaeleen felt her face redden. "Cole!"

He put his hands in the air in mock surrender. "I'm not saying it's wrong, Shaeleen, but I see the way you look at him."

"Well, he is a good man and probably too good for me. As you've said before, trouble follows me and probably always will. I'm just the daughter of a carpenter."

Cole laughed. "Shae, you will never be 'just' something. Don't you realize that you are one of a kind? Kings and queens bow to you and nobles want to be your friend."

"That's just what Keeper Melindra said when she first gave

me the TruthStone." Shaeleen shook her head in disbelief. "It really is quite amazing. Me, a TruthSeer! Can you believe it?"

Cole dropped his remaining oats on the ground and started to brush his horse. "I can't believe you've learned to tell the truth so well. That was never your strong suit."

Shaeleen began brushing her own horse beside Cole. "Don't I know it! It's a cruel joke the stones play on me."

Cole turned quiet for a moment. "The stones play with all of us sometimes."

She knew what he was referring to. The first time he had set eyes on Diamonique, he had been instantly smitten—but she was betrothed to a prince. "Don't give up hope, big brother. One thing I've learned is, where the power of the stones are concerned, anything can happen."

Cole smiled. "You're right, Shae." He put down the brush and tied the horses with a long tether. "Now let's get some food."

"What I wouldn't do for a sweet right now," Shaeleen said as they gathered some wood for a small fire.

Cole pulled vegetables out of his bags and unwrapped some salted venison. In a few moments, he had a fire going, and the sweet, smoky scent of the cooking meat made Shaeleen's mouth water with anticipation.

"Almost done," Cole said sometime later. "Grab some plates for us," he motioned to Shaeleen.

She walked over to her bag and pulled two tin plates out of a side pocket. She saw something buried beneath. She yanked it out and brought it over by the fire.

"What have you got there?" Cole craned his neck to see

better.

"I don't know." Whatever it was felt soft, and it was wrapped in a light cloth. Pulling the last corners of the cover away, she laughed and cried at the same time. "Oh, Cole!"

Her brother stood and came over to her. He joined in her laugh. "Someone must really like you!"

In her hands, Shaeleen held a perfectly shaped sweet roll. How had Basil done that? She wiped the tears from her eyes. He definitely was too good for her.

"I guess when it comes to the stones, anything *is* possible." Cole bent back down to pour the vegetables and meat onto their plates.

* * *

For the next two days, they rode hard in a northwest direction toward Lake Myr where they would cross over into Antioch on their way to Shema. Shaeleen thought about using the power of the SpeedStone, but it would be hard on the horses, and for the time being wanted to keep them along. She couldn't use her powers indefinitely, and using the horses made it easier to take along their provisions.

"I hope Orin and Marcus got to the river safely," Shaeleen said as they neared the Myr River.

"They would have been far south of here," Cole said.

Shaeleen nodded her head in agreement. On the other side of the lake, she could see the outline of Lakeside rising up in the afternoon sky. She wiped her brow and was glad for the slight relief from the warm weather as they neared the lake. A small breeze blew across its surface.

A few boats were tied up next to a smattering of buildings at the eastern shore. She was sure after riding for over two days, and before that escaping from Stronghaven, they smelled horrible. She was looking forward to a warm bath and a soft bed at an inn in Lakeside. If not, she might have to bathe in the lake. Glancing at it, she wasn't overly excited at that prospect.

Cole approached a group of men that sat on the ground in front of a ketch, the largest of the three boats at the edge of the lake. She could hear him ask about the fare to cross. Their response was an outrageous amount.

"Sir, that seems an extreme price," Cole growled.

One of the men stood up. He was only an inch taller than Cole, but weighed at least fifty pounds more. His head was shorn, and his neck and arms were thick with muscles rippling across them. "That is the going fare for those from Galena. Are you calling me a liar?"

Shaeleen mumbled words under her breath that a lady shouldn't say as her stomach clenched. It had been nice traveling with her brother, who never lied or misled her. Now they were back around other people, and the lies would start— it was just so natural for everyone. *I used to be like that.*

"He may not be, but I am." Shaeleen strode forward, her dark blue cape swirling around her small body.

The other two men on the ground chuckled.

"Hey, Clyde, better watch out," a younger man said. "You might have met your match."

Clyde glared at the other two, then back at Shaeleen.

Turning to Cole, he said, "You need a little girl to do your work, boy?"

"Sir," Cole said, looking from Shaeleen, then back to Clyde. "We just need passage to Lakeside, if you don't mind. We've been on the road for days."

Clyde squinted at the two of them. "You're not more of them runaway nobles from Stronghaven, are you? We've heard about the trouble there."

"We are not nobles," Cole stated.

The man gazed at their clothes and clearly didn't agree, but he told the other two to get up and get the boat ready.

Shaeleen looked south along the lake, toward the river. She spotted a disturbance in the distance. She put a hand over her eyes to shade the sun and wondered why there wasn't a SeeingStone to be able to see farther. That could come in handy. Next time she saw Melindra, she would have to ask her about that.

She glanced over at the men. They would be another thirty minutes getting things ready. "Cole, watch over me." She motioned him to follow her behind a building—away from the sailors, but still in the sunlight. "I need to check on something," Shaeleen pointed to the cloud of dust and low rumble to the south.

Cole nodded and stood guard.

Shaeleen thought about the TruthStone in its familiar pouch under her cloak. She was familiar enough with its power now that she didn't need to touch it to pull on its power. Closing her eyes, she felt the familiar power filling her entire soul. Letting the warmth of the sun touch her face, she drew herself into the light. It was still a marvel to realize that truth and light worked together with each other. Rising up in the light, she glanced down and saw the men preparing the ship. The captain barked orders to the two crewmen, and they obeyed.

Turning south, she flew along the sunlight. A few stray clouds floated across the blue sky, but nothing that would stop Shaeleen from seeing what she needed to see. The lake and river sparkled, and the grass grew green on either side. At one point, she saw a small herd of deer grazing on the long summer grass.

She moved south and focused on movement there. It was men, and they were moving fast along the eastern bank of the broad river. Red capes flew around them, and Shaeleen realized who it was. *Gabor!* They had obviously not found Orin or his father, and having also missed Basil, they were scouring the edge of the river for signs of their escape. At least they weren't in the east causing trouble. But at the rate they were driving their horses forward, they would be at the ships about the same time as the crew would cast off with Shaeleen and Cole.

She needed to head back and warn them, but then she saw a lone man at the back of the three columns of men. *Erwin! That weasel!* Maybe she had some time for a little fun. Shaeleen dropped down closer to them and flew above the men until she found herself right above Erwin.

Shaeleen wondered how much she could do outside of her body. "Stop!" she yelled.

Erwin and other soldiers in the back of the company looked around. One horse stumbled and threw a rider to the ground. Erwin swerved around him and slowed down. Shaeleen went lower and reached her hand out to touch the top of Erwin's head.

Pain! Shaeleen felt herself yell out back in her body, and Cole touched her and tried to call her back.

Erwin stopped and grinned. Looking around him, he yelled, "TruthSeer, where are you? Are you trying to hide from me? I'm coming for you."

Shaeleen still hurt from touching him. It must have been her TruthStone reacting to the evil power of the ShadowStone.

"You're not so strong outside of your body, are you?" Erwin snickered, his belly shaking with mirth. He drew something from his pocket, and dark strands of shadow swirled around him. A new cloud appeared overhead, and the sky grew darker.

Shaeleen tried to pull herself back to the light and to her body but couldn't get away. Reaching inside of her, she felt the power of the TruthStone and pulled more of it into herself. The air around her lightened, and she smiled with relief.

"Erwin, I missed you!" Shaeleen said. It caused her some pain, but without her body, it was not enough to be a problem. Even though he couldn't hear her, the lie hung in the air around him, and he bent over with pain. She laughed and continued, "You are the greatest TruthSeer, Erwin. I will worship you forever. You will rule all of Gabor and Galena."

Each statement hurt Erwin deeper and deeper. A roar escaped from his lips as he fell off his horse and onto the ground, rolling around in constant pain from each of Shaeleen's lies. Soon, the shadow around her lifted, and she was free of his hold. Pulling the light into the TruthStone, she gathered up her power and threw a bolt of light at Erwin's ShadowStone. It flared up brighter, causing Shaeleen a modicum of pain.

Erwin grabbed the stone and held it wrapped in both hands. Shaeleen's ability to reach it diminished. The column of soldiers had stopped and circled around Erwin on the ground. The captain dismounted and tended to the TruthSeer apprentice. Soon, Erwin stood back up.

Shaeleen knew she better leave while she still could. She had learned something valuable: lying when she was away from her body didn't hurt her much. She moved along the light and rose up above the soldiers and started north toward her body, Cole, and the ship. The closer she got, the sicker she felt. Her stomach hurt, and her head pounded. She found it hard to concentrate, and the light began to dim around her.

"Cole," she called out to her brother. As her wizard guardian protector, he heard her and pushed his own protective strength into her.

It was enough. Shaeleen fell out of the light and back into her body on the ground. She rolled in sudden and intense pain, then leaned over and vomited.

"Shae!" Cole reached for her. "What's wrong?"

"The lies!" Shaeleen realized. She hadn't felt the lies when in the light, but her body responded just the same. She had spoken multiple lies to Erwin, and now her own body was paying for it. It took her some time before she could stand.

By then, the small sailing ship was ready, and the captain was calling to them. Shaeleen let Cole help her to the ship. She heard the sound of horses and looked south. Erwin and his army were only a few minutes away.

"Captain, we need to leave now!" Shaeleen yelled.

"We'll leave when I say we are ready to leave."

Shaeleen pointed at the approaching soldiers.

"Gabor!" the captain said. "What are they doing here?"

"They want to kill us, so you better be ready to leave right now," Shaeleen said.

The soldiers stopped and spread out in two rows on the shore in front of them. The captain ordered the crew to push off without Shaeleen and Cole, but Shaeleen sloshed through the water and grabbed the back of the boat. She and Cole jumped in.

"Hurry, Captain!" Shaeleen yelled at him.

The man gave her a dark look, but he motioned for his men to get rowing. The front row of soldiers pulled bows off their backs, nocked their arrows, and shot.

"Cole!" Shaeleen yelled.

Cole drew his sword and waved it in the air in front of them—yellow lightning flew out of its tip. The fire met most of the arrows, a few falling short into the water just behind the boat.

One of the crew struggled to get the sails to catch a wind. Another volley of arrows came toward them. Cole blocked them with fire from his sword.

Shaeleen moved to the back and pushed out against the water, creating a strong wind that propelled the boat forward. The boat jumped in the water and sped away from the shore. However, the force of the push had two crew members falling out of the boat and into the water.

Shaeleen stopped propelling the boat. They were out of bowshot, but Shaeleen could hear the raving screams of Erwin. The captain maneuvered the boat around to pick up his crewmen while giving Shaeleen daggered looks. On the shore, the soldiers lit arrows on fire and shot them into the remaining boats, catching fire instantly.

"What a waste," Cole said under his breath. "Just like Freetown."

"My boats!" the captain roared. He pulled a knife and came at Shaeleen. Cole was suddenly in front of her, using his power of speed as her wizard. He took the knife from the captain and threw it in the water.

"Who's going to pay for my boats?" he raised his voice as he looked from Cole to Shaeleen.

"No one!" Shaeleen said, angry at the captain. They would all be dead if not for her powers. Of course, a small voice in the back of her mind reminded her, it was her fault they were in danger. She pushed it aside for now and glared at the captain.

Cole shook his head at Shaeleen, then turned back to the captain. "We will pay for all your boats, Captain, and any harm to the buildings and your crew."

The captain sighed. "You better."

"We are not thieves, sir," Cole said. "We are honorable."

The captain rolled his eyes at Shaeleen, and she growled at him. He jumped back, and Shaeleen laughed. "Scared of a girl?"

"Shae!" Cole chastised. "Don't tease. It's our fault their livelihood has been threatened. We will pay for what we did."

Everyone stayed quiet for the next hour and a half until they reached the far western shore and set foot on land once again.

Cole turned to the captain. "Arrangements will be made for payment." He raised his eyebrows at Shaeleen, signaling her to be nice.

Shaeleen smiled and bowed slightly to the captain. "Thank you for a wonderful trip. I will send a letter to your king advising him to pay for your boats."

"The king?" the captain stuttered. His crewmen stood next to him, mouths open, still soaking wet. "Who are you?"

"I am Shaeleen," she said. Then added to herself, *The TruthSeer who is trying to save your kingdom and all of Wayland.*

CHAPTER NINE

Shaeleen and Cole sat eating a plate of roasted pork and potatoes later that night. They'd found an inn near one of the nicer districts in Lakeside. She felt clean for the first time in a long time. Her hair was still damp from washing it out. They had stopped to get traveling clothes at a local shop where Shaeleen had bought a dress—dark blue-dyed leather fit tight on top and through her waist, then dropped straight around her legs with a long slit, affording her the ability to move and ride easily. She still wore her old knee-high boots over new black hosen.

Cole sat back with a big grin on his face. "Best food I've had in a while." He wore black leather pants and a full leather vest over a cotton shirt. They also purchased cloaks with hoods to keep the sun off their heads as they continued their journey west, but they were not needed while eating.

"I agree." Shaeleen smiled and glanced around. "Seems kind of a somber place though, don't you think?"

"The world has grown more dangerous lately."

She nodded her head. A small group of men in their twenties stared in Shaeleen and Cole's direction. Locals by the look of it. Shaeleen glared back.

"Let it go, Shae," Cole said to her. "They've probably been talking to the captain of the ship that you so conveniently angered."

"Hey, we offered to pay for all his ships," Shaeleen defended herself.

"Yes." Cole nodded. "But news still travels."

Within the next few minutes, two of the men approached the table where Cole and Shaeleen sat. One of them, with too much drink on his breath, leaned in close.

"I hear you're magic users," he said in disgust, his words slurred.

"What if we are?" Shaeleen snapped back. She heard Cole groan next to her.

"We don't like magic around these parts," said the other man, smaller and skinnier than the first.

"I'll take care of this, Finn," said the first man.

"Sure thing, Brody." Finn stepped back in deference.

"The power of the stones is what Wayland was founded upon," Shaeleen said. "Magic is everywhere."

Brody put his hand on his hip just above his sword. "You telling me how to think, miss?"

Shaeleen stood up and faced him. "I'm telling you that magic is everywhere. To say you don't like it is to say you don't like your friends over there."

Brody turned and looked back at the two remaining men at their table. Shaeleen pulled upon the power of the SpeedStone and StrengthStone and raced over to one of the men, lifted him up and deposited him on a small dance floor next to where some musicians were preparing to play.

"How . . ." Brody turned from his friend and back to Shaeleen, who'd returned to her table as if nothing had happened.

Cole coughed, trying not to choke on his drink. "Shae, let's go."

Shaeleen turned to Brody and pointed to the man standing on the dance floor. "You better go and talk to your friend about using magic like that in front of you. He must have the power of the SpeedStone. It is strong here in Antioch, is it not?" Shaeleen felt her stomach tighten again, and she grimaced but stayed standing through the lie.

Brody, too full of drink to think clearly, marched over to his friend and started arguing. Shaeleen turned to Cole. "Let's go to our rooms."

He turned, and they walked up a flight of stairs. They reached their rooms and both walked inside Shaeleen's room first.

"I'm not sure if you should be in here alone," Cole said. "Maybe I should sleep on the floor."

"I'm not afraid of those men."

"Well, maybe you should be. You shouldn't have done that. The power of the stones is not anything to trifle with."

Shaeleen sighed. She'd told Orin that same thing multiple times. "I know. But sometimes I get so frustrated with people. How do you not want to knock them on the floor from time to time?"

"Who says I don't?" Cole said.

Shaeleen spun around. "You? Mr. Etiquette? Wanted to hit them?"

Cole stared at the floor, clearly embarrassed. "Yes," he said, but then looked back up with fire blazing in his eyes. "But

I don't. I have more control than that."

Shaeleen sat down hard on the bed to test its bounce—there wasn't any. "Don't you get tired of being honorable and strict and right and following every procedure to its fullest? Sounds like a hard life."

Cole put a boot up on a chair and began to unlace it. "A proper life is worth living, Shae. If we don't follow our own principles and stay true to that, then who are we?"

Shaeleen shook her head, then began to unlace her own boots. "Isn't it hard to keep track of it all?"

"If you tell no lies, then there is nothing to keep track of," Cole said.

"Ouch!" Shaeleen reacted to his uncharacteristic insult, then reached over and grabbed a pillow and threw it right at his head. He had not expected that, and it hit him fully. Shaeleen laughed.

"Hey!" Cole said.

"The great wizard cannot even protect himself from his dainty little sister?" Shaeleen laughed and threw the other pillow.

Cole moved his hand and, without touching the pillow, turned its direction in the air. It headed for Shaeleen. She put her own hands up to her face but didn't get there in time, and it hit her and knocked her over on the bed.

Shaeleen sat up, grinning. "See? It's fun, Cole."

Cole laughed. "You mean you're having fun?"

Shaeleen nodded, but then before she knew it the other pillow came racing toward her head. Before it got there, Cole swirled his hands in the air, and it began to spin so fast that

Shaeleen could hardly see where it was. Then she yelped in surprise.

"Cole, put me down!" Shaeleen cried out as she felt her body lift up into the air. Cole began to spin her around above the bed. She was getting dizzy and a little sick to her stomach. "Stop!" she cried out in a fit of giggles. "Before I throw up on you."

Without warning, she stopped spinning and fell to the bed, both pillows landing on top of her. She rolled on the bed so dizzy she couldn't sit up straight. She laughed uncontrollably.

"Shae, stop," Cole warned her as he tried not to laugh. "You're going to draw attention to us. We're not ten years old anymore."

"I can't stop." Shaeleen giggled and broke out in another fit of laughter. Then Cole joined in, and they both laughed for a good three minutes. It felt good to laugh and feel something besides fear and pain.

A loud knock sounded on the door. In a flash, Shaeleen and Cole stopped laughing and stood facing the door, Cole with his sword in hand. All mirth was gone from the room.

"Who is it?" Cole asked.

Shaeleen stood behind him and wondered who else knew they were here. Only Basil and Lord Gregory in Freetown knew their ultimate direction, and there was no way Erwin and his red army from Gabor would brave trekking into another kingdom.

"Treats for our guests," said a male voice on the other side of the door. "It's the innkeeper."

Cole turned to Shaeleen to verify the man's words. She

nodded her head. She detected no falsehood there. Cole slowly opened the door. In front of them stood a man in his fifties, a bald spot in the middle of his head. He was dressed nicely and in his thin hand he held a plate holding two sweet pastries. Shaeleen's stomach growled, and her mouth dripped with anticipation.

The innkeeper laughed. "Sounds like the young miss here likes her sweets."

Cole took the plate from the man. "You have no idea, sir. Thank you for your consideration. Could you make sure our horses are fed well and ready at first light?"

The innkeeper gave a short nod of his head to Cole and turned back down the hallway.

"Nice man," Shaeleen said as she grabbed the plate from Cole and took a sizable bite from one of the pastries. "Mmmm." She closed her eyes and savored the soft, fluffy bread. There was a hint of cinnamon baked inside—and lots of sugar. Without taking a breath, she took a second and third bite, hardly chewing before the next bite went in to her waiting mouth.

"Hey, only one for you." Cole grabbed the plate and brought the remaining pastry to his lips, but before he took a bite, Shaeleen doubled over in pain.

"Aaargh." Shaeleen felt her stomach spasm. Sharp pains spread through her insides, and she fell back on the bed.

"Shael!" Cole raced to her side. "What's wrong? Is it a lie?"

Shaeleen shook her head back and forth, shutting her eyes hard and clenching her teeth. This was no pain from a lie. This was different. This was something more physically induced. It spread through her entire body, and she involuntarily curled up into a ball. "Cole! Cole." She groaned through her teeth. "I'm going to die."

"You're not going to die," Cole said.

"Aaargh," she cried out. It would be better if she did. Death would be a comfort after what she was feeling. Her stomach clenched, and she rolled over on her side and vomited down the side of the bed. Cole jumped away, but she was sure his feet were splattered with bits of pastry and dinner. There was a slight relief in her gut, but pain still lingered. She now felt hot and sweaty and wanted to rip her clothes off—though she knew in the back of her head that doing so would be very inappropriate.

"You've been poisoned," Cole stated.

Shaeleen knew it for the truth and nodded her head. She tried to sit up, but a new round of pain racked her body and she laid back down. Cole ran to a small table in the corner. A pitcher of water, a cloth, and a small basin sat there. He poured some water on the cloth and brought it over to her. Sitting down next to her, he dabbed her warm brow with the cool cloth. It felt good, and she tried to take a deep breath.

"The innkeeper," Cole whispered. "He poisoned you."

Shaeleen groaned again. "Don't lie, Cole. Please, I'm already in enough pain."

"I'm so sorry," Cole apologized. "But who?"

Shaeleen had a hard time thinking straight and at the moment didn't really care who it had been. She just wanted it to go away. Her stomach cramped up again, and another bout of sharp pains spread from her intestines to her heart. She sat up on her elbow, pushed Cole away, and vomited again. After heaving a few more times, she laid back on the bed. Cole gave her the cloth, and she wiped her mouth.

"Water?" Shaeleen whispered. She was so thirsty.

Cole brought her a cup of water, and she drank it greedily. He touched her forehead and frowned. "You're burning up!" Cole stood. "I need to find a healer or herb woman."

Shaeleen nodded at him. "Go. I'll be all right."

Shaeleen heard the door close, and Cole's loud footsteps running down the hall. She hoped she could stay lucid until he returned.

CHAPTER TEN

S haeleen went in and out of consciousness. *What is taking Cole so long?* She couldn't tell how long it had been. It could have been minutes or hours. She reached inside of her to find her familiar powers, but the poison dulled her senses and she was barely able to sense them there.

The door finally opened. She heard multiple footsteps enter the room. Her brother had found someone to help!

"Cole!" Shaeleen whispered. She opened her eyes and tried to sit up.

Before she did, rough hands grabbed her arms and held her down. Shaeleen tried to scream. It was the men from the dining room. Cole's warning not to interfere echoed in the back of her head, and she promised herself that if she survived this, she would listen to her brother more often.

"Get away." Shaeleen tried to push back, but she was too weak. Two other men joined the first by her bedside.

"Ahh, the magic user," said Brody, the apparent leader. "What do you think, boys?"

Finn, the skinnier one, snarled at her. "Poison only works on those with magic, Brody."

The other one nodded his head. His head was shaven, and he wore a sword at his waist. "Where's the other one?"

Brody squeezed Shaeleen's arm harder. "Good question,

Lyman."

Shaeleen tried to call up her power of the StrengthStone, and even though she could feel the power in the stone hanging in the pouch at her waist, she couldn't access it.

"Where is the man?" Brody moved his face closer to hers.

Another bout of cramping tore through her body. Her stomach heaved again. "Move." She groaned, trying to sit up and lean over, but Brody held her down. The best she could do was to turn her head and spew any last remnants in her stomach all over the front of the big man. Somewhere in the back of her mind, she found some consolation with what she had done.

Brody jumped away with a yell. "You foolish girl!"

Finn snickered, but with a murderous look from Brody, he stopped and looked away.

Brody grabbed a blanket from the bed and wiped himself off the best he could. "Where is the other one?" He turned back to Shaeleen.

Her head hurt now, and it was so hot in the room. She needed to give Cole time to return, so she said nothing. This only made Brody angrier. He slapped her hard on the face. The sting brought tears to her eyes.

"Where did you get the poison from?" she croaked.

"We don't answer to you," Lyman said.

Shaeleen tried to reach her hand out to touch him, but she was too weak. She didn't think a TruthSpell would work right now anyway. "What are you going to do with me?"

Brody sneered at her. "We are going to turn you in and collect our reward."

"Yes, our reward," Finn rubbed his hands together, and his eyes opened wide in glee.

"I'm just a girl. A nobody." Shaeleen tried to think clearly, but it was getting more difficult. The poison had weakened her mentally as well as physically. "Who would pay for me?"

"Those that don't want magic around anymore," Finn said.

"Shut up, Finn," Brody turned to his companion.

"Shadow keepers," Shaeleen mumbled. How had their influence spread so far so quick?

"What did you say?" Brody asked.

"You are under the influence of the shadow," Shaeleen said, still trying to stall for time.

"What is she talking about?" Brody turned to the other two. They shrugged their shoulders.

"Maybe she's delirious," Finn said. "They said it would disable her magic. Maybe we gave her too much."

Brody shot Finn another dangerous look. "Go outside and look for her companion."

After Finn left, Brody glared at Shaeleen. Lyman took a small pouch out of his pocket. "Maybe we should give her more."

Shaeleen watched him finger the small packet, and he opened it up. A puff of dark shadow floated out of the bag. Lyman took a deep breath and scowled down at her. His eyes had grown darker, and his mouth sneered at her.

"The shadow." She took a deep breath and tried to move her body to the far side of the bed.

"Put that away!" Brody said. "They want her alive."

Shaeleen felt the first stirrings of hope since the ordeal

started. *Where is Cole?*

"Grab her." Brody motioned Lyman to help. "We're taking her now."

Shaeleen struggled while the men lifted her up, causing them to drop her.

"Stay still, girl," said Lyman, "or we'll knock you out." He brought his fist back, and Shaeleen cringed. "There were no directions on the shape we had to deliver you to her in."

Her? Another shadow keeper.

Shaeleen stopped struggling. She would rather be coherent and observant as they took her—waiting for a chance to escape. The two large men picked her up and left the room. They took her down some back stairs and into the early evening air. The sticky humidity, though not as bad as Stronghaven, made her feel even hotter. She craved a drink of water.

Finn met them there, and the three of them placed her in a small handcart, covered her with a blanket, and pushed her down the rough streets. Her body became bruised every time they hit a bump, and her skin burned under the blanket. She pushed it off once, only to have Brody throw it back over her again.

"Are you trying to hit every bump?" she yelled at them, but her voice came out not much more than a squeak.

"Shut it, girl," Lyman said.

They pushed her down the main street for what felt like fifteen minutes, then through a few side streets to a part of town that had no streetlamps. Shaeleen couldn't see much else from her position in the cart. Finally, they stopped, and she heard a knock. After a moment, a creak signaled to her that a door had opened. A few whispers ensued, but Shaeleen couldn't hear what they said. Brody came over, picked up Shaeleen, and threw her over his shoulder. She stifled a gag. The scent of her own vomit on him mixed with an obvious lack of bathing was appalling.

She was taken through the threshold and dropped roughly onto a chair. She scooted herself around and tried to sit up, but her body hurt anytime she moved. She brought her hands up and wiped the sweat from her forehead and tried to look around.

Only one candle burned in the corner on a small table sitting between two other chairs. None of the chairs matched. The shelves behind them were empty of anything personal and appeared to hold months, if not years, of dust. Glancing at the floor, she noticed their footprints in the dust. This home was abandoned and hadn't been used in a long time.

"You may go," came a woman's voice from the end of a hallway. She held out a pouch to Brody. "Your payment."

Brody began to open the pouch as if to check its contents, but the woman swatted his hand.

"It's all there," she said. "Don't you trust me?"

Brody shrugged.

The three men left the room, and the woman walked toward Shaeleen. Now she would finally see who her abductor was. The woman walked slowly with grace, almost floating across the floor. Even in the dim room, Shaeleen could see tendrils of shadow around her feet as she moved closer. The woman sat down in a chair opposite Shaeleen and pulled back a dark hood from her head. Her thin, medium-aged face was framed by long, brown hair—but it was the glasses, which were rare among Verlynians, that made Shaeleen remember who she was.

"Solanna!"

The woman smiled, and her eyes were filled with delight. The last time Shaeleen had seen her was at Melindra's and Aeron's home. She worked in the archives of Sylvermoor and reported to Prince Brevin—the man Shaeleen knew was the head of the shadow keepers.

"Surprised to see me, TruthSeer?" she sneered at Shaeleen. Her face was older, and her eyes darker than before.

"You turned Melindra and Aeron in," Shaeleen said, quickly putting together a few things from her time on Verlyn. She hadn't found out how Melindra had ended up in the dungeon in the palace at Sylvermoor, but now she knew.

"Prince Brevin showed me the way."

"The way of the shadow," Shaeleen whispered and put her head back against the chair. She was so tired. At least her stomach didn't hurt anymore—except from the lack of something in it—but her skin burned, and her thinking was muddled.

Solanna stared at her. "Not much without your power of the stones, are you? Now you understand how all of Wayland will soon feel."

Shaeleen was too tired to answer.

"The gathering of keepers voted," Solanna said with a voice void of inflection. "It is now unlawful for those in Wayland to hold magic."

"You have no right," Shaeleen said, trying to sit up. She forced her muscles to obey her will and felt a small semblance of her normal strength return, but not much. "You more than anyone should know the history of the stones of power. They were given freely to King Wayland. You have no right to make laws that govern our use of them."

"Ahh." Solanna laughed and shook her finger at Shaeleen. "You were not a very good student, were you?"

Shaeleen glared at the woman. She didn't appreciate being told the truth about her studies. She had always found them quite boring.

Solanna continued speaking as if reciting from the many books she must have read in the archives of the ancient library. "Yes, the stones were given freely to King Wayland, but"—she put up a finger—"only on the condition that the power of the stones was used wisely."

Shaeleen's eyes opened wider, and she sat up, trying to concentrate through her fever.

"Ah, I see you didn't know. I assure you, there is an original signed copy in the archives, and"—Solanna seemed very proud of herself—"the council in Verlyn is the body that decides if the stones are used wisely."

Shaeleen groaned and closed her eyes again. She was getting very tired.

"The magic poison is working on you."

Shaeleen shook her head and opened her eyes. "Magic poison?"

Solanna scooted to the edge of her seat and pointed a thin finger at Shaeleen. "And this is a perfect example of how the stones of power are not being used wisely. You, who call yourself a TruthSeer, hardly know anything about magic at all."

"But . . ." Shaeleen tried to argue. *It isn't fair. The TruthStone was thrust on me!* Part of her knew that Solanna was right. It was the same argument she had heard from Georrod.

Shaeleen!

Cole's voice in her head made her twitch. *Cole, help me!* She tried to answer back, but she felt so weak. She pushed all the power and thought she still possessed into calling for him. She hoped it was enough.

"Now what?" Shaeleen croaked.

"Now we sit and take pleasure in watching you fade away," said a new voice coming into the room.

"This is Amara," said Solanna. "One of the original five to hold a ShadowStone. With direction from Prince Brevin, she has now shared a portion of that stone with me." Solanna sat back in her chair, grabbed a glass, and brought it to her lips.

Amara sat down in the only other chair in the room and took a drink from Solanna. Shaeleen wanted a drink of something so bad. Her mouth was dry and her lips chapped. She still felt so hot . . . and weak. "Water?"

Solanna laughed. "Oh no, that wouldn't do. Water would dilute the poison."

Shaeleen groaned and closed her eyes again. Thoughts of her family came to her mind— how excited they had been when she was first invited to the castle to meet with Prince Basil. *Oh, Basil!*

Shaeleen realized that Solanna was still talking.

"You vomit, then your body gets a fever, then you feel

weak and have a hard time concentrating. The poison eats away at the power of the stones inside you. And then you will surely die."

Shaeleen stopped listening as a deep, sluggish thought came to her. The stones of power. She still had them on her. The StrengthStone, SpeedStone, and IntelligenceStone sat embedded in the large TruthStone that hung by her side in a small pouch—a pouch that stopped others from seeing the stone, even those with the power of the shadow.

Thoughts of how she had received each stone came to her, intermixed with hopes that Orin had made it back to Mistport and that Taegen had fought against the shadow. Dreams of lakes of stones came to her . . . a mountain—Mt. Eyvindr. She must go there! These thoughts jumped around her head, and she wondered which part were lucid or hallucinations, but she hung on to one bit of Solanna's words.

She had said that the poison eats away at the power of the stones. Unlike others, however, her stones of power were not in her blood. What if she gave the stones away? What if they weren't hers anymore?

CHAPTER ELEVEN

Shaeleen found her mind wandering more and more. She had no idea how long she had been sitting there with Amara and Solanna. She tried to ask questions to keep her mind alert.

"Amara, when did you get your ShadowStone?"

Amara looked at Solanna for a moment, then back at Shaeleen and shrugged. "I guess it does no harm—as you will be gone soon. An afternoon a little over a year ago, just before the gathering of keepers. Keeper Dunstan, upon orders from Prince Brevin, gave each of us a stone."

Shaeleen tried to really concentrate, trying to pull upon the powers of her IntelligenceStone, but it was too hard—her mind too foggy. But she was able to put something together. "Ah, so you and Georrod and Hutchin and Dunstan had stones." *I'm missing one of them.*

"And Cailu," said Amara. "You haven't met him yet. He is in South Bay and, from what I hear, having so much fun with the queen there."

Shaeleen ground her teeth together.

"Why is this taking so long?" Solanna finally said as she stood up. "She should be out by now. The poison should be destroying the powers in her."

Shaeleen had to stifle a laugh. They thought the power was

just internal, part of her blood, but she was different than anyone they had encountered before. She physically had stones of power in her possession—and more than just one!

Amara waved her hand. "She is powerful. It will take time."

Solanna walked around Shaeleen and stared hard at her. "No. There is something else here. Something we are missing, Amara."

"You mean the ShadowStone is not all powerful?" Shaeleen mocked them.

Solanna slapped her hard on the right cheek, causing Shaeleen to tilt, almost falling out of her chair. "Insolent child." She leaned down to gloat in Shaeleen's face. "You play with powers you know nothing about. The ShadowStone is a reflection of the stones of power—an equal balance. They are pure stones from Verlyn and more powerful than any pathetic piece of stone you were given."

Spittle flew into Shaeleen's face, and she sat herself back up straight in the chair, at least as straight as she could. It was getting more and more difficult to move.

"Where is the stone Melindra gave you?" Solanna said. "Where have you hidden it?"

"What stone?" Shaeleen said. "I don't have any stone." No pain! It actually felt good to lie again, and a small giggle spilled from her lips.

But Amara took a deep breath, and her face filled with pain. She stood up and approached her. Laying a hand on Shaeleen's head, she brought forth the power of the ShadowStone. "Tell us the truth, Shaeleen. Where is your stone of power?"

Shaeleen screamed with pain. The compulsion of the ShadowStone tried to make her speak. Tendrils of its dark power swirled off of Amara's hand and down Shaeleen's face. She arched her back and yelled out again. "You're killing me!"

"That's the point!" Amara said with a sneer.

Solanna slapped her again, and Shaeleen fell over once more, this time to the other side. She could feel the TruthStone and the powers of all the other stones it held just out of reach. It was immense and wonderful, but not accessible to her at the moment. Her hand moved to where the pouch was hidden under her cloak. They had searched her earlier but had not found it. The power of the ShadowStone worked deep into her mind, trying to force her to obey the shadow keeper's words. A sudden thought jumped through her mind.

"Your ShadowStone is a reflection of a TruthStone," she mumbled.

Amara stepped back for a moment and smiled. "Good. Good. You recognize the power. Now tell me where your TruthStone is."

Shaeleen fought back as hard as she could. Her mouth opened, and her hand moved to the pouch. She wanted to obey the shadow. She really did, but in the back corner of her mind—a part not accessible consciously, but there, nonetheless—she saw a flare of blue, red, and orange. She realized something about the ShadowStone. She had the strength of four stones, and they only had one.

She knew what she should do: lie. "I. Do. Not. Have. A. TruthStone."

Amara fell back and grabbed her head. Solanna leaned over and seemed about to vomit. Their stone was a shadow of a TruthStone and, in some twisted way, couldn't stand a lie either. But Shaeleen could—for the moment.

"I am not a TruthSeer. I have never been to Verlyn. I have no other powers," Shaeleen mumbled lie after lie after lie. She felt her life slipping away and couldn't even sit back up. Her mouth was dry and her throat raw, but she continued the lies. "I hold a ShadowStone. I love being a TruthSeer."

Both women were on the floor vomiting and yelling. Neither had much experience with managing the pain of a TruthStone. Amara shot out a bolt of blackness against Shaeleen, and she slumped even further in the chair, her head hanging over the side of the faded red armrest, her brown hair hanging in front of her face. Her breathing became labored. The more she lied, the quicker the poison seemed to work on her, but the more delight she got from seeing the shadow keepers reeling with pain.

"Stop it. Stop the lies," Solanna yelled at the top of her lungs, her voice screeching and echoing in the room. She crawled on her hands and knees toward Shaeleen's chair, a murderous look in her eyes.

"I love the shadow keepers," Shaeleen said with every ounce of strength she had. The two women screamed out again, but Solanna inched closer and reached out her hand toward Shaeleen's neck. "I love Melindra for giving me the TruthStone. I love Georrod for trying to drain my blood." She stopped for a moment, tears coming to her eyes. She knew she was dying but vowed to take the two shadow keepers with her.

Solanna reached around her neck with one hand—it was stronger than Shaeleen would have thought. "Shut your mouth!" she howled in pain.

In the end, only one face came unbidden to Shaeleen's fevered mind, and she moved her lips to force out one more whispered lie. "And I love Prince Basil."

Both Melindra and Solanna stopped their screaming for a split second, and their eyes cleared. Solanna's hand slipped off her throat.

That's not a lie!

Both women laughed and slowly stood up. Shaeleen was too weak to even move her head. She couldn't think. What had she last said? Was she out of lies?

The next moment, the door crashed open and a bolt of light flashed through the room. Shaeleen saw the two women's feet shift away from her.

"Shae!" Cole yelled.

Shaeleen had never felt happier to see her brother in all her life. She had no voice left to yell out, and her head sat still on the cushioned armrest. Crashes, bolts of fire, light and dark, raced around the room, but the two shadow keepers in their weakened state were no match for an angry wizard.

Everything went quiet, and Cole was at her side, tenderly lifting up her head. "Shae? Shae?" She blinked for him and managed a small smile. He scooped her up in his arms and held her.

With the last ounce of strength she had, she reached to her side and grabbed hold of the pouch. Pulling on it, she whispered to Cole, "Take it!"

Cole shook his head. "No. No, Shae. You're not thinking clearly. You need your powers."

"No," she said so softly that Cole had to lean in to hear. "They are killing me right now. Take it or I die. I give it to you freely."

Cole's face was a mask of emotion—fear, worry, strain, and a hunger for more power. Then it smoothed back over, and he steeled his face to determination. He took the pouch from her and gasped. Green light burst forth from the pouch and filled the room.

Looking up into his face, Shaeleen grinned mischievously. "Now we'll see how you fare."

"This isn't a joke, Shaeleen," Cole said. "I found a medicine man."

"We need to go to Lightfort. I need the power of a full HealingStone."

"Not like this, you don't. You just need some rest," Cole said, then he grimaced in pain for the lie he told, although unknowingly. "How do you stand this, Shae?"

She knew what he meant. The pain of lies. She almost laughed at it now. She was free, and it felt wonderful!

"We have to go now," Cole said. "You need a HealingStone."

"That's what I said," Shaeleen said weakly. "But first, I need water. Lots of it. It will help dilute the poison."

Cole carried her outside, and they found a small neighborhood well. In the dark night, no one was using it. He laid Shaeleen on the ground and pulled up a bucket of water. He held it to her lips, and she drank her fill.

"Can you stand?" Cole asked.

"No." Shaeleen shook her head. "Not yet. You'll have to carry me."

Cole shook his head at her. "You don't ever make things easy, do you?" He picked her up in his arms, and she felt the power of the StrengthStone in his muscles.

"Run, Cole," Shaeleen whispered. "Use the power of the SpeedStone."

CHAPTER TWELVE

The next two days were a blur. They raced toward the kingdom of Shema and city of Lightfort. Cole now held her significant powers along with his own—most likely making him the most powerful wizard around. However, as powerful as he was, his physical body still grew tired, and he was able to use the power of the SpeedStone less and less.

At first, he pushed himself as hard as he could out of sheer determination to help her, but after multiple uses of the SpeedStone, his bursts were shorter and shorter. Currently, they sat resting a few hours from the famed island city of Lightfort. Shaeleen couldn't believe they had made it there so quickly. Cole must be exhausted. Shaeleen could barely sit up, and she leaned against the side of her brother's body.

"It's beautiful," Cole sighed a moment later.

"What is?"

"Lightfort," Cole answered. "The way the river runs around it."

"I can't see it, Cole," Shaeleen almost sobbed. "Where is it?"

He pointed. "Right there, to the northwest—a few more hours of walking."

Shaeleen squinted, but she still couldn't make anything out but the trees and grassland around her. "Cole, I can't see it."

Her voice sounded panicky. "My eyesight is failing now."

"I'm sorry, Shaeleen." Cole shifted his body to stand up. "I'll go faster."

Shaeleen lifted a weak hand, stopping him from standing. "No, Cole. You need rest. We don't know what we're going to face there, and I need you to protect me and get me to the king."

"We need to get you healed first, Shaeleen!" Cole said, his voice rising. A few birds nearby scattered from a tall pine tree and flew away from them.

"I can manage," Shaeleen said.

Cole leaned over in obvious pain. "Shae, how did you take the lies?"

Shaeleen knew what that meant. She didn't have many days left. Maybe Cole was destined to take over for her. "Cole, if I don't make it—"

"Stop—don't say it." Cole waved his hand at her. "We're going to fix this. The healers in Lightfort are famous, but we will go straight to the king. He must have the HealingStone."

Shaeleen smiled weakly. "See? I told you we should go to the king first." She laughed, but then started coughing.

Cole turned to her and stood carefully, then bent and picked her up. "Still as bossy as ever," he said.

Shaeleen smiled weakly and leaned her head against his shoulder for support. She didn't know what she would do without him. She knew he didn't like carrying the TruthStone and all the implications that brought, but they had to face the fact that she might not make it out of this alive. He would have to carry on without her.

Cole started walking down the last hill leading to the Cadyn River surrounding Lightfort in a circle of water. Shaeleen's breath grew more shallow with every step he took. After some time going in and out of consciousness, she finally drifted off to sleep.

* * *

"Shae! Shae!"

Shaeleen opened her eyes and looked into the worried face of her brother. "We are almost at the river. There is a dock and boat launch to take us to the city, but there are guards all around, and things seem very tense."

Shaeleen scooted around in her brother's arms to see better. Past a few feet in front of her, the scenery got blurry. It cleared a little as she concentrated and as they got closer. She could finally see the wide river and a huge gleaming city rising up in the middle of it, almost as if out of the river itself. Tall spires disappeared in low-hanging fog, and the muted sounds of the bustling city met her ears.

Cole walked up to the docks where small boats stood ready to take passengers to Lightfort. As he approached, six men moved out to intercept him. All wore crisp white uniforms edged with green and blue. Their piercing green eyes took in everything around them. One, with bands of color on his right arm, took a step in front of the others and with a firm stance, drew his sword.

"What is your business here?" the man said. His voice was deep and gruff, belying his young age. He looked hardly a few years older than Cole.

"My sister needs a healer, sir," Cole said with a short nod of his head in deference to the officer's obvious rank.

"There are no healers here," the man said.

Shaeleen felt Cole's stomach tighten against her body, and he did all he could to stay standing. She was amazed at his strength. He knew the man lied.

"There are always healers in Shema, and Lightfort is known for having the best," Cole said evenly.

The man nodded his head. "That may be true, but they are not available now. Lightfort is closed to all visitors."

"Closed?" Cole's voice was tight, and Shaeleen knew he teetered on a dangerous edge that he was not used to being on. "I have carried my sister for over two days from Lakeside. She is dying."

A few men behind the leader laughed, and one said, "You lie. Lakeside is at least five days away in good conditions—and carrying someone . . ."

Cole took a step forward. "I do not lie, sir. You can be sure of that." Shaeleen felt power crackle from his body.

The men took a step back as they too felt something from Cole. The head man hesitated and looked around, obviously out of his element now. An older man walked up. He was mostly bald with brown hair around the fringes. His arm held numerous swatches of colors. This newcomer stepped up to the group, and all six saluted him.

"Captain Tucker, what seems to be the problem here?" the newcomer said.

"General Archer, this man is insisting on going to

Lightfort."

The general turned to Cole and Shaeleen.

"Sir." Cole nodded deeply to the man. "My sister is dying, and we need a healer and to see the king."

General Archer raised his brows. "No one sees the king, young man."

"Archer," Shaeleen said. Her voice squeaked out in a weakness she berated herself for having. "We will see the king."

The general's face grew more stern. "No one sees the king," he repeated.

Cole almost dropped Shaeleen. He stumbled under the pain of the general's lie. He laid Shaeleen on the ground and leaned her gently against an old tree stump. He stood back up, one hand resting on the pommel of his sword, and glared at those around him. "What has happened to the renowned hospitality of Lightfort?" Cole asked, fire blazing in his eyes.

"There is trouble in the land," General Archer said. "As your presence indicates. We are protecting ourselves and our king. Lightfort is no longer open to visitors. I am sorry about your sister. You may continue on around the lake, then to West Bay. You may find a healer there."

Shaeleen tried to sit up, but her head spun and she fell to her side with a groan. Breathing hurt, and everything around her grew darker. She shook her head and pulled upon her stubborn resolve to stay coherent.

"Cole!" was all she could say.

Cole went down on his knees next to her and shook his head. "I can't do this, Shaeleen." His voice pleaded with her. "How do you stand the power of the stones?"

"You have to." She tried to appeal to his honor. "You are my guardian protector. That is your role above all. You swore to protect me."

Tears filled Cole's eyes. "I want to, but I don't know what to do. I'm not like you. I can't just burst my way in. There are rules."

"There are no rules for us, Cole." Shaeleen reminded him of their true standing. "Use the stones!"

Cole's eyes went wide, and he stood up slowly. The general, captain, and their men still stood blocking Cole and Shaeleen's way to any boats.

"I serve the truth," Cole said with a firm voice, the power in his words causing a stillness in the air around them. Shaeleen watched the men step back. The general gave a questioning look, but his feet stayed rooted.

"I admire that, young man, but you must leave," General Archer said. "I insist." His hand moved to the hilt of his sword.

Cole drew his blade and held it out in front of him; fire danced along the length of it. For the first time, General Archer appeared worried.

"Measure my words well, General," Cole spoke. "My sister Shaeleen is the prophesied TruthSeer to save all of Wayland. I am her guardian protector wizard."

Shaeleen saw Cole breathe in deeply, his back straighten. She smiled knowingly. He was pulling on the powers of the stones. The general seemed to falter at Cole's words, and small snippets of conversations began among the rest of the people on the docks who had gathered near to watch.

"Go on, Cole," Shaeleen said softly. She knew it was hard

for him to set aside his honor and use his powers to force their way in.

The general said nothing.

"You say that none other than Shema are allowed to enter, that you are closed to outsiders?" Cole repeated what the general had told them.

The general nodded his head and Shaeleen saw his hand resting on his sword hilt, now a few inches out of its scabbard, ready to be used if needed.

"By virtue of the TruthStone and as TruthSeer and Wizard, we are above the law of any one kingdom. As a true citizen of Wayland, we serve all its kingdoms. As such, by being a citizen of none, we are a citizen of all, and so I claim we are both legal residents of all of Wayland's kingdoms, including Shema."

The general's eyes were round with surprise, and the other men whispered among themselves, confused at his words. Shaeleen smiled at her brother's obvious use of the IntelligenceStone.

"What are you asking then, young wizard?" The general's tone had softened, but still held firm.

"I claim the right to enter Lightfort as one of her citizens," Cole said firmly.

"He's a spy," came a voice from the back of the growing crowd.

The pain of the lie caused Cole to lean over with a grunt, the tip of his sword hitting the ground.

A wave of nausea and pain swept through Shaeleen, and she wondered if it was the poison or something else. She knew she only had hours left to live.

"Cole, hurry."

Cole stood back up and faced the general. "We demand an escort to Lightfort now, sir. My sister needs to be healed for the sake of all of Wayland."

"And you declare what you said to be true?" the general asked.

Cole nodded his head. "By the power of the TruthStone, I so swear." Green light burst from the tip of Cole's sword and wrapped itself around the group of men standing in front of him. They gasped at the show of power, but by the looks on their faces, Shaeleen knew they felt the truth of it also.

The general called out to two men. "Gather the girl, take these two to my personal boat, and ready the rowers."

"Thank you, General," Cole said, sheathing his sword. He wavered on his feet before gaining control. Two men carried Shaeleen farther out on the dock and toward a long boat.

"Always a pleasure seeing a man of honor," General Archer said to Cole with a salute.

Cole saluted him back and they all stepped onto the general's boat. Rowers took their places on each side and began to row.

"Faster!" General Archer bellowed out, his booming voice filling the air. "We carry the hope of Wayland."

CHAPTER THIRTEEN

Shaeleen sat on a bench in the boat, leaning against her brother, barely able to maintain her balance.

"We're almost there, Shae," Cole said in soft tones. "Hold on."

She smiled weakly. "I'm not deaf or dead yet, though my eyesight is dimming. Tell me what you see."

Cole continued to hold her securely in place. "It's amazing, Shae. The city of Lightfort sits in the middle of the lake, its towers reaching far into the sky. A huge wall and towering pines wrap around its perimeter between the city and the lake."

Shaeleen nodded. She could see a blurry shape looming closer in front of them, but its detail was lost on her. The lap of the water against the boat brought a soothing and comforting sound to her ears. "Can you see the docks yet?"

Cole shook his head. "No."

General Archer turned toward them. "There are no docks on Lightfort."

"Then how do the boats land?" Cole asked.

Shaeleen noticed that he had reverted back to his proper ways once the general relented to give them passage. She knew that demanding something from a person in authority was foreign to her brother, but it had been the only way. Sometimes people didn't respond to niceties.

The general chuckled. "Ah, so you haven't been to our kingdom before, I see. The only way into the city of Lightfort is through the tunnels."

"Tunnels?" Shaeleen asked, growing curious.

"You'll see." General Archer smiled. "In a few minutes, you'll see why Lightfort is named so."

Shae looked at her brother, and he shrugged. After a short time, Shaeleen blinked and put up her hand to shade her eyes from the brilliant light in front of them.

"Shae, it's amazing," Cole said. "The setting sun is reflecting off the rooftops and spires of the city, and it looks like the entire city is on fire."

"The city of Lightfort," General Archer explained, "has panels of mirrors and glass on the top of many of its buildings and on every spire of the castle. Each day at sunset, they reflect the sun and cause the city to shine. If we are ever attacked, each mirror and glass can be turned to blind our attackers. Of course, that's if they can get close enough."

Shaeleen squinted her eyes and wished she could see the marvelous sight better. She closed her eyes and tried to revel in the light. *Such power in the light.* It lifted her spirits. Suddenly, it went dark, and she opened her eyes. The opening of a large cave was directly in front of them, forming a tunnel from Lake Cadyn and into the island itself.

"There are two tunnels—east and west—into and out of the island and the city," General Archer said.

"It would be hard to attack," Cole said.

"That's the idea," the general said. "When King Wayland's daughter, Shema, was given the land, she knew immediately where to build her castle. The capital has stood here ever since."

Shaeleen wondered if its defenses would be enough against the shadow keepers. She frowned as the darkness grew. Rock walls surrounded them on both sides and above. The rowers continued, and soon they emerged from the tunnel and came to a landing. A dozen other boats lined the wooden dock next to the water, and a lawn sat behind it.

Just being in Shema and close to the city that held healers and the HealingStone lifted Shaeleen's spirits, and she found that she could even see around her better. Flowers and trees were interspersed in what Shaeleen supposed must have been a park. People in simple clothes strolled along walkways throughout the park and down past the water.

As they pulled up, two men saluted the general, then pulled the boat in and secured it.

"We must get to the king," the general barked out. "Bring the carriage."

Soon, a simple brown carriage was brought down to the water's edge, and General Archer motioned for Shaeleen and Cole to board.

"Can you walk?" Cole asked.

She took a step, still holding on to his arm. "Some." The effort was difficult, but with so many people watching, she wanted to appear in control of herself. They didn't have too far to walk. A footman held the door open, and between Cole and him, they were able to get Shaeleen into the carriage. She fell onto the seat, exhausted after the short walk.

"This is stupid," she mumbled. "I'm going to kill those

shadow keepers." And she meant it. Solanna and Amara had tried to kill her. She was lucky her power came from the stones and not her blood. She wondered how Cole was faring with them. She looked at him, sitting across from her. His forehead was furrowed, and his eyes grew concerned. "Cole?"

"Just trying to keep from hearing all the lies. They're everywhere."

Shaeleen nodded her head. "It's funny how quickly I got used to the constant pain."

Cole gave her a look of compassion. "They should have asked you before giving you this burden."

Shaeleen tried to smile, but it came out more like a grimace. "That's for sure." She laid her head back and closed her eyes again. They were so tired and heavy. Her right side leaned against the inside of the carriage, her left hand holding on to the seat, too weak to move.

The carriage moved uphill on smooth roads, winding its way toward the looming castle. Shaeleen could see it now and again through the side window, between enormous pines that grew thick around the houses and businesses. It felt like a city in the mountains. The general and a few men rode their horses in front of the carriage as an escort. Soon, they came to broad iron gates. The twilight of the late summer lingered, and Shaeleen could barely make out the castle in front of them.

"It's bigger than the castle in Stronghaven," Cole said.

"And Riverton and Mistport, from what I can tell," Shaeleen said.

The carriage stopped. A man rushed up and opened the door for Cole and Shaeleen. Her brother helped her out and put his arm around her. General Archer was off his horse and joined them shortly.

"Would you like to freshen up first, TruthSeer?" he said to Shaeleen.

She glanced down and had to keep from laughing. Her dress was filthy, and there was a rip in her cloak. She hoped she didn't smell too bad. "No, I'm afraid I need to see the king, wizard, and TruthSeer as soon as possible."

General Archer nodded at her briskly. He gave a questioning look to Cole as if asking if he would like to freshen up also. Cole only shook his head. "My sister needs a healer."

"The king is a healer," General Archer said, but then hesitated. "Though, I am not sure if he will use his powers or not." He opened his mouth to say more but stopped and closed it again.

"He must," Cole pleaded.

The general nodded and led them forward. Luckily for Shaeleen, there were only two steps to reach the front door. The double doors opened for them as soon as they approached.

"I have sent word ahead," the general said. "Hopefully you won't have to wait long, but . . ."

"But what, General?" Cole asked.

General Archer shook his head for Cole to be quiet as a servant led the three of them into a waiting room. The servant helped Cole lay Shaeleen on a small couch, then left the room.

"What aren't you telling me, General?" Cole's eyes blazed at the man. "You owe us the truth."

"I don't owe you anything, young man." The general's face

grew hard. He rubbed at the scruff of beard on his chin. "You demanded to see the king. You never asked if the king would actually see you or not."

Cole opened his mouth, then closed it again. "Is the king well?"

"The king is fine," the general said.

Cole's face went white, and he did all he could to stay standing. Shaeleen knew the feeling of a lie all too well. Her brother grabbed the pommel of his sword for strength.

"The king is sick, isn't he?"

Shaeleen was amazed at her brother's use of the IntelligenceStone. He had a natural propensity for using it that she didn't. General Archer lowered his eyes. Before he could say anything more, the door opened. Shaeleen sat up on her elbows. Into the room strolled a man that Shaeleen supposed was in his late twenties, but his shoulder-length hair was prematurely graying, and he walked with the use of a gold-topped cane. His face was ashen, but his green eyes still sparkled with life.

The general bowed low. "King Haelen."

The king nodded his head to General Archer. "Uncle, you know the law."

Uncle? Shaeleen glanced back and forth between General Archer and King Haelen.

"My lord." General Archer frowned at the king's censure but moved on. "These two claim to be a TruthSeer and a wizard."

The king nodded his head and took a step toward Shaeleen and Cole.

Cole bowed low. "King Haelen, thank you for seeing us. My sister is in grave danger and needs a healer."

"There are many healers in Shema," the king said. "Why come here?"

"Because there is more at stake than just a healing," Shaeleen croaked, the words no more than a whisper. "The poison was a magic spell, and only someone with great healing powers can save me."

"Please, sir, it's been three days since we left Lakeside," Cole pleaded. "She doesn't have much longer."

The king's eyes opened wide. "Three days?"

"Yes, sir," Cole responded. "I used the power of the SpeedStone as much as I could."

King Haelen nodded. "Still, my uncle should not have let you in. There is danger in Wayland, and we want nothing to do with it. We have closed ourselves off from the world."

Shaeleen closed her eyes and moaned. She could feel her heartbeat slowing. When she opened them again, all three men stood around her. She motioned the king closer—she knew her voice wasn't very strong. All three leaned in.

"Haelen," Shaeleen said with as firm a voice as she could muster. "You can't hide from the shadow keepers. They will find a way in eventually—unless you heal me. I am the prophesied one!"

The words had the intended impact on the king. She could tell King Haelen knew the prophesies, as the other kings and queens did. He stopped short and stared at her, then shook his head. "Myths," he said and turned away.

What? Shaeleen couldn't believe it. "Where are you going?"

"To get my TruthSeer," the king said as he put his hand on the door. Before he opened it, he turned to General Archer with hard eyes, then walked out the door, slamming it behind him.

CHAPTER FOURTEEN

As soon as King Haelen left the room, Shaeleen let out a long breath and turned to General Archer. "The king's uncle? You failed to mention that fact."

The general grimaced. "It's not something I advertise. As you can see, he doesn't think too highly of me."

"And why is that?" Cole asked.

"I didn't think it was right to close us off from the world and spoke up about it."

Cole nodded his head in understanding. "But he is the king."

"Yes." General Archer stood up from his chair and walked to the window. Shaeleen couldn't see him, but she could still hear him.

"His father was my older brother. He recognized early on that I had a knack for leadership and put me over our armed forces in Shema, eventually giving me the rank of general. Both of us were young and had grand visions for our kingdom." The general paused for a moment.

Shaeleen could see Cole watching the man. She shifted on the couch and could now see him at the window. She imagined him looking at the lights of the city and possibly out over the Cadyn River.

"My brother, King William, began to grow sick. No one

knew what was happening. The healers couldn't help him, and his own healing powers grew dim. He passed away two years ago. Then his wife, Haelen's mother, passed away last year. As you can see, Haelen is also very sick. He is a good boy, but he's afraid. He has a wife, but no heir yet."

Hearing about Haelen and his father's sickness filled Shaeleen with dread. "The HealingStone," was all she could muster to say. She hoped it wasn't gone yet.

The candles in the room seemed to dim.

"Cole, I don't feel too well." It was hard for her to admit it. She had always been strong, but she knew she was dying now. "You must continue on. You need to gather the other stones."

Cole leaned down next to her on his knees and touched her forehead lightly. His hand felt cool on her burning skin. Tears filled his eyes. "I can't do this without you, Shae. You've always been the strong one."

"You can. You must," Shaeleen tried to raise her voice, but it only brought on a cough. "You are stronger than you think. The magic you now hold—yours and mine."

"But I don't want to be defined by my magic." Cole shook his head. "It's not who I am in here." He thumped a finger on his chest. "I can't play the games you do or threaten people or"—he smiled through his tears—"make irrational decisions."

Shaeleen smiled at his attempt to lighten the situation. *I don't want to die. I want to see Mom and Dad, Alva, Orin, Taegen, and . . . and . . .* Tears blurred her dimming vision. "Basil."

"What?" Cole asked. "What did you say?"

"Tell Basil . . ." Shaeleen tried to stay strong. Her voice

wavered. "Tell him . . ."

Before she could finish her sentence, the door opened. General Archer moved back into the middle of the room. Cole turned his head, but stayed at Shaeleen's side. Shaeleen tried to see who was there, but the room was growing darker. *Shouldn't they light more candles? The sun is down.*

"Cole, Shaeleen," King Haelen said with pinched lips. "This is TruthSeer Julianna and her wizard, Martin. They will do what they can for you." With that, he turned to leave the room.

"No!" Shaeleen raised up on her elbows as much as she could. Her words were not a plea, but a command. Her body shook with the effort, and her head pounded. She could barely see the king, but she knew which one he was by his movements. He whipped his head around. The TruthSeer and Wizard sucked in a breath at the command from Shaeleen.

"How dare you?" King Haelen said, his voice quivering with anger. "I am the king here in Shema."

Shaeleen motioned for Cole to sit her up. Her vision blackened, and she took a ragged breath. "Cole, I can't see." She shivered, and tears dripped down her eyes.

"Shae, Shae," Cole whispered next to her, and she felt his arm around hers. "Hold on."

"My dear," the Wizard Martin spoke for the first time, and Shaeleen felt him touch her shoulder. "Let me help."

Shaeleen felt warmth from his fingers on her shoulder. It then spread through her arm and up to her neck, face, and down to her chest. As his magic spread throughout Shaeleen, her vision began to return. She saw King Haelen standing and glaring at her, but he remained in the room.

"Ahh, what is that?" Martin pulled his hand away, and he looked from Shaeleen to TruthSeer Julianna, then back to Shaeleen. "What is wrong with you?"

"Poison," Shaeleen said, feeling a bit more energy, but still not enough. "Magic poison from a shadow keeper."

"There are no shadow keepers," Julianna said with a stern voice. As she said the words, Julianna herself and Cole both bent over in pain. Cole held his well, but Julianna was not expecting it and put a hand on Martin's arm to steady herself.

"I wouldn't speak those lies anymore," Shaeleen said with a grimace.

Julianna scowled at her, but then spoke to Cole. "Why are you feeling pain if she is the TruthSeer? If what you have told General Archer is true?"

Cole bowed his head slightly at the TruthSeer. "You know it is true, TruthSeer. When the magic poison began affecting my sister, it would eventually affect the stone she held, so she entrusted it to me." He glanced at Shaeleen. "Temporarily."

"But I have not heard of a new TruthSeer apprentice," Julianna said.

Shaeleen slumped back down on the couch. The poison that had been held at bay momentarily by Martin's powers was now affecting her again—and faster. She gasped, cried out, and clutched her chest with one hand. Cole leaned down next to her again.

"Please." Cole turned to the king. "Help my sister. She is dying."

Julianna moved Cole out of the way. "The king cannot

waste his powers on you. Let me do what I can." She grabbed
Shaeleen's face in both her hands and peered deep into her
eyes. "I have considerable healing powers, besides the power of
the TruthStone."

Shaeleen felt the warming sensation again but knew right
away it wasn't going to be enough. Julianna's healing
strengthened her heartbeat somewhat, and her vision cleared
again.

"I've done what I can for you," Julianna said. "You can
stay here for a few days to recover, then the general will escort
you from Lightfort."

"Cole?" Shaeleen called to him, and he leaned down close
to her. Even though her words were for him, she knew that the
others were listening carefully. "I need you to be strong. We
need the HealingStone."

Julianna, Martin, and Haelen all gasped at once. General
Archer looked at Shaeleen, and she nodded her head slightly.
She knew he believed them, but it would be hard for him to go
against his king's wishes—as hard as it would be for Cole to do
what he had to do.

"My lord," General Archer said to the king. "She is the
prophesied one. You know the prophesies. All in the royal
house do. And you recognize the HealingStone is failing."

The king swung his head toward Archer, his face turning
red. "How dare you speak to me of such things."

General Archer walked closer to the king. "I have followed
you faithfully ever since my brother died and done everything
you have asked, even when I didn't agree with it, but you must
do what is right now. This girl is our only chance."

"You would go against your king, Archer?"

"I know you are afraid." General Archer put a hand on the king's shoulder.

The king pushed his hand away. "You're a traitor. You will be banished for this."

Shaeleen watched Cole's eyes smoldering at the way the king was treating his uncle. With a pat on Shaeleen's arm, he stood and then quickly appeared at the king's side. The king yelled out as Cole grabbed his arm. The door opened, and two guards came rushing in.

"Is everything all right, sire?" one of the guards asked.

Everyone in the room tensed and waited for the king's answer. He looked around the room, then fell into a coughing fit. Cole dropped his hand, but still stood close by.

When the coughing was over, the king pointed to General Archer. "Take the general to the dungeon, then prepare rooms for these two." The king pointed at Cole and Shaeleen. "And post two guards at each room at all times."

The guards moved to the general with an apologetic look. He held his arms out for them to take him.

"Stop," Shaeleen yelled, using all the strength she had left. "General Archer is not the traitor here."

"He defied me, and I am the king." King Haelen stomped his foot.

"And an immature one at that," Shaeleen said to the surprise of everyone, but she pushed on before anyone could interrupt. "Archer is following the directions of a higher authority."

"No one else is of higher authority here," Martin said

looking around the room.

Shaeleen took a deep breath, but it hurt. The pain was returning again. If she didn't get the HealingStone soon, she wouldn't last through another weak healing. "I'm surprised at you, Martin and Julianna. The TruthSeer was set up to support the king and the stone he holds, with the wizard guardian to protect the TruthSeer, but the TruthSeer is not under the king's commands."

Julianna's eyes went wide, and she nodded her head slightly. "She is right, but I have not given any directions contrary to the king."

"But I have," Shaeleen said, her head plopping back on the headrest of the couch. She closed her eyes and tried to breathe, but it was getting more difficult. Everything in her body hurt— her stomach, head, heart, feet, and arms. Her vision was dimming again.

Cole was by her side. His hand touched her forehead again. "She's burning up." With two quick steps, he was at the king's side, glaring at the two guards holding General Archer in place. Cole pulled a pouch from his side and opened it. Green light escaped and flew around the room in circles of light.

Cole reached into the pouch, pulled out the TruthStone, and held it reverently in his hands. The embedded StrengthStone, SpeedStone, and IntelligenceStone let off their weaker lights of red, blue, and orange. Everyone in the room gasped.

"The stone is so large," Julianna said quietly.

"The prophesies are true," General Archer said, a green glow lighting his surprised face.

Power sizzled around Cole. He reached his hand out to the king, hesitated, then touched his arm.

"No," Shaeleen whispered.

He turned his head to her. She knew he was about to force the king to know the truth and obey him—everything that his personal code was against. But he would do it for her. She couldn't bear to know that she had destroyed her brother this way.

"Don't do it, Cole." Tears flowed from Shaeleen's eyes. "It's not worth it. I'm not worth it."

Cole's voice choked. "Shaeleen, you are worth it all—all my honor, if I can save you." Fire crackled down his arms and to his fingertips. "Not because you are the prophesied TruthSeer, but because you are my sister."

Cole turned back to the king, and his face hardened. Shaeleen couldn't bear to watch her brother give up everything for her.

Before Cole let go of his power, the king's shoulders dropped, and fear spread across his face for the first time. "I didn't know." His eyes darted around the room, then settled back on Cole. "What do you want from me?"

"We need the HealingStone."

CHAPTER FIFTEEN

Cole's words caused chaos in the small group. Arms went flying, voices were raised in anger, and Shaeleen listened to it all as her eyesight faded away, this time leaving her in total darkness. She took a deep, rattled breath and tried to figure out what was going on.

"This is ridiculous," TruthSeer Julianna yelled over the din, her voice a higher pitch than the men in the room. "The HealingStone belongs to Shema and has always stayed under the protection of the royal family."

"We don't even know who these two young people really are," shouted Wizard Martin, his voice low and bellowing across the room. "They only bring trouble to our city."

"Young man," the king said, quieter than the other two, but just as firm. "I'm afraid I cannot give you the HealingStone. It must stay protected."

Shaeleen could hear Cole groan in frustration. Even without the TruthStone in her possession, she knew the king was lying.

"Cole," Shaeleen whispered so soft that she wondered if her brother would hear her. But he did, and she felt him at her side.

"Shae?" Cole put his hand on her arm.

"Can you feel the stone—the HealingStone?" Shaeleen

asked. "Use the power of the TruthStone and feel it. It must be close." She coughed and grabbed her chest. It was on fire and hurt with every breath she took.

The king, wizard, and TruthSeer continued to talk loudly on the other side of the room, while Cole grew quiet. After a brief moment, he spoke to her again. "You are right," Cole said. "It's close by, but it is very faint. Almost as if—"

Shaeleen interrupted him. "Almost as if it hardly exists. That's why he doesn't want to give it up. He's embarrassed. Look at him. He can't even heal himself any longer."

"But will it be enough for you?" Cole's voice was pleading.

"It will have to be."

Shaeleen felt Cole reach his arms under her and lift her off the couch. The proximity of his power and the TruthStone restored her sight again somewhat, and she could see a bit around the dimly lit room. Cole walked toward the door with Shaeleen in his arms. The others in the room stopped talking and watched. Martin stepped forward, blocking Cole's way to the door.

"Where are you going?" he asked.

Cole moved his head to the side with a quick motion, and Wizard Martin went flying across the room, landing in a heap against the far wall.

TruthSeer Julianna grabbed Cole's shoulder, and Shaeleen could tell she was about to use her power on him. Cole barely looked at her. Green fire shot out from the ends of his fingers and engulfed the TruthSeer, freezing her in place. An incredulous look crossed her face, words frozen in her mouth. Cole now turned his focus to the king. The two guards that still stood by General Archer moved to guard their king, swords pulled out in front of them. Cole pulled upon the power of the SpeedStone and StrengthStone, and the two were knocked to the ground, their swords spinning away from them across the floor.

King Haelen put his hands up in front of him. "Don't hurt me," he pleaded.

"I'm not going to hurt you," Cole said, his voice devoid of emotion. With a turn of his head, he directed the king to walk in front of him. "Open the door."

Shaeleen was struck with a strange sense of normalcy as Cole carried her out into the hallway. Servants and nobles walked along, content with their daily duties. The distant smell of something sweet cooking in the kitchen caused her stomach to rumble with desire. No one was aware that the fate of their known world hung in the balance.

The king led them down the hall, and Cole followed, although Shaeleen surmised he knew exactly where they were going. General Archer followed silently behind them. A few nobles tried to stop and talk to him, but he waved them away with a flick of his hand. They stepped aside and looked at the small procession with questioning looks. One glance from Cole had them scattering away to whatever errand they had previously been doing.

Soon, they came to a door where two guards stood at attention. Without moving her head, Shaeleen faintly took in the gold inlay and fine carving details in the door. One of the guards saluted the king and pushed the door open.

"Will you require anything, my lord?" the guard said stiffly.

The king shook his head. "Make sure we are not disturbed."

The guard saluted again and closed the door behind them. They stood in a sitting room of the plush quarters of the King of Shema. Dark wood polished to a high shine ran the length of the walls, breaking only for two grand windows and a fireplace. A set of stuffed chairs and two couches were centered around a small table on which sat a tray of glasses and a silver pitcher.

"Water," Shaeleen croaked.

Cole motioned his head to the king. "Pour her a glass."

The king seemed put out but walked to the tray and glasses nevertheless. He picked up a curved glass and poured water out of the pitcher. He brought it to Cole, his long white robes swishing around him. The king's eyes shot daggers at Cole, and Shaeleen thought for a moment he might throw the cup in her brother's face, but instead he brought it to Shaeleen and held it there for her to take a few sips.

The cool water tasted good on her parched and burning lips. She felt it go down her throat and into her stomach. A brief respite of thirst brought a moment of peace to her. She nodded her thanks to him, and he returned the glass to the table.

"The stone," Cole said, walking over to a shelf on the far side of the room. The shelf stood behind a large mahogany desk and next to a door that Shaeleen surmised was the king's private bedroom. The shelf held a few books, vases, and other decorative trinkets. The king came up beside them and put his hand up toward the shelf, then hesitated a moment.

"Put me down, Cole," Shaeleen whispered to her brother.

He nodded to her and walked back to the sitting area and deposited her gently on the small couch, pushing a plush red cushion under her head. "You all right?"

She could only nod. As soon as his touch left hers, the dimness returned, and her eyesight began to fail again.

"Bring the stone here, sir." Cole spoke to the king. Shaeleen realized, by the lack of honorific title, how tired Cole actually was and how much the stone was taking from him.

Shaeleen heard a few clicks, then the king's boot stepped across the floor back toward them. He let out a deep sigh, and she could see he held something in his hand.

"Open the pouch," Cole directed.

As the king did so, he sighed and whispered, "I'm sorry."

She heard her brother gasp as only a very faint pink glow filled the air above the king's hand. "It's hardly more than a few grains of sand."

Tears leaked out the corner of Shaeleen's eyes as she saw the pained look on her brother's face. He reached his hand down to his own pouch and pulled out the TruthStone. Its glowing green light brightened the room, and Shaeleen could feel the power of the stones strengthen her. The red, blue, and orange glow of the other stones joined the green and flew up in the air above Cole. The power moved around the air between the king and Cole, then moved toward the tiny pink Azeztulite HealingStone the king held in his outstretched hands. The HealingStone raised out of his palm and joined the bright light, its pink light a minuscule addition to the rainbow of colors already there. The stone of power was carried on the light back to the TruthStone Cole held, then it shot forward and embedded itself in the stone alongside the others.

The entire stone flashed bright, and Cole gasped. "So much power!" His voice roared, and Shaeleen watched him struggle to hold it all. "It's going to kill me." Flames danced across his eyes, and colors swirled around his body. A few stray flashes of lightning crackled around the three of them in the warm castle air. Shaeleen heard the door crash open behind them and the voices of guards trying to tell someone the king was not to be disturbed.

"If the king dies, I'll have your head, guard," Wizard Martin yelled.

Julianna cried, "Shut the door."

Cole turned his head toward the interruption and pointed his hands at the two. "Stay away!" Crackles of power ran through his arms and to his fingertips. His eyes were ablaze with anger, and his body shook with power. Shaeleen feared for her brother now. It was too much power for one man to hold; never had a wizard held so many stones of power at once. She could see the hesitation in the way he held his jaw. His soul was a struggle of anger and honor.

"Cole," she whispered to draw his attention away from doing something he might regret.

He looked down at her but didn't seem to recognize her. *What have I done to my brother?* Would this be the end? Would he keep the power for himself now? Everything in the world around them seemed to grow quiet as Shaeleen watched her brother struggle to come to grips with the power, choices flickering through his mind in rapid succession.

When she thought all might be lost and she would surely

die right then and there, she saw a slight shake to Cole's head and his eyes cleared back to their normal color.

"The stone," Shaeleen croaked out her words. "Give it back to me now."

CHAPTER SIXTEEN

Cole took a deep breath and nodded to her. He knelt and gently laid the TruthStone in her hands, placed them on her chest, and closed her fingers around it. Then he stood with a sigh of relief.

Shaeleen gasped. The familiarity of the TruthStone's power coursed through her body. At its presence, the poison flared up in response and tried to attack it. Shaeleen groaned but held on tightly. With barely coherent thoughts, she pulled on the power of the tiny HealingStone now embedded there. Its own power, although smaller than the other stones embedded there, washed over her immediately, giving her real hope for the first time. She felt warmth rush through her body, running through each organ and vein, trying to wash out and destroy the poison there. Shaeleen almost laughed for a moment as she felt it working, but then as sudden as her joy came, the stone began to falter. *It's too small!* The poison was pushing back at the HealingStone.

No!

"Fight it, Shae!" Cole's voice came from beside her. "Use the power of the stones."

The power of the stones!

She used the IntelligenceStone to instinctively see what to do. Reaching deep inside of the power of the TruthStone, she grabbed the StrengthStone and used it to bolster the potency of the HealingStone. Then she called up the power of the SpeedStone and pushed it with the others, causing the healing to spread throughout her body more rapidly. She felt it working! But it wasn't enough.

She grabbed the significant power of the TruthStone and focused it on the eastern window. The light of the large moon was rising above the horizon. It wasn't as bright as the sun, but she remembered what General Archer had said about the reflectors. She reached out her mind and found herself in the moonlight itself. Looking down on the castle and the town, she sped around, turning each of the reflectors toward the castle, focusing their light on the window there. Finally a bright white stream of light now shot toward the eastern window

With a loud crash, the window blew open, and Shaeleen rode the light back into the room and into her body. She gasped, and her body sat up in a rigid jerk. Cole reached over and held her up.

Shaeleen opened her eyes and saw the stream of blinding white light filling the window, the room, and wrapping around her and Cole. The king was on his knees. Martin and Julianna had jumped away from the stream of light but still remained on their feet. General Archer stood to the side, a small smile on his face. The fire seared through her and began to scorch the poison from her body, but it still wasn't enough.

"Cole," Shaeleen said, her voice stronger now. "I need your power."

He gave her a questioning look. With one hand on the TruthStone, she laid the other on Cole's arm and called up a powerful TruthSpell. She could feel Cole's wizard powers racing through his veins. She knew all his thoughts and concerns. He gasped at the intrusion and tried to pull his hand away.

"I'm sorry, Cole." Tears came to Shaeleen's eyes as she realized once again she was going to use her power on someone else she cared deeply for. *What kind of monster am I?* She wondered briefly if she could do it, but she had to. *I am the kind of monster who has to save the kingdoms from the shadow keepers!*

And with that last thought, she dove deep into Cole's mind and the source of his power. She saw his honor holding strong, but with cracks in its defenses—cracks she knew the previous few days had caused. *Will he ever be the same again?* She saw his desire to do what was right. The previous hour had hurt him deeply, and he wondered if he was still a worthy person. Then she saw a spark of light and was drawn to it—his love for Diamonique and the pain of knowing she was Calix's now. She left that alone and didn't dig too deep. That was too personal.

Through the light, Shaeleen felt the power of the IntelligenceStone guiding her to Cole's source of power—a power that had been dormant until she'd named him her protector and guardian, that came to him from distant relatives from Verlyn. The thought surprised her. She knew their eyes and slightly swept up brows were indicative of Verlyn heritage, but she hadn't realized his wizard powers, as well as her ability to hold the TruthStone and its additional powers, had come from their line of ancestors.

With as much finesse as she could muster, she directed the flow of his power to her hand. At first, she felt him fight it, but then he let go and let her direct it at will. She drew upon the stones of power he held in his blood and brought it into her, giving her the additional power she needed to reject the magic poison that had been given to her.

The poison grew smaller and smaller. Cole slumped down next to her, and she realized she had to be careful and not take too much from him. A thought of how to destroy the shadow keepers came to her, and she locked it away in her mind for future use. *Maybe I can draw the shadow powers into me and drain them of their power too.*

Shaeleen destroyed the last bit of poison in her body with all the powers she held and let out a loud scream. She took her hand from Cole's arm and brought it back to hold the TruthStone with both hands.

It is done!

The powers of the TruthStone receded as the sun set, and the room went dark from both the magic and the sun. The only sound breaking the silence was the curtains billowing in front of the broken window.

Cole lifted his head. "Is the poison gone? Are you healed?"

She smiled and wiped her eyes. "Yes, Cole. I'm sorry I had to do that."

Cole only shook his head, honor and decorum returning to his eyes. "I am your guardian wizard, sworn to protect you with my life."

She reached over and gave him a long hug. "Thank you."

"I am also your brother, Shae," Cole whispered. "I would do anything for you."

"I know. I know," she cried.

He pulled back and looked at her. "Just don't ever, ever give me that much power again. I told you when we left Stronghaven for Mistport to never tempt me with that again."

Shaeleen laughed and wiped her eyes with her hands. General Archer stepped forward to give her a handkerchief, and she wiped her nose. Shaeleen stood up. Her legs wobbled for a moment as her strength continued to return. The general and Cole were quickly at her side to help her.

Cole glanced at the king, wizard, and TruthSeer, then back to Shaeleen. "Now what?"

Shaeleen pursed her lips and thought a moment. She sniffed the air and smiled. "I need something sweet to eat. I'm starving."

Cole laughed first, but the tension broke and the rest joined in. Though the king, wizard, and TruthSeer looked to be forcing theirs, concern and fear apparent on their faces.

CHAPTER SEVENTEEN

King Haelen directed a guard to show Cole and Shaeleen to a room in which they could get a meal, then he turned to his uncle, General Archer. "Please make sure the two are not disturbed, General."

Shaeleen knew that the king was really telling Archer to have a guard watch over them. At that moment, Shaeleen didn't really mind. She felt as if a fog had lifted from her mind, as well as her body. She felt better than she had in a long time—even before the poison—and she surmised it was the now-constant influence of the HealingStone. Small as it was, besides the TruthStone, it was the most powerful of the stones of power.

As she was ushered out of the room by General Archer, Shaeleen stopped at the threshold and turned back around. The king, his TruthSeer, and the wizard had moved together and were talking in quiet tones.

"Haelen," Shaeleen said. Gasps sounded around her, and Cole elbowed her in the ribs. "Your Highness," she added more sweetly. "We are not done talking yet. Before we leave, there are words you need to hear." The king opened his mouth, but she cut him off with the wave of her hand. "Later, after we eat."

She turned and followed Cole and the guards into the hallway. She was surprised at how bright the castle appeared now that her full vision was back. Candelabras hung every dozen feet or so down the hallway outside of the king's room. They were led down a broad staircase, a different one than they had come up earlier. Shaeleen ran her hand over the smooth banister, appreciating the fine workmanship. Soft carpet cushioned her steps as they descended. As they reached the main floor, curious onlookers stopped and tried not to stare, but Shaeleen could see them talking in low voices to each other as she walked by.

She and Cole were escorted to a private dining room. A table that would normally seat at least thirty people ran the length of the room, high-backed chairs around its perimeter. Word had run ahead of them, and two place settings were set in the middle. The general pulled a chair out for Shaeleen, while Cole sat down opposite her. She faced the window, and though it was dusk outside, bright lights close to the castle showed her a small flower garden around the patio adjacent to the dining room.

"Are you not eating with us, General?" Shaeleen asked.

General Archer shook his head. "No, but I will be outside the room if you need anything."

Shaeleen smiled. "Keeping us from being disturbed or keeping us prisoners?" She cocked an eyebrow up at him.

The general let out a bark of a laugh. "Keeping you safe, miss."

"Safe from whom?" she teased.

His demeanor grew serious. "You really should be more careful, young TruthSeer. The king is not as compliant as you may think he is."

Shaeleen opened her mouth to respond, but a trio of servers came through a side door with plates of steaming food. The general nodded his head to Cole and left through the door they had entered, closing it behind him.

"He is a good man," Cole said.

Shaeleen looked at him questioningly as the servants placed platters of sliced beef, fried vegetables, and fresh baked rolls in front of them.

"General Archer is a man of honor," Cole said. "He will keep us safe."

"How do you know?"

Cole smiled but said nothing, apparently waiting for the servants to leave. Right before the last one left, Shaeleen called him back.

"Sir, would you happen to have anything sweet in there?"

The man smiled, and his eyes lit up. "You could smell it, couldn't you?"

"Oh, yes." Shaeleen sniffed the air around her. "If I would guess, some kind of fruit pie with a very sweet filling."

The servant laughed and clapped his hands. "Very talented nose you have there, miss. Maybe you should be a chef."

Shaeleen's smile dimmed slightly. "Oh, if life were that easy."

The man nodded his head as if he understood. "Well, we can't all have the privilege of creating masterpieces. I'll go and fetch you a piece."

Shaeleen smiled her thanks, then turned back to Cole. "Sometimes it would be nice to create something good. I feel like all I do is destroy."

Cole glanced up from shoveling a generous forkful of meat from the tray to his plate. "Shae, don't think that. You don't destroy things."

Shaeleen shook her head and stabbed a fork into a tasty spear of summer squash. She took a few bites and chewed slowly, thinking about what she had done. "I've taken stones of power from four kingdoms, hurt Orin, caused a mess in Verlyn, left Basil alone, and almost destroyed you. Everywhere I turn, I seem to bring trouble."

Cole chewed his own bites of beef, took a drink of chilled juice, and sat back. With a twinkling in his eyes, he tried to lighten the mood. "You were always trouble, sister—that didn't start with the stone."

"Hey," Cole yelled when Shaeleen picked up a roll and threw it at him. He dodged it with speed, and it hit the wall behind him. He surveyed the room and looked toward the doorway. "Shae, you can't do that."

Shaeleen stuck her tongue out at him, and they returned to their food. The two ate in silence for a few minutes, enjoying their first good meal in days. Faint sounds of the evening bustle of the castle could be heard behind the doors. Shaeleen took a deep breath and felt the powers swirl through her.

"Do you really trust Archer?" Shaeleen finally asked.

Cole nodded and swallowed a last bite of bread. "I held the TruthStone. I could tell he was a good man. He serves his king well, even if he doesn't think everything he is doing is right. That takes a lot of honor and inner strength."

Shaeleen nodded, feeling the truth of Cole's words, now that she held the TruthStone again. "Then I think I will ask for him to accompany us to South Bay. We could use an ally."

Cole seemed to agree with her.

The side door opened, and the servant from earlier came in with two plates of pie. Shaeleen clapped her hands in joy and smiled wide. She looked down at the confection as he set it in front of her. Sweet berries poked out from under a browned crust, and a generous dollop of whipped cream covered the top. After setting down the two plates, the servant reached into his apron pocket and pulled out something else. Shaeleen lifted her head up as high as she could to see what it was.

"I thought you might appreciate this," the servant said. "I have a feeling you have had a hard day." He reached his hand out, and Shaeleen put hers forward and took a piece of chocolate from him. It was about the size of a walnut and had white icing drizzled on it. He nodded for her to take a bite.

"Mmmm," Shaeleen hummed. A soft caramel middle with bits of nut slid out of the hard chocolate shell. "That's wonderful!"

Cole laughed. "She does have a sweet tooth." The man offered Cole one also, but he shook his head. "The pie is more than enough for me, sir. Thank you for making my sister so happy."

Shaeleen popped the rest of the chocolate into her mouth, relishing the taste on her tongue. Before swallowing, her eyes brightened up. "We should take you with us."

The servant laughed heartily. "It's enough to know that my creations are appreciated, miss." He reached over to take their food plates. "Now let me take these out of the way."

Shaeleen and Cole finished their pie and sat quietly for a

moment. Then Shaeleen let out a long sigh. "I guess we can't stay here forever."

"You want to talk to the king again? Is that wise? He's not very happy with us."

"He needs to hear what I have to say. I need to warn him like all the others. His actions may not warrant it, but he needs the warning just the same."

"Why, Shaeleen," Cole said with a smile as he stood, "that's the most honorable thing I've heard you say in a while."

Shaeleen shot him a mock look of anger. "I'm not doing it for him, but for his people."

"Aww." Cole laughed. "You've spoiled it already." He moved to the door and knocked on it. General Archer immediately opened it. Shaeleen left the room first, turning to the general as she passed.

"We require your presence when we meet with the king, Archer," she said with a smile. "My brother informs me that you are an honorable man, and I need an ally right now."

General Archer coughed and glanced at Cole for help. Cole shrugged his shoulder and followed behind Shaeleen.

"I would do as she asks, General," Cole said. "She usually gets her way in the end."

"So I've seen," General Archer mumbled and motioned with his hand for them to follow him. Before going to the king's chambers, he brought them to another room where two servants greeted them.

Shaeleen grew suspicious. "What is this, Archer?"

"I think a change of clothes will go a long way as you meet with King Haelen again."

Shaeleen let out a sigh of relief and nodded her agreement. She and Cole took a few minutes to change into newly supplied clothes and wash their faces. When they left the room, rather than going upstairs to the king's chambers, they moved farther down the hall on the first floor. They entered another room, this one more like a small office. Half a dozen chairs sat in front of a desk. A colorful tapestry hung behind the desk, a smaller version of the one upstairs. Shaeleen studied the embroidery in the tapestry and tried to guess how they made it with such detail. It was a scene of Mt. Eyvindr on Verlyn, its snowy peak contrasting nicely with a bright sky. She was drawn to it and took a step forward.

"Exquisite, isn't it?" General Archer said.

Shaeleen nodded. "What's on the other side of the mountain, do you think?"

Both Cole and the general gave her a questioning look.

"The south and east side of the island are desert," the general answered. "So I have heard. I have never been there."

"Hmmm." Shaeleen felt drawn to the mountain for some reason.

"What is it, Shae?" Cole asked.

"I don't know. Something I need to understand is right on the tip of my mind," Shaeleen said.

Before any more discussion could be had, the door opened and in walked King Haelen, with the TruthSeer and wizard in tow. Their countenances didn't look any friendlier than before.

The king moved to the chair behind the desk and motioned them all to sit in front of him. Cole sat down next to Shaeleen and whispered in her ear, "Take it easy on him. He's sick."

Shaeleen nodded and turned to the king. She took a deep breath and tried to be more diplomatic than she had ever been in her life—it was not easy. "Sire," she began with a small smile. "I am sorry that things turned out like they did. The gathering of stones from the other kingdoms has gone more smoothly. But time was of the essence, and my life hung in the balance."

The king, looking even more haggard than earlier, nodded. "Now that you have taken our HealingStone, what happens to me? To my life? I have no heirs."

It finally clicked with Shaeleen. All this time the king was reluctant to give up his stone, small as it was, because he thought it was the only thing keeping him alive. The only thing keeping the kingdom from falling to vying factions.

"Sire, we have healers," General Archer said.

The king gave him a look that said he should be quiet. It irked Shaeleen, and she let it show a bit. "Why do you hate your uncle so, King Haelen?" Shaeleen asked.

The question caught all in the room by surprise.

"I . . . I don't hate him," the king said.

Shaeleen felt the familiar pain in her gut at the same time as Julianna did. They both looked at each other, then back to the king.

"Try again," Shaeleen said.

The king let out a long sigh, then spoke. "My father, myself, and my uncle"—he waved an arm toward the general— "were up north in Fisher's Landing a few years ago. My father hadn't been feeling well and wanted a relaxing weekend of fishing. The second day we were there, Archer wanted to venture farther out in the sea, where larger fish were. My father and I disagreed, as it looked like the waves were growing rough—the sign of an incoming storm. But Archer took us out anyway. A great storm arose, and we were tossed around, barely holding on for our lives."

Shaeleen watched Archer, who held his head in his hands, looking down at the red and gold carpet beneath his feet.

"A huge wave came along and pushed us back toward the shore," the king continued. "Archer lost control of the ship, and we continued to be pounded by larger and larger waves. The salt cliffs loomed up in front of us. Our boat turned sideways, and the next wave smashed us into a huge rock. The jolt threw both me and my father to the side of the ship about twenty feet apart, then the ship began to turn over. I yelled for Archer to save my father—the king of Shema." King Haelen paused, as if reliving the scene in his mind.

Shaeleen sat on the edge of her seat. Cole gave her a questioning glance. She nodded back to him. Every word spoken so far was true.

The king continued, speaking softer now. "Archer froze as the ship tipped further. He took a step toward my dad, then seeming to betray him, moved back as my father began to fall off the boat. Instead, he raced over to me and grabbed me, pulling me back safely into the boat. I yelled at him to save my father, but he didn't do it. He let him fall off the boat." Tears appeared in the corners of the king's eyes. "He was smashed between the rocks and ship and died instantly." The king turned to Archer, who still had his head down. "Why did you hate him so?"

A hush filled the room. There was something unsettling to Shaeleen at the end of the king's story. Something wasn't right. She glanced at the TruthSeer and saw a similar question in her own eyes.

Slowly, as if moving through thick mud, General Archer raised his head. Tears filled his bloodshot eyes. "I loved your father, Haelen. I worshiped the ground he walked on. He was the best of all of us. He was kind, strong, fair, honorable, but he was always sick—like you. He hated it. He struggled to appear strong to our people, but he felt like they talked about him behind his back. It broke his heart. He loved them all so much."

The king hung on Archer's every word.

"Your father wanted that trip to be special for you. He knew it might be the last trip he would be able to make. You see, he was terribly sick, and as you know, the HealingStone had been stripped small through the years to keep our people strong and healthy. He hid it from you and your mother, but he was dying." Archer struggled to find his words for a moment before continuing. "I don't know if he had days, months, or a year to live—none of us know our time for certain."

The king opened his mouth to ask a question, but Archer held up his hand to still his words. "Let me finish. It is time you know." Archer stood up and paced the room a few times. "When our boat crashed and your father was thrown to the side, I wanted nothing more than to save him—my brother that I had grown up with for almost fifty years, my lord, my beloved king—but he was hurt badly when he hit the side of the boat.

When I moved to help him, he spoke to me in a whisper. He ordered me—as the king—to . . ." Archer stopped pacing and stood behind his chair, hands gripping the back of it, trying to gain control of his emotions. "As his last act as king of Shema, he ordered me to save you, Haelen. In his final act, he thought not of himself but of his beloved kingdom. He knew he didn't have much longer to live, even if he did survive the shipwreck, and he couldn't take the chance of you falling overboard and dying, leaving the kingdom without a king."

The king stood up, tears streaming down his tired face. His mouth opened and closed a few times, but no words came out.

Archer faced him. "I never hated your father, Haelen. I loved him enough to let him go and save his son instead."

King Haelen took a few steps forward, hand moving on the desk for support. Archer took a few steps forward as well. With a last quick step by both of them, they embraced and let years of misunderstanding melt away.

CHAPTER EIGHTEEN

Shaeleen felt her own heart soften at the embrace between Haelen and Archer, and a sudden realization came to her—whether through the IntelligenceStone or just through her own heart—that she may have misjudged others the same way that Haelen had. The thought brought shame, and she vowed to judge others better and give them the benefit of the doubt.

The king walked back and sat down behind his desk. Archer returned to his chair. After taking a few moments to compose himself, the king looked back at Shaeleen. She knew instantly the question that was still on his mind.

"My lord." She bowed her head more reverently to the king this time. "I was given this TruthStone only a few months ago. I was never given any training, other than a small book of notes by former TruthSeers. I was given a charge by a keeper of the stones from Verlyn to gather all the other stones of power across Wayland. My task is to restore the full power of the stones to Wayland once again—but I don't really understand how that will happen."

The king nodded, then TruthSeer Julianna spoke. "You are a very dangerous young woman, Shaeleen," Julianna said. "The amount of power you now hold is staggering. How can you not have a plan for what you will do with it? You could destroy us all with your power!"

Shaeleen sat forward on her seat and turned to look at Julianna. "Don't you think I haven't thought about that?" *I don't want to be the monster,* she thought to herself before continuing. "I can be dangerous, you are right, but only to those who oppose me and the task I've been given."

Her words seemed to send Julianna back into her seat further, a look of fear crossing her face as she looked down.

Shaeleen stood up and walked over to Julianna. Bringing the power of the TruthStone down upon Julianna, Shaeleen had to make sure she wasn't tainted by the shadow. "Whom and what do you serve, Julianna?"

The TruthSeer's head whipped up, almost as if by Shaeleen's willing it so. She glared at Shaeleen for ten long seconds, then let out a puff of air, and a resigned look spread across her face. "I serve the truth, TruthSeer Shaeleen, and I acknowledge your supremacy in this."

Wizard Martin let out a gasp next to her. "Julianna?"

She turned to him. "It is true, Martin. All of it. She tells the truth and has more power than me or you or anyone else I know. She is—"

"The prophesied one," the king finished the statement. "The one to bring the stones of power back."

Shaeleen nodded. "But there are those who oppose that. This is what I must warn you about. There are shadow keepers —keepers who serve a ShadowStone, a power that wants to bring all power back to Verlyn. Recently the gathering of keepers, as well as the council of Verlyn, have outlawed magic in Wayland and are not allowing those from Wayland into Sylvermoor. The shadow keepers are wreaking havoc in the kingdoms of Wayland and want to take all magic back for themselves."

"So we are right to shut ourselves off from the outside," the king said, looking at Archer.

Archer stayed silent and watched Shaeleen.

"I don't know," Shaeleen said. "It may take us banding together to win, but maybe you will be safe here. I really don't know. I have to get to South Bay in Althea and retrieve the HearingStone—the last stone—before returning to Verlyn."

"But isn't that what the shadow keepers would want you to do—bring them back all this power?" Julianna said. "It's better to keep it on Wayland."

Shaeleen shook her head. "I don't know yet how to defeat the shadow keepers, though I have a few ideas, but I do know I need to get to Verlyn to replenish the stones. As you well understand, they have shrunk and barely have any strength remaining."

The king nodded. "I know that all too well. We need to restore them again. We need the full power of the stones." He coughed, as if to emphasize the point of his own sickness.

Shaeleen smiled with compassion. "Use the healers you do have for now. I hope to return here sometime in the future with better news for you."

The king nodded and stood. "What else can we do for you?"

Shaeleen noticed the new reconciliatory tone of King Haelen's words now that they all had a better understanding of things. "I would ask two things. First, do you have any men available to send to the aid of Prince Basil in Galena? He is trying to hold part of Galena for himself against his cruel brother, Calix, and Commander Kerr from Gabor."

"Shae," Cole spoke up. "Calix is the rightful heir by law. You can't supersede the law. It's not right."

"I agree," Archer said with a nod of acknowledgment to Cole. "If we are to keep Wayland intact, we must work within the bounds of law."

Shaeleen let out a deep breath and mumbled, "Honorable men." She thought to phrase it differently. "Basil has said as such. However, there is nothing unjust about standing up against a tyrant and protecting what you have from being taken or destroyed unfairly."

Cole nodded. "I can understand that."

"Me too," Archer said.

It was hard sometimes for Shaeleen to live among men with such a strict honor code. "All right then, a battalion of men to hold the line at Basil's camp and to make sure that Calix or Commander Kerr stop rampaging across the land and destroying towns."

The king nodded. "I can do that and still stay safe here in Lightfort. As you have seen, it is difficult to get to."

Shaeleen only grunted, still thinking about Galena. "When the time comes, I might have to do something about Calix if he won't see reason in this." Cole gave her a harsh glance, but she ignored it for now. "Second thing." She returned to her requests for King Haelen. "We would like supplies and for General Archer to accompany us to South Bay in Althea. I need to retrieve the HearingStone."

General Archer turned to her, surprised. "Why me?"

Before Shaeleen could answer, King Haelen said, "Because the best general in all of Wayland should accompany the prophesied TruthSeer and help to protect her. This will help to offset some of the trouble we have caused her today."

Shaeleen smiled at the king. "Thank you, sir."

"I can see reason, when it is pointed out to me in the right way," he said, a bit of censure in his voice.

Shaeleen looked down for a moment, then brought her head up, all business again. "Do we go by sea from West Bay or down the Cadyn River?"

"The Cadyn," the general said right away. "It is full and fast this time of year and easy to navigate. It is the most direct route."

Shaeleen smiled and clapped her hands. "Already showing your worth, Archer. Well then, we leave first thing in the morning." She stood up as if to dismiss the group.

A hiss came from Wizard Martin, but King Haelen waved his hand in the air.

"It's all right, Martin. She is the hope of Wayland, and as I heard from General Archer originally, they are outside of the law and not beholden to any authority or king."

"A dangerous woman for sure," said Julianna, then her eyes softened somewhat. "Just be careful, my dear. Not everyone is as understanding and accommodating as we are."

Shaeleen laughed. "Accommodating, indeed. I've had enemies that have treated me better." Her mind went instantly to the young Shadow Keeper Taegen. She still hoped to be able to turn him back to the light. *Just one item on a long list of things to do to save the world!*

* * *

By midday the next day, Shaeleen, Cole, and General Archer stood on the shores of Lake Cadyn at the mouth of the Cadyn River going south. Shaeleen turned around and looked at Lightfort sitting in the middle of the lake. She could see it brighter and clearer than when they had first arrived. It was a beautiful city, and she hoped it would stay that way before the shadow keepers found a way to infiltrate it.

They had a medium sized rowboat full of supplies. They would all take turns rowing, though the flow of the river would do most of the work for them.

Shaeleen was anxious to leave, as it could take their group five to seven days to reach South Bay in good conditions. A summer storm, raiders, or any number of other things could lengthen that time frame. An anxiousness was rising inside her day by day. The confrontation with the shadow keepers was growing closer.

Just one more stone.

CHAPTER NINETEEN

The Cadyn River emptied out of Lake Cadyn at a fairly good rate. Shaeleen hoped the small rowboat they were in would get them safely to South Bay. General Archer sat in the back of the rowboat with a tiller and steered, while Shaeleen and Cole sat in the middle and front of the boat, respectively. Periodically, Cole would use a double handled paddle to help steer around an outcropping of rock or navigate a small bend in the river.

Shaeleen, without much to do at the moment, took in the scenery around her and thought about what might lie ahead. Her left hand hung over the side of the boat, and she let it skim the top of the water. The river was wide and flowed originally from the northern Myr Mountains on the border between Shema and Gabor, then into Lake Cadyn, splitting around Lightfort before flowing south all the way to the sea at South Bay. It was the only landmark that ran the entire length of the continent of Wayland.

Since Shaeleen had gathered the HealingStone into the TruthStone, her strength from the poisoning was returning remarkably quickly. She knew there wasn't much left of the HealingStone, which told her how potent it actually was. The combined strength of all the stones together was almost a constant buzz in her head now. Well, not exactly a buzz. *More like a restless energy that is building and won't stop.*

Thoughts of the shadow keepers—Georrod, Dunstan, Hutchin, Amara, as well as others tainted by the shadow whether they had a ShadowStone or not—ran through her mind. There was Solanna, Erwin, and maybe even Calix and Wizard Faegon, Orin's mother and the other founders at the compound. With Prince Brevin their leader, how many more were there on the island of Verlyn? Her thoughts turned to Taegen. In her mind, she hadn't named him as a shadow keeper—because she hadn't wanted to admit that—but he was.

The boat hit a rough spot, and Shaeleen grabbed the side with both hands while the general yelled orders to Cole on how to steer through the rapids. Water sprayed up on them. It was a nice respite from the hot summer day. To Shaeleen's left, lush grasslands went on for as far as she could see; to her right, they were approaching a thick bunch of trees.

"The forest will continue until we pass through the Great Mountain Divide," the general offered, noticing Shaeleen's attention on the trees.

"It's so large," Shaeleen said, taken in by the sheer size of it all. Having grown up on the coast, she hadn't been around much forest—until being shipwrecked in the jungles of Verlyn, but that was different.

The general chuckled. "You obviously haven't been to the Myr and Cadyn forests up north. You could be lost in there for weeks without ever finding your way out."

Shaeleen shivered. "Up until about two and a half months ago, I had barely traveled off the peninsula of Stronghaven."

"And you, Sir Cole?" asked the general, raising his voice to be heard over the water.

"We're just the humble children of a carpenter, General," Cole said, glancing back with a smile for Shaeleen. "Before Shaeleen named me her wizard, I was quite shy. It was Shaeleen who encouraged me to learn the sword. I wanted to join the king's guard or the army when I turned eighteen and serve Galena."

"Now he serves me instead," Shaeleen said with a laugh.

The general joined in the laughter. "From what I can see, that could be much more difficult than the king's guard."

"You have no idea," Cole said.

Shaeleen dipped a hand in the water and flung it back into General Archer's face and then a scoop forward to Cole's back. Both men yelled out but laughed. The first part of the day passed quickly, and soon they were past the rough spot. They continued to float down the river.

Shaeleen was thinking about the last few months when an idea came to her. "What if we use the power of the SpeedStone to propel us forward faster? Orin rowed with his powers to get us to the shore in Gabor."

"I don't know, Shaeleen." Cole turned around to face the other two.

"This man, Orin, is a friend of yours?" General Archer asked.

Shaeleen glanced down for a moment. She still felt bad about what she had done to him in Mistport. *But I didn't take his powers away. That was a shadow keeper!* "Yes, he is a good friend," Shaeleen said. "A young man really, not even fourteen yet, but in line for the throne of Antioch behind his father, Marcus."

General Archer nodded, clearly not understanding the entire story, but not pressing any further.

"Give me the paddle, Cole." Shaeleen reached her hands out. "I'll do it."

Cole arched his brows at her. "Don't you think it would be better for me—"

Shaeleen cut him off. "No, I don't. Your powers come with need. Mine are more stable."

"But you've never rowed before," Cole continued to argue.

"Yes, I have. I've rowed around the shore at Stronghaven."

"That's not the same," Cole said. "The water there was smooth and deep."

"I can do it, Cole," Shaeleen pushed. "Now give me the oars."

The general stayed quiet during the argument, but now he cleared his throat. "Miss Shaeleen, the river is different than a bay or a pool of water. There are rocks and sudden rapids. I still need to tend the rudder."

Shaeleen waved a hand in the air at him. She was sure she could do it. If Orin could, she could. *How hard can it be?* She just had to spin her arms quickly using the power of the SpeedStone and their boat would move downriver, saving them hours or maybe days if she could keep it up. With obvious misgivings, Cole handed her the long oar and sat down in front of her on his seat.

"Turn around and face the front," Shaeleen said to him as she lowered the oars into the water. "Let me know if anything is coming that I need to steer around."

Cole grumbled but turned around. "Just take it slow."

Shaeleen took a deep breath. She was a bundle of nervous energy and needed to use it on something. All this power in her and nothing to do had been driving her crazy. *I can do it!* She lowered the oar into the water on her right hand side and kept it there for a moment, feeling the pressure of the current on them. She drew upon the powers of the StrengthStone and felt the muscles in her arms grow tight, her veins rushing with the power. Looking ahead of them to a long, straight stretch, she pulled upon the power of the SpeedStone and began to turn first one arm and then another. The oar whisked through the water, up and out, then back down again on the other side. The boat lurched forward for a moment, rocking from side to side.

"Shae!" Cole turned back around and stared at her.

She smiled at him and began to row faster. The rocking settled down as the boat shot forward on the water. *I'm doing it!* Euphoria filled her. It felt wonderful, almost as if she were flying. She sped her arms up even faster.

"Steady there," she heard General Archer say from behind her.

It really was a breathtaking experience. The boat skimmed along the top of the water. The forest on her right was a blur of green and brown.

Shaeleen laughed out loud, her giddiness driving her forward. The power in her was truly amazing. It filled her and made her want to shout. *Is there anything I can't do?*

"Rapids on the left," Cole warned her.

She let General Archer turn the rudder while she kept rowing even faster.

"I can't turn it fast enough," the general yelled. "Slow down!"

The rapids didn't scare Shaeleen. If she rowed faster, they could just fly over the top of them.

"There's a turn in the river up ahead," Cole yelled. The boat tipped to the left, and he had to grab on to stay upright.

Shaeleen had another sudden thought—the blue IntelligenceStone at work. Hot sun and sunshine filled the air. While continuing to row from side to side, she briefly closed her eyes and drew up on the power of the TruthStone and pushed her spirit out into the bright light. She looked down and saw the three of them in the boat. She couldn't believe how fast she was rowing. The strength and speed she held was incredible. The power of the HealingStone kept her body from getting tired.

She glanced ahead. From this vantage point, she could foresee any obstacles in her way and compensate for them ahead of time. It was perfect. Looming to the south on both sides of the river, the Great Mountain Divide rose, its snow-capped peaks remarkably high in the air. She saw the turn ahead of them that Cole had warned of. The river narrowed somewhat, but if she stayed to the center, she should be fine. Keeping her body rowing down below in the boat, she scouted the area ahead of them in her mind.

Coming to the turn, General Archer yelled, "Slow down. You're going too fast."

But General Archer didn't understand the power she held. Something in the back of her mind pricked her consciousness—it was definitely the power of the

IntelligenceStone—and she realized that what she had felt earlier was not the stone itself, but her own desires. Looking down, she saw they were indeed taking the turn too fast. She wouldn't be able to stay in the middle of the river as it turned right. The boat now was moving at a startling speed toward a huge rock rising out of the water next to the left bank.

"Shaeleen!" Cole screamed.

"Hold on!" Archer bellowed.

Shaeleen tried to stop her arms from spinning, but by being outside of her body, she lost control. She tried to release the power of the stones and return to the boat. Everything was happening so fast she became confused about where she actually was. Below her, she saw the boat about to strike the rock and knew she had made a horrible mistake.

Her spirit returned to her body, and she stopped rowing. It was too late. They hit the rock hard, and the sound of shattered wood filled the air. Archer and Cole yelled out at the same time as the boat slammed sideways into the monstrous rock, throwing all three of them into the air.

No, I can't die! Thoughts of everything she had done flew through Shaeleen's mind at incredible speed. She had been greedy and wanted an outlet for her power. She hadn't listened to Archer or Cole, and now they were all going to die because of her poor choices. Was this how it all ended? Would the shadow keepers win after all because of her own foolishness?

It was a harsh reality to face.

CHAPTER TWENTY

Shaeleen felt herself fly up out of the boat and, out of the corner of her eye, she saw Cole falling toward the water and Archer, hands flailing, heading toward the rock they had smashed into.

What good is all this power if I can't use it to help people? The thought raced through her mind, and she pulled upon all the stones of power—their power coming to their master without reserve or complaint. The IntelligenceStone directed her actions without conscious thought. She pulled upon the SpeedStone, took the speed, and reversed it—slowing them down instead of speeding things up.

Time stopped around Shaeleen.

It was a strange experience. She hung in the air, five feet above the boat. Her brother was flying out toward the water, arms outstretched and fear across his face. The general still hung in the air behind her, his head mere feet from shattering against the sharp, brown rock. Splinters of the boat froze in midair, and white droplets of rushing water around the rock suspended around the three of them, waiting for gravity to complete their motion. But the stones of power were stronger than gravity.

With Shaeleen's next thought, the power of the TruthStone coupled with the HealingStone formed a blanket of green and pink light that wrapped itself around each of them individually, a slim strand connecting them back to Shaeleen. Taking a deep breath, she saw the grassland on the eastern edge of the river and directed the strand of light that connected them toward the grass. They sped toward the shore.

With a final thought, the sounds of the river, the crashing of the boat, and the yells of the men came back full force as time resumed.

Shaeleen put her arm forward and used a spell of opposing speed to slow their descent. She didn't have time to do much, so she still hit the ground hard. She rolled a half dozen times before coming to a stop. With a grunt, she pulled herself to her feet and looked around for Cole and Archer. Both men were on their backs several feet away. Archer had hit a tree, while Cole lay on a patch of grass.

"Cole! Archer!" she yelled. "I'm so sorry. Are you all right?"

She ran to Cole first and kneeled next to him. She shook him twice, and he opened his eyes. He looked at her with relief, but it was soon replaced with anger. He shoved Shaeleen's arm and got up on his knees.

"Where's Archer?" Cole said. His distress was apparent when he didn't use the general's title.

Shaeleen pointed, and both of them ran over to him. Cole leaned down first and moved him away from the tree. The general groaned with the movement, and his eyes flickered open.

"My back!" he bellowed, his deep voice filling the air around them. "I think I broke my back." Then his eyes closed, and he went still, but his chest rose and fell with light breaths.

Shaeleen leaned down to him and moved her hand toward his back.

Cole swatted her hand. "Haven't you done enough harm already?"

Shaeleen had never seen her brother so livid before. Veins popped out on the side of his neck, his eyes flashing dark and dangerous. He shook with barely held rage.

"I . . . I . . ." Shaeleen stuttered and looked down. What could she say? She deserved all of his anger. She had been foolish in trying to use her powers to speed the boat, with no thought for anyone else's safety.

Cole continued to glare at her, but she took a deep breath and turned back to Archer. "You can yell at me later, but right now, I might be able to heal him."

Cole shook his head as if he didn't believe her but moved back a bit to give her room. Shaeleen could hear his heavy breaths behind her. Shaeleen pulled the TruthStone out of its pouch and cradled it against Archer's chest with one hand while putting her other hand under him. His cotton shirt and leather vest were wet with water and sweat. She closed her eyes and summoned her powers. She felt warmth around both hands.

Reaching deep inside of Archer with her powers, she could feel the workings of his body. His breathing was strong, but his mind kept him unconscious to hold him from feeling too much of the pain in his back. The man was strong for his age—the effects of living in the kingdom of the HealingStone. People in Shema were known for living longer than people in other kingdoms. Archer didn't have access to an actual HealingStone, but the powers were strong in his blood. Shaeleen centered her focus there and used the small specks of the HealingStone she now had to bolster his own healing.

Opening her eyes, she saw the familiar green glow of the TruthStone surrounding the top half of his body. Feeling for the StrengthStone and SpeedStone, she used them to speed up his recovery. Shaeleen felt the stirrings of exhaustion. The hour of using the SpeedStone and the subsequent use of the other stones to get them out of the dangerous situation she'd caused were beginning to dampen the previous boundless energy she'd had earlier in the day.

With one hand still under Archer, she felt his muscles pull his bones back together. The warmth of the HealingStone rode on the StrengthStone and SpeedStone to begin fusing them back together. Shaeleen could feel it all working deep in her mind.

Lightheaded, she swooned and almost fell over, but Cole was at her side and used a strong arm to hold her up. She gave him a grateful look, but he ignored her.

"How is he?" Cole said, looking only at General Archer.

"He is healing," Shaeleen said, still concentrating. "I think my powers will be enough."

Cole grunted.

"Don't worry," Shaeleen said. "I won't steal your powers again."

"Shae!" Cole's voice raised in a warning. "Don't go there right now. Just heal Archer." His voice fell quiet, then a moment later, he sighed and in a softer voice said, "If you need my powers to heal him, you may."

Shaeleen wondered how her brother had so much good and compassion in him. She knew what it had cost him when she'd taken some of his power to heal herself, yet he was willing to do it again.

"He is a good man," Cole said to her questioning eyes. "He doesn't deserve this."

And that's what it came down to for Cole. Black and white. Good and bad. Right and wrong. Honor and injustice. How Shaeleen wished life was so easy for her. Being a TruthSeer required her to see things differently. The truth wasn't always right, and honor wasn't always good. Good people did bad things, and bad people did good things. *Am I a good person or bad?*

Suddenly, Archer's back came up off the ground. He opened his eyes, and a long wail came from his lips. Shaeleen pulled her shaky hands away from Archer, placing the TruthStone back in its pouch. "It's done."

With those words, she let the exhaustion take her. She fell backward to the ground, and darkness overcame her.

* * *

Shaeleen opened her eyes and looked up into the branches of an enormous oak tree. The sun still shone in the sky—she could see it through the leaves—but it was much lower than before. The faint sounds of the rushing river filled the background with a constant roar. Sniffing the air, Shaeleen smelled the smoky scent of fish cooking close by.

After blinking a few times and making a quick survey of

her body with her mind, she decided that she was all right and sat up. Less than a dozen feet away, Cole sat in front of a small fire, turning three fish on a homemade spit of sticks. Archer was resting on a flattened patch of grass opposite him, propping himself up on one side with his elbow. When he saw her looking over, he raised his eyebrows in greeting, the barest evidence of a grin on his lips.

Shaeleen groaned inside but stood up and walked over to the two men, bracing herself for the lectures that were sure to come. She knew she deserved harsh words and would accept them honorably. She would make her brother proud of her.

First, she walked to Archer. "General Archer, how are you feeling?"

"Why so formal, young Shaeleen?" The general gazed up at her. His eyes held pools of wisdom but also compassion and humor.

Shaeleen was surprised by the question. "It's just that . . . Well . . ." She stumbled on a correct answer. "It's just after all I've done . . ."

The general moved to sit up, a wince crossing his face. "I would think after all we've been through in the last few days, we should be on a first-name basis." He said this to Shaeleen, but also glanced at Cole, who nodded back at Archer. Shaeleen followed their looks. When Cole saw her watching him, he turned back to his task.

"Smells wonderful," Shaeleen said, trying to draw Cole into the conversation. His quiet demeanor was worse than yelling would've been. But thinking about it, when had Cole ever yelled at anyone?

"I hear I have you to thank for healing my back," Archer said, moving his body to sit with his legs in front of him. He leaned back and placed his hands on the ground behind him.

Shaeleen grimaced. "You're welcome," she said with embarrassment. "But I'm afraid I wouldn't have had to heal you if I had listened to you and my brother in the first place. I'm sorry."

"It's a hard lesson for anyone to learn, but especially those in leadership positions of power or responsibility," Archer said.

Shaeleen sat down at a place on the grass where she could look at both Archer and her brother. "But I'm not a leader."

Archer barked out a laugh.

"And that's been one of your problems, Shae." Cole spoke for the first time since she'd awoken. "You think you can be the same carefree person you were before . . ."

Shaeleen started to interrupt, but Cole flashed her a look that made her hesitate. She took a deep breath and listened instead.

While talking, Cole took the three fish off the spit and set them on a small pile of large leaves he had gathered. "The moment you were given the TruthStone, your life changed, Shae. A TruthStone! Have you ever thought of that? Of the five kingdoms and Verlyn, there are only five true TruthSeers; even if you were one of them, that would be amazing. Five out of the entire continent. But you are so much more. You are to be one of the greatest TruthSeers ever in our history—outside of all kingdoms, beholden to none."

He paused while he passed each of them a fish on a large leaf. Shaeleen tried to take in what she was hearing. The things he said frightened her to the bone. After giving the fish out, Cole sat down near her. Archer moved closer.

"You now have a TruthStone embedded with the IntelligenceStone, StrengthStone, SpeedStone, HealingStone, and in a few days, the HearingStone will join them there in your pocket. In your pocket, Shae!" Cole's voice grew louder. "Do you understand that? Do you really understand who you are?"

Shaeleen wiped her eyes. If he'd simply yelled at her, that would've been better. Anger and blame she could deal with. But responsibility . . . That was hard.

Cole peeled a piece of fish away from the bone and popped it in his mouth. "Shaeleen, when this started, I pledged my life to your safety and the pursuit of truth. That pledge still holds; I would not dare waver on my oath. But I need you to step up and be who you are meant to be. You are the prophesied TruthSeer—the one to gather all the stones and restore their glory to the five kingdoms. As part of that, it seems you are also going to destroy the shadow keepers, saving Verlyn along the way. All of us look to you to save us."

Silent tears streamed down Shaeleen's cheeks as she faced the gravity of the situation for the first time since being given the TruthStone. She was only fifteen years old. Why did this responsibility come to her? How could she do all of what Cole said?

Cole reached over and tenderly wiped the tears from her cheeks. Her body shook, trying to keep from sobbing. She turned to Archer, who seemed to be purposefully looking down at his fish instead of at her and Cole. She didn't blame him. He was most likely laughing at her inside. *How could this young slip of a girl save us all?* was what he was probably thinking.

"Shae," Cole called her attention back to him.

Shaeleen took a deep breath. What more could he say? Hadn't he said enough to make her feel overwhelmed and undeserving of the power she held?

"Shae," he began again. "There is one more thing."

Shaeleen braced for more responsibility.

"Out of all the people in the five kingdoms or in Verlyn, I am glad it is you who have been given that responsibility. Because I know of no other fifteen-year-old woman who could do what you have to do. I believe in you, Shae! I always have. I told you I didn't want your power before; I couldn't handle it. But you . . . you keep going, no matter what happens. You've been to four kingdoms and Verlyn in less than three months. Who else could manage that? You are incredible, and I am happy to be your guardian protector wizard and your brother."

"Oh, Cole!" Shaeleen let out a sob and threw herself into her brother's arms, hugging him fiercely. "I don't deserve such a good brother."

After a moment, Archer wiped his hands on the grass and spoke. "Quite a speech there, young man. I think greatness runs in your family, and not just with your sister. You are destined for a high calling also, I would guess."

Cole laughed. "Me?"

Shaeleen felt similar stirrings of the truth at Archer's words. The stone revealed to her a brief image of the future, and she smiled and wiped the remaining tears from her eyes. "Archer speaks the truth, and the truth is one thing I know for sure."

CHAPTER TWENTY-ONE

That night, the three of them decided to sleep under the stars on the grassy plain. They took turns keeping watch, but nothing bothered them. Early in the morning, Cole brought up more fish from the river.

"How are you catching those?" Shaeleen asked. She knew her brother didn't have any fishing gear. Both boats had been lost downstream, and they had no supplies with them at all.

Cole blushed and sheepishly studied the fish in his hands.

"Cole?"

He looked back up at her and grinned. "I used speed and strength to catch them and started the fire with the power also."

Shaeleen was surprised. "I thought you didn't have much control over your powers unless you were protecting me."

Cole shook his head. "You still don't get it all, do you? Everything we do right now—*everything*—is for you, Shae. You need to be fed and stay strong so that you can accomplish your tasks. That's why it works."

Interesting.

"So now what?" she asked the two men.

Archer pointed downriver toward the canyon that opened up between the Great Mountain Divide. "Even after resting last night, we made good time down the river with your speed."

Shaeleen tried not to smile, but it was hard to hide her grin.

"It still wasn't right, Shae," Cole said to her, but he wasn't angry.

"There is a settlement a bit before the mountains," Archer said. "We can walk there by nightfall and find boats. We are technically in Antioch on this side of the river, but I know a few men who live here. There is a lake on the other side of the mountains that, if we get a small sailing boat, we should be able to make good time on. After that, it's just a short trip down the rest of the river through the forest and into South Bay. There are small villages along the way to get supplies and food."

"So two to three days to South Bay?" Shaeleen asked.

"At the longest," Archer said with an affirmative nod.

* * *

True to Archer's words, later that day, they came upon a small village where they were given a boat. They took the river to a small lake and traded that boat for a small sailboat the following day. Now they were in Althea. Once across the lake, they went back to the use of a rowboat, which carried them swiftly down the river and through a thick forest on the way to South Bay.

During this stretch of their trip, Shaeleen was quieter than usual. There was a lot to think about. Her brother was right about her attitude, but was he correct in what lay before them? Could she *save the world?* The TruthStone that sat so comfortably by her side seemed to say she could. Shaeleen jumped up with the excitement of it all.

"Shaeleen!" Archer yelled. "What are you doing?"

Cole turned around and gave her a bewildered look.

Feeling embarrassed, she slowly sat back down, careful not to rock the boat like she had when she stood up. "Sorry, I just realized something."

Mile by mile, as they grew closer to South Bay, her resolve grew harder and more determined. She remembered Cole's words about her destiny and had never felt any pain during his remarks. Cole was right; a lot of people did depend on her, even if they didn't know it. She needed to take this seriously.

I can do it.

The forest closed over them like a canopy, and the river took their boat forward, fast and smooth.

"There was talk at the last village of trouble in South Bay," Archer said.

Shaeleen rolled her eyes. *Why should it be any different here?* "What kind of trouble? I admit I don't know much about Althea."

Archer sat at the tiller and steered the boat, while Cole still sat up front, using the paddle when needed to keep the boat steady in the fastest part of the river. "Queen Emmony has recently married. Her previous husband met with an accident at sea about a year ago—got caught in a storm off the point of Hightower. Since she has remarried, she has been seen less and less."

Shaeleen had a feeling who her new husband might be. *A shadow keeper.* "Is she sick?"

"I don't know," Archer said with concern. "The people in

the village I spoke to said she hasn't been seen in a few weeks. She has twins—a girl and a boy—who have also disappeared."

Cole turned his head around to join in the conversation. "How old are the children?"

Archer thought for a moment. "They should be somewhere between your two ages. Sixteen or a bit older, I would guess."

"Hopefully the HearingStone is still safe," Shaeleen said. "I need to get to Verlyn soon."

"Let's take things easy this time," Cole said to Shaeleen. "I don't think it's the time and place to go storming in and demanding things."

Shaeleen bristled at the insinuation, but Cole smiled, and she realized he hadn't meant it as a criticism. She nodded to him. "You're right, my guardian wizard, though I have come to grips with who I am. Storming the castle and declaring who I am sounds somewhat fun." She winked at her brother and laughed.

"And dangerous," Cole said.

"Can't handle yourself, Wizard?" Shaeleen teased.

Cole shook his head at her and turned back around to paddle away from the edge as they wound around a curve in the river.

"I know people here," Archer offered. "Let me get some information first, then we can plan on how to proceed."

The forest thinned around them, and in another mile, the river began to grow wider. Up ahead, they could see the outlines of South Bay. A significant wall surrounded the city, but houses and farmlands had grown up outside of it. The city sprawled up the banks of the Cadyn River and spread west. Archer waved at a group of fisherman on the banks of the river, but they just turned inward, speaking to each other and pointing at the three of them.

"Not a very welcoming bunch," Shaeleen mumbled.

"Take us to the bank, Cole," Archer suggested. "Let's get out here."

About a mile from the city, they left their boat on the bank of the river and began walking into town. They passed a few other travelers who looked at Shaeleen and Cole, then picked up their pace and hurried on their way.

"We seem to be making people nervous," Archer said. "I surmise not many from Verlyn make it over here, and you two hold some resemblance to them."

"I would bet the queen's new husband does also," Shaeleen said, feeling the effects of the IntelligenceStone.

Cole looked over at her.

"Shadow keeper," Shaeleen said with a sigh.

"General," Cole said. "What do you think we should do?"

Archer glanced around nervously. "Don't call me that here, Cole. I have a feeling that we don't want any of our identities known right away. Let's find a place to clean up, eat, and get a change of clothes. Then I'll see what I can find out."

A ruckus was heard up ahead, and Shaeleen noticed a group of men and women blocking the road in front of them.

"Stay behind me," Archer said as they went to the edge of the group.

Shaeleen stood up on tiptoes to try to see better. "What's happening?"

"Shh," Cole said to her.

Shaeleen grunted and moved a bit to her right to find a place to see better. Jumping up and down, she finally saw a small group of what seemed to be soldiers, all dressed in black, holding two people between them. One of the captives was a young boy and the other a young girl. She couldn't see their faces, but they struggled against the soldiers.

"They're just children," a women in the front yelled. "Let them go."

The commander of the group put his hand up in the air to quiet the crowd. His broad shoulders and closely shaved head made him look even more menacing. "They have broken the law and will be dealt with accordingly."

What does that mean?

"What law?" yelled a man from the back, shaking his fist in the air. "We know of no law that makes it legal to take children away."

"King Cailu has informed us that it is now against the law to practice magic on Wayland," the captain said.

"He is not our king," yelled another man. "Where is Queen Emmony? Where are the twins?"

The crowd began to surge closer, and the captain's men who weren't holding the children stepped forward, swords out in front of them. Shaeleen glanced back to where Cole and Archer stood. Should they help these people? Cole could tell what she was thinking and shook his head at her not to interfere. She sighed and continued watching.

"The queen is unwell, and King Cailu has our best interest at heart," the commander tried to explain. "Magic is fading and no longer needed in Wayland. It is old-fashioned, a thing of the past. Embrace the new future!"

"Embrace the future!" the other soldiers repeated.

Shaeleen gasped, and a few heads turned her way. One man glared at her and pointed in her direction. "She's one of them," he yelled.

Shaeleen took a step back. Without noticing him moving, Cole stood by her side.

"What about lying low and not using our powers?" she whispered to him.

"I am here to protect you," Cole said. "It seems by doing nothing, you still find trouble." He smiled at her, but his eyes darted around the crowd.

Others turned from the captain to her and Cole.

"He's one of them too!" shouted a woman. "Witches from Verlyn. Just like the king."

"What have you done with our queen?" another woman, older than the rest, stepped closer to Shaeleen.

"Clear the way," the captain said. "What have we here?"

The broad-shouldered commander with two other guards in tow pushed through the growing crowd. People parted, allowing them to pass. Shaeleen looked past them to where the other soldiers held the children still. With the crowd to the sides now, she could see the children more clearly now. The girl turned her head and looked straight at Shaeleen.

"Abby." The word escaped her lips before she could think. The last she saw of the ship captain's daughter was when her father had taken them from Verlyn back to Stronghaven.

What was she doing here?

CHAPTER TWENTY-TWO

Abby smiled at Shaeleen and pulled against the soldier holding her, but the man held her tight. The commander looked from the girl and back to Shaeleen, taking in her eyes. A slight look of annoyance spread across his face. He clearly didn't know what to do or who Shaeleen was.

Standing as tall as she could—which wasn't much—she gave the commander a haughty look. "We are here to take the prisoners," Shaeleen said.

The commander eyed her up and down and laughed. "You?"

Cole stepped forward, following Shaeleen's lead. They looked enough like Verlynians that she hoped these men would follow their orders. Her brother put his hand on the hilt of his sword, and a faint light traveled up his arm.

"He has magic," said a younger man. "They're from Verlyn."

The crowd surged forward, closer to Cole and Shaeleen. General Archer had moved around and was now stationed at their back.

"Witches! All of them," a skinny lady yelled. A man next to her picked up a rock and threw it at Shaeleen.

Cole reached out with his power of speed and plucked the rock from the air. The crowd gasped. Another rock came flying, and he swatted it away. The commander of the soldiers looked around nervously. His six men were clearly outnumbered now. He slid around behind the group as they paid more of their attention to Cole and Shaeleen.

"Help is coming, Shaeleen." Abby's voice came out clear and loud over the group.

Shaeleen glanced around but didn't see anyone coming. A woman reached out her hand and grabbed Shaeleen by the wrist. Shaeleen's power was ready to strike, and strike she did. Pulling her arm away from the woman, she brought her other hand out in front of her and sent a blast of air, pushing the front of the group back against the others. They fell into each other, and everyone scrambled to get up, fear spreading across their faces.

"Shaeleen, help!" Abby's voice cried out again.

Shaeleen tried to run around the side of the gathering and saw the soldiers climbing on their horses, preparing to use the distraction to take the children away. At the same time, a low rumble ensued, and over a small rise to the west, a group of at least twenty horses came into view. *That's what Abby heard.*

Swords were raised in the air, and before the soldiers could get away, they were encircled by the newcomers. The crowd turned from Shaeleen and Cole to the newcomers. Two horses stepped forward—ridden by a young man and woman.

"The prince and princess," someone from the crowd cried out.

Cheers ensued, and the crowd gathered close around the commander and his soldiers. Shaeleen and Cole shrunk farther to the back.

"We should go," Archer whispered to them.

Shaeleen nodded, and they turned, walking quietly out farther west. They began walking up a small rise.

"Let them go, Commander," the prince ordered, his voice carrying in the air over the crowd to where Shaeleen, Cole, and Archer now walked.

Shaeleen stopped and turned around to watch the exchange.

"I'm sorry, Prince Raimund," the commander spoke. "The king has ordered all persons using magic to be cleansed."

Shaeleen's heart missed a beat.

"Shae." Cole grabbed her hand. "Let's go."

Memories of the time she and Orin had been cleansed by Shadow Keeper Georrod came flooding back into her, and her feet stayed glued to the ground. She couldn't let Abby go through that. It had taken Orin's power of speed and left him tainted by the shadow. She took a step back toward the group. Cole pulled her arm away, and she resisted.

The princess spoke up then. "They're just children, Commander." Her voice was high and smooth. "Surely, you can let them go into our care."

The commander turned back and forth between his own soldiers and the twenty men and women sitting on horses behind the twins. Fear crossed his face.

"Let them go," the crowd began to chant. "Let them go."

The commander nodded his head. "As you wish, Princess Noelle." He motioned to his men, and they let the children go. "But the king will hear about this interference."

The commander and his men jumped on their horses,

turned around, and raced back toward the city. The young boy went running to the crowd, where he was taken in a hug by a middle-aged woman. Abby stood still, unsure where to go.

"Shaeleen, think of the bigger picture," Archer said to her from farther up the rise. She turned to him and nodded, letting Cole pull her along. She hated being a leader if it meant leaving her friends behind, but Archer was right. If they returned to the crowd, they would be in danger. Obvious strong sentiments of hate existed between them and those from Verlyn—most likely brought on by the workings of their queen's husband during the last year.

They cleared the small rise, putting some distance between them and the crowd before turning south again toward the city.

"You two will have to lie low somewhere while I go into the city," Archer said.

Shaeleen pointed to a copse of thick trees to the southwest of them. "We can stay there. Just bring us some food when you get a chance and some clothes." She looked down at her own pants and shirt. They were dirty, and rips and stains covered them. She had been looking forward to a warm bath and a meal at an inn. "Doesn't seem fair that I am the most powerful person in Wayland, yet have to hide out in a thicket of trees," she mumbled.

"You need to get the HearingStone," Cole said. "But we have to keep you alive, too. Have you forgotten Lakeside so soon?"

Shaeleen grunted and turned with Cole to walk to the trees. But before they went more than a few steps, a low rumble was heard. As soon as Shaeleen's brain registered what it was, Raimund, Noelle, and their people rode over the small rise.

"Stop!" Raimund said to the three of them.

With twenty horses coming down on them, Shaeleen didn't have much choice. Archer walked back over to them. He and Cole drew their swords and stood in front of Shaeleen, while Shaeleen readied a spell. She hadn't left the crowd only to be taken by another group that hated her for her eyes.

A younger voice cried out, "Shaeleen!" Abby stuck her face out from behind Princess Noelle and waved at Shaeleen. Her smile ran from ear to ear.

Shaeleen put her hand on Cole's arm. "Lower your sword."

He glanced at her, then back at the group of riders in front of them. He lowered it, but still kept it drawn and in his hand.

Shaeleen studied Raimund and Noelle. Their faces were thin but healthy, and they held themselves in a way that let others around them know who they were. Their arms were toned and fit. Both had blond hair and tan skin, indicative of someone who spent much of their time outside on the coast. South Bay had a temperate climate that was nice most of the year. Shielded from the fog and storms by the peninsula of Hightower, Shaeleen had heard it was a favorite vacation spot for much of the nobility on Wayland.

Archer stepped forward and gave a nod. "Prince. Princess."

Surprise ran across the faces of the twins, but it was Noelle who spoke. "Uncle Archer! What are you doing here?"

"Uncle?" Shaeleen said to Archer.

He shrugged and said, "Later."

Shaeleen grunted, but now understood why she had been prompted to bring him along. She wondered briefly how many of her thoughts were her own these days and how many came from the stones themselves. She bristled a bit at being manipulated by anyone or anything.

Prince Raimund turned to a few of the other men. "Double up and give these people horses."

The men did as he asked. Shaeleen, Cole, and Archer each grabbed the reins of a horse and jumped up into a saddle. The prince motioned them forward. Shaeleen looked at Archer for confirmation, and he nodded. She trusted him, so they joined the group riding west, farther away from the city. After about twenty minutes, they turned north and entered a small trail into the forest. A few men stood waiting beside the path and, as soon as they passed, covered up the trail markings and their tracks. They rode slower now, having to bend around huge trees and duck under low-hanging branches.

After another hour of riding, they came to a sizable clearing in the middle of the woods. Shaeleen gazed around in surprise. A small village had been built here. A few crude buildings filled the area with dozens of tents interspersed throughout. Small vegetable gardens and a pen holding pigs and cows sat off to one side. The prince and princess dismounted, handing their horses over to a small boy. The others took their own horses to care for. Shaeleen, Cole, and Archer dismounted, and the prince motioned for a few other younger boys to take their horses for them as well.

Abby came running up to Shaeleen and gave her a big hug.

"What are you doing here?"

"Still trying to save the world." Shaeleen laughed. "And you? Last I saw, you and your father were in the Stronghaven harbor."

"We barely got out of there before Commander Kerr and King Calix closed the port," Abby said.

Shaeleen frowned at the news and wondered how Basil was doing. She shook her head to clear the thoughts.

"My father is securing a new ship at the port. I was out in the market and overhead someone talking—you know, with my powers," Abby said with wide eyes. "Someone noticed and told a guard. I ran, but you saw how that ended up."

"I'm sorry, Abby." Shaeleen felt anger beginning to rise again. "I'm here to take care of all that."

Abby nodded. "The prince and princess want to talk to you."

Shaeleen gave the young girl a quizzical look. A moment later, the prince and princess motioned for the three travelers to follow them. Shaeleen said her goodbyes to Abby and followed her brother and Archer. A clear creek ran in front of them, and the prince motioned for them to drink. After they drank, he smiled broadly at Archer and spread his hands to his side.

"What are you doing here, Uncle?" the prince asked.

Archer motioned to the twins, while speaking to Shaeleen and Cole. "This is Raimund and Noelle. Their father, the queen's first husband, is my younger brother."

Shaeleen nodded. "So Haelen is their cousin?"

Noelle's eyes flashed darkly at Shaeleen. "Yes, King

Haelen is our cousin. And who are you to speak his name so familiarly?"

Shaeleen realized the princess didn't seem to like her. It didn't matter to Shaeleen. She was not here to make friends, but Noelle better not get in the way of her mission. Archer paused a bit in the introductions and looked at Shaeleen. She nodded for him to proceed. Might as well let them know who she was.

"This is Shaeleen and her brother, Cole," Archer said. "Shaeleen is a TruthSeer and Cole, her wizard."

Cole bowed low to the twins. "Prince Raimund and Princess Noelle. It is our pleasure to meet you."

Noelle's face softened at Cole's gesture and words. Shaeleen let them all have their moment of decorum. She was more anxious to get to the HearingStone than share niceties.

"I hadn't heard one of the esteemed TruthSeers was traveling in such a disguise." Noelle laughed with a slight sneer, while looking Shaeleen up and down.

Shaeleen took a step forward. *Why, that little* . . .

Archer put a hand on her arm and pulled her back, then turned to Noelle. "Have some manners, Princess. Shaeleen may be the only person standing between you and the destruction of your people." Archer eyed the camp around them in the clearing with his eyebrows raised. "I take it things are not going well for your kingdom at the moment."

Noelle grunted, but Raimund laughed and motioned them all over to a crude table to sit down. "Let's talk civilly here." He smiled at Shaeleen. "I'm sure we've all been under a lot of stress."

CHAPTER TWENTY-THREE

A crude rectangular table had been set up at the edge of the small community. Planks of wood hammered carelessly into a few tall logs. Shaeleen looked up at Cole, who sat next to her and shook her head.

"Don't worry about the woodwork, Shae," Cole whispered. "We have bigger things to worry about. I have a feeling your special abilities may be tested during this conversation."

Shaeleen nodded her head. Across the table from her sat Noelle, Raimund, and Archer. Noelle seemed to have a permanent scowl on her face, while Raimund was more relaxed. She wondered who was older and hoped they wouldn't have a debacle in the succession of Althea like they had going on in Galena.

Archer turned to his nephew and niece. "First of all, do you know where your mother is?"

Raimund opened his mouth, but Noelle shook her head slightly and he closed it again. Well, now Shaeleen knew who was the oldest. *Too bad. Raimund has the better temperament to be a good ruler.*

Noelle glanced at Shaeleen and Cole before answering her uncle. "We don't know."

Lie! Shaeleen knew it as soon as the girl opened her

mouth. Bending over in pain—the first she had felt in a while—she placed her fists in her gut and tried to sit up straight.

Both Cole and Archer gave hard looks at Noelle. Archer spoke. "I told you she is a TruthSeer, Princess. You might want to watch your words."

"So you do know where your mother is?" Shaeleen asked the twins, glaring at Noelle.

"We suspect she is being held at an old family estate just off the castle grounds," Raimund said.

Noelle frowned at him but didn't stop him from talking.

"And I assume it is guarded well?" Shaeleen asked.

Noelle nodded. "King Cailu has some of his men there. He holds a tight rein on them, which isn't all that bad."

"Like the commander back on the road," Cole said.

Noelle and Raimund nodded.

"What are your thoughts on this law outlawing magic?" Shaeleen asked, the power of the IntelligenceStone and TruthStone pushing her forward.

"I don't care about magic." Noelle waved a hand in the air.

It was the truth.

"My mother kept that old wizard and TruthSeer around for years. I didn't see much good come of it," Noelle continued, not afraid to share her thoughts. "The power of the HearingStone is a weak power compared to others. Althea has always been at a disadvantage compared to the powers in the other kingdoms, and we've gotten along just fine."

"And Rai?" Shaeleen asked, not really sure why she shortened his name such. "Do you have thoughts different from your sister?"

Noelle's face turned red at the use of Raimund's name in so familiar of a fashion, and Cole sucked in his breath.

Raimund himself stumbled, trying to come up with a coherent answer.

"That's what his mother calls him," Archer explained, trying to hide a grin.

"I like it," Shaeleen said with a smile. "So what do you think?"

"I don't think what the commander and my mother's husband is doing is right," he said. "We have pride in our heritage and our use of the HearingStone. The powers of the stones are to help others. We are as much a part of Wayland as any kingdom is."

Shaeleen glanced around and saw Abby with some other children. She pointed in her direction. "That young girl there saved the lives of all on her father's ship because of her power. She also alerted me and others to the impending attack by Commander Kerr in Stronghaven. All of the stones have their purpose, and they work together in a way that none of us really understand. All are important to the balance of magic in Wayland and Verlyn. That is what Cailu and others are trying to disrupt—the balance of magic. They want it all for themselves."

"I really don't care about the magic and the stones," Noelle said, slamming her hand on the table. "The king is just trying to maintain control of the land while our mother is ill."

"Is that what he's told you?" Shaeleen asked, following a pain that firmly told her the queen was not sick.

"I just want to find my mother," Raimund said. "She is the

leader of Althea, not Cailu."

Noelle and Raimund exchanged heated looks. Shaeleen didn't like or really trust Noelle. She wasn't acting rationally, but Archer had been put with them for a reason—here was an in to the queen and to the castle in South Bay.

"I need to find your mother also," Shaeleen said quietly. "I need her stone."

Noelle and Raimund stood up in quick succession and glared down at Shaeleen.

"You could've said that with a little more tact," Cole said out of the corner of his mouth, standing up himself. "My sister is the hope of Wayland, Your Highnesses. The truth guides her. She has been tasked to gather all the stones and restore them to their fullest once again." He turned his head to Archer. "Your uncle can assure you that she will get the stones, one way or another, and it would be much better to cooperate with her."

Archer motioned to the prince and princess. "Please sit down. You don't want the entire camp seeing this, do you?"

The two sat back down, seemingly chastised. Archer glanced around and lowered his voice, afraid of someone overhearing them. "Now," Archer continued, "I can attest to the fact that this young woman will go to lengths you haven't imagined to retrieve the last stone, so let's not argue any more on that fact. When the time comes, she will get it."

Noelle glared at her uncle then at Shaeleen. Raimund leaned back a bit, and a small grin pushed up the corners of his mouth. "So how can we help?"

"We need a diversion," Archer said. He waved his hand around the camp. "How many have you got here?"

"We have about fifty horsemen here and more come each day. There are also another fifty or so archers and swordsmen." Raimund grimaced a bit. "Many of the people are afraid, but few really agree with Cailu and what he is doing. We try to intercept his men as much as possible, though some magic users have been taken."

Shaeleen grimaced with thoughts of the cleansing. "We must act quickly. Archer is right. We need a diversion that will draw as many guards away from the castle grounds as possible. Cole and I will find your mother and return her to the castle."

"What about Cailu?" Noelle asked.

"I can take care of the shadow keeper," Shaeleen said firmly. She was tired of all the trouble they were causing. What if Abby hadn't been rescued today?

Noelle lifted her eyebrow, as if not believing Shaeleen's words.

"Don't worry, Princess." Shaeleen winked at her. "I'm stronger than I look. I'll try to keep the castle intact for you to rule there someday."

Noelle stood up again. "I will not have this woman telling us what to do. I will decide when we rescue my mother and how to deal with things in Althea. She has no authority here."

We're wasting too much time here.

"Ouch!" Noelle gave a yelp, her hand rubbing her backside.

Shaeleen barely moved on the bench. Cole shook his head, though she could tell he was trying to suppress a grin.

"What did you do?" Noelle asked Shaeleen.

"I gave you a spanking like the spoiled child you are."

"What? How?" Noelle sputtered. "You didn't even move."

"Oh, I moved. You just didn't see me," Shaeleen said.

"Focus, TruthSeer," Archer growled from across the table. "Remember who you are."

Shaeleen gave him a dark look but relaxed. "You're right, Archer." She turned back to the princess and nodded her head slightly. "Noelle, I am sorry I did that to you. I'm tired and have had a long journey, with more to come. We don't have much time." Shaeleen flicked her fingers at the young princess. "Now, can you run and get your captains and commanders and bring them back here? We have plans to make, and I have directions to give."

Noelle's face turned red. Raimund stood up next to her, his face a mixture of mirth and concern.

Noelle stomped her foot. "I am in charge here."

Shaeleen let out a long breath. "All right, here it goes." With one smooth motion, Shaeleen jumped up on the table and waved her hands in circles around her. Swirls of green, blue, red, orange, and pink flew around her head. Then she clapped her hands, and the lights sped off through the camp in a dazzling display of color.

"Gather in," Shaeleen spoke softly, but the sound echoed and reverberated through the colors and throughout the camp. "The TruthSeer needs your help."

The colors gathered around each man and woman in the camp and pushed them closer to where Shaeleen stood. Once they were all assembled together, she raised her hands over her head and clapped once. Thunder sounded overhead from a clear sky, and the trees shook around them.

"Is everyone here?" she asked.

"Yes," said a man in the front. By the look of his uniform, he was a commander of sorts. His hand rested on his sword.

Shaeleen winced at the man's lie and studied the camp around her. Finally, she pointed toward a tent in the back. "I feel that someone is missing."

A woman spoke up. "That's the abbot, the leader of our local monastery. He was hurt protecting his people and an infection has settled in. His granddaughter attends him."

"Bring him to me," Shaeleen said.

The woman looked at Noelle and Raimund for confirmation.

"Don't look at them," Shaeleen said. "I am in charge here."

A gasp went through the crowd, and the man up front drew his sword. Cole stepped forward, and with a wave of his hand, the man's sword went flying to the side, hitting into a nearby tree.

A few others drew their swords when a voice from the back spoke up. "Put your weapons down."

An old man scooted forward, accompanied by a young girl. The crowd parted in reverence, allowing him to walk through. He stopped in front of the table that Shaeleen stood on.

"Are you really the TruthSeer?" he asked her. His gray hair hung down the side of his weathered face. One hand held his side as if in pain.

"How did you know?"

"I heard your conversation from my tent." He smiled at

her.

The HearingStone! She should have been more careful.

"A TruthSeer?" someone else in the crowd said.

Shaeleen moved to jump down off the table, but first drew upon the power of the SpeedStone and used it like she had before to slow herself down. She floated out past the table, then lowered herself to the ground. The crowd gasped. Some backed up, while others moved in closer. She took a few steps to reach the man and put her hand out to touch his arm. Closing her eyes, she drew upon the power of the HealingStone and lent it strength. She pushed away the man's fever and closed the wound in his side. Opening her eyes, she saw that his face was ruddy and healthy. Even his hair seemed a bit less gray.

"Bless you, child," the abbot said. "You are more than a TruthSeer, it seems."

Shaeleen nodded her head. "I am the TruthSeer that will save Wayland from the shadow keepers and restore the power of the stones. In this, no one holds authority over me."

She glanced intentionally at Noelle, whose face was carved as if in stone. Anger flared from her eyes, but she said nothing.

"Now, let's plan on how we restore your queen to her throne," Shaeleen said in a loud voice.

Cheers broke out around the camp as they all moved in closer to hear Shaeleen's plan.

CHAPTER TWENTY-FOUR

The next day, Shaeleen wondered if the plan was brilliant or utterly stupid. They were going to walk directly into the lair of the shadow keeper.

The white sandstone castle stood on a rise overlooking the bay. Palms lined the well-maintained road, and Shaeleen marveled at its beauty.

"Play your part well, TruthSeer," Archer growled at her from behind. "It's not my intention to be caught." For emphasis, he pulled on a rope that held her and Cole.

The plan was for Archer and the two other soldiers with them to bring Cole and Shaeleen in as captured magic users. They hoped then to be taken to where the other prisoners were being held, including the queen. They would free them, then return to the castle for the HealingStone before facing the Shadow Keeper Cailu.

Shaeleen knew from experience, however, that not everything would go according to plan. Most likely, it would fall apart in the next few minutes, if past history was any indicator of her luck. The five of them stepped up to the castle gates, and guards stepped in front of them.

"What is your purpose here?" a large fellow with bulging muscles and light hair asked.

"We have apprehended two criminals and are bringing

them in," Archer said, pulling the rope tied around Shaeleen and Cole's hands.

The guard glanced up and down the street. "Are you stupid, man? The prisoners are taken around to the back entrance. We can't have this up here."

Shaeleen was impressed by the way Archer kept his cool after being called stupid.

"Yes, sir." Archer bowed and turned to go the way the guard had instructed. A loud voice came from inside the castle grounds.

"What do we have here?" a man said, striding forward. He was thin and wiry, late in years, but with a strong voice and quick gait.

Archer groaned behind Shaeleen and whispered, "TruthSeer Wain. He's a weaselly one. Watch out."

Here goes the first glitch in the plan.

Shaeleen and Cole kept their heads down. Out of the corner of her eye, Shaeleen watched as TruthSeer Wain stood in front of them, his head tilted to the side.

"I told them to take the prisoners to the back gate, sir," said the guard, hanging back behind the group.

TruthSeer Wain waved the guard back to his station, then walked closer. Shaeleen kept her head down, watching his shoes. They were black and shiny. He lifted a bony hand up to her chin and pushed her head up. She looked at him defiantly. Obviously, the color of her eyes caught him off guard, and he let out a small hiss. He then walked to Cole and did the same.

"They are obviously magic holders, TruthSeer," Archer said with a small bow. "We are bringing them in to be cleansed."

Wain, still not saying anything, held his chin in his hand and seemed to be studying Shaeleen and Cole and from toe to head. Shaeleen held her breath and hoped he couldn't tell what powers they really had.

"Are you from Verlyn, here to cause problems?" Wain said.

Shaeleen sighed at the easy question. She shook her head.

He studied them for a moment longer, then nodded his head. "What are you doing here in South Bay? Were you doing magic?"

How could Shaeleen answer those questions without giving herself away? Before she could speak, Cole tried to step forward, but Archer, playing his part, pulled him back.

"Stay away from him," Archer growled.

Cole's eyes flashed back at Archer, then to Wain. "We had trouble up north and came down the Cadyn," Cole spoke carefully. "My sister can't always control herself with her magic."

That was true! Shaeleen bit her lip to keep from smiling.

Wain stayed quiet, thinking. He stared at Archer longer, and his eyes bore into him as if trying to figure something out. "We've met before?"

Archer jerked a bit but kept his face straight. "I am a relative of sorts to the queen," he said smoothly. "You might have seen me before."

The man is good with his words, Shaeleen thought.

"The queen . . ." TruthSeer Wain seemed to blank out for a moment. "Where?" he mumbled.

"What was that, sir?" Archer asked.

Wain shook his head a few times, as if trying to awaken out of a dream. "Oh, nothing. I just haven't seen the queen in a while."

He's under some type of spell.

"I'm sure she is all right," Archer said.

"Of course. Of course," Wain said with a frown. "Why wouldn't she be? Either way, King Cailu has everything under control." The man seemed slow of thought, his mind in a fog.

"Does he?" Shaeleen said. They needed to get to the prisoners.

"What does that mean?" Wain stepped back in front of her.

She tried to hold her hands in front of her, pulling on the rope that held her to Archer. "What about these rules against magic?"

"Magic?" Wain said, shaking his head. "Magic is bad, my dear. We all know that. It corrupts people. It's been weak here for years, and it's better to just let it go away."

Shaeleen couldn't believe what she was hearing. She pulled up the power of the stones and hoped Wain couldn't tell. He didn't move but continued to look at her. She tentatively reached out her mind to feel his magic . . . but found nothing.

He's been cleansed!

Shaeleen gasped and looked to Archer and Cole with wild eyes.

"Shae, what's wrong?" Cole tried to move closer, but Archer pulled him back.

Cole turned and glared at Archer. "Let me help my sister."

Archer turned his head back to Wain. "Sir, please, I need to take these two to be cleansed. They are dangerous."

Wain waved his hand at him and nodded. "Of course, good man. Don't let me detain you any longer."

Archer pulled their ropes hard, and the two other guards pushed Cole and Shaeleen from behind. The ropes chafed around Shaeleen's wrists, and she whimpered a bit. Cole gave her a look of sympathy. Soon, they were outside the gates and heading around a corner to the far side of the castle grounds.

"What was the meaning of that?" Cole turned to Archer, his eyes blazing.

Archer glanced around, but no one was close enough to hear—though you never knew in Althea so Shaeleen brought her rope-tied hands to her lips and shushed the two.

Both men seemed to understand, but Archer whispered softly, "I had to play the part. The TruthSeer almost recognized me. We've met multiple times. He's not himself."

Shaeleen nodded her head and leaned in close to her brother and Archer. "He's been cleansed. He is no longer a TruthSeer."

Archer gasped, and his face paled. "They can do that?" he spoke, this time more loudly.

Shaeleen examined her surroundings and nodded. Then she started walking toward the rear of the castle, forcing Archer to start walking with them, keeping the rope in tow. Soon, they arrived at a small back gate to the castle grounds.

"Shae, are you sure about this?" Cole said in a whisper. "What if they try to cleanse us?"

Shaeleen shivered. That was not something she would go

through again.

A guard ushered them through the back gate and escorted them toward another building a hundred yards or so behind the castle. With each step, Shaeleen's anticipation grew. How were they going to free the other magic users? Would they be too late? If they had cleansed the TruthSeer, then anyone could be cleansed.

The back wall of the castle estate lay another hundred yards behind the building they were heading to. Shaeleen stared hard at it, waiting for the next part of the plan to begin. But nothing happened, and a sick feeling crept into her stomach—not from the TruthStone, but from her own sense of wariness. The man leading them brought them up to the building. Two other guards stood to either side of a light wooden door. The rest of the building was a white sandstone, a similar color to the castle itself, but newer.

"We have prisoners for you." Archer pushed Shaeleen and Cole forward.

A man at the door reached inside a sack and pulled out a small pouch, then threw it to Archer. He caught it in the air with a sound of coins clinking together. He opened it up to look inside.

"It's all there," the man said. "You can leave now."

Archer glanced at Shaeleen and she looked at Cole. A distraction was supposed to be occurring, but the air around them grew quiet.

"Is there a problem here?" the man said to Archer.

Archer motioned the other two guards away with a shake of his head. "No. We're leaving."

Shaeleen noticed that Archer walked slowly. He turned back once then with a frown as he headed to the gate. The man grabbed Shaeleen and Cole's rope with a laugh.

"Two more for cleansing!" he yelled into the building, pulling them inside.

As soon as they entered, Shaeleen knew something was wrong.

My magic is gone!

With panic rising inside her, she looked at Cole and could see a similar horror mirrored on his face. She tugged on the ropes and tried to run, but they were pulled tighter. Cole lashed out and tried to hit someone, but the ropes held him.

Why hadn't I thought of this?

"Now, now," said the man. "We'll have none of that. We can cleanse you conscious or not; it's your choice."

"You have no right to do this!" Shaeleen pulled again and tried to get away.

Cole kicked his foot out and caught a guard in the gut. He fell back, and Cole swung his tied hands around and connected with the jaw of another man. This gave Shaeleen an opening, and she headed toward the door. All she had to do was to step outside, and her power would be restored. She could take the entire building down from there, if need be.

Coming to the door, it opened in front of her. Shaeleen skidded to a stop as a tall man with long, dark hair and light blue eyes stood staring at her, a black cape swirling around him in the silhouetted doorway. Someone else stood behind him, but she couldn't tell who it was.

"Well, well." The man put his arms out to block Shaeleen.

"What do I have here?"

Shaeleen tried to get around him, but it was of no use. She turned around and saw that Cole had been subdued by three other guards. The rest of the men knelt on the ground, facing the man in the doorway.

"King Cailu," they said in unison.

The shadow keeper!

CHAPTER TWENTY-FIVE

"Some plan," Shaeleen growled under her breath. Nothing was working out. She had never considered that the building would block her magic; it was similar to the compound she and Orin had been in outside of Mistport.

A guard came up behind Shaeleen and held her tight with the ropes. The man who had brought them in turned to Cailu and bowed. "Your Highness, two new magic users to cleanse."

Cailu laughed, then took his slender finger, put it under Shaeleen's chin, and brought it up. He was tall, and Shaeleen had to look almost straight up. His face was angular, and his brows swept up like hers and Coles. She could see his ear on the left side where his long hair split around them; they were pointed. She shivered at his touch.

"I will cleanse this one personally, Garyth." Cailu said. "She has caused me and my fellow keepers enough problems." He ran his finger down Shaeleen's cheek to her neck.

"Leave her alone." Cole struggled and kicked out again.

Cailu waved a hand in the air, and Cole crumbled to the ground.

"Cole!" Shaeleen tried to pull away and get to her brother, but her size and strength were no match for the men holding her and the ropes around her hands. Tears formed in the corners of her eyes as she turned her head back to Cailu. "So much for magic being outlawed."

Cailu laughed. "It's not outlawed for me, my dear. I am from Verlyn and a rightfully raised keeper of the stones."

"A shadow keeper!" Shaeleen spat.

Cailu shrugged and opened his palms up in front of him. "Semantics. The ShadowStones are just reflections of the other stones. They are a mirror of the same thing."

Shaeleen tried to think of what to do, but without the use of the IntelligenceStone she had gotten used to, her mind seemed sluggish and slow. Cailu motioned for Garyth to take her away.

"Prepare her for the cleansing," Cailu said. "Then we will see if I let her live or not. Keep her away from the others. I have other business to attend to first, then I will return." He turned and walked out of the building.

When he moved out of the doorway, Shaeleen gasped when she saw who was behind him. "Noelle."

Noelle lifted a hand and shielded her eyes against the sun. With a look of satisfaction, she smiled from ear to ear. Then she took her other hand, lifted it up, and slowly dragged it across her throat while staring at Shaeleen.

Shaeleen pulled against the ropes. "Traitor! How could you do this?"

Garyth pulled her back and closed the door. Shaeleen turned and saw Cole still slumped on the floor. Her chest began to beat harder. "What are you going to do with him?"

"Cleanse him, just like you, witch!" Garyth said. He motioned two others to carry Cole away, but he took Shaeleen down another hallway. "You must have really angered the king."

Shaeleen stayed quiet, trying to think of a way to get out. Princess Noelle had sold them all out. That's why there was no distraction to help them free the prisoners. That's why the shadow keeper knew she was there. Shaeleen berated herself for not seeing Noelle's duplicity. Her recovery from using too much power on the river and the quick pace they had been keeping had made her careless.

They passed three rooms on the way down the hall. The doors were partially opened, and Shaeleen could see three to four people in each room. "Are they cleansed?" she finally asked.

"Some are," Garyth said as he pulled her toward a door at the end of the building. Another man stood close by. "Clear the storage room, you two. This one is to be held separately from the others."

With another man helping, the two men took fifteen minutes to bring crates and barrels of what seemed like food and supplies out of the room, stacking them on the side of the hallway. Finally, Shaeleen was pushed in and the door closed. Darkness filled the room. Only the small light under the door shone in.

"Two guards at all times," she heard Garyth say.

Sitting on the floor, Shaeleen leaned her head back against the wall and banged it a few times. How could she have been so stupid? She screamed out in frustration.

"Quiet in there," said a guard outside of the doorway.

"Make me," Shaeleen yelled in frustration.

She heard a laugh outside the door, and another guard

joined in before he spoke. "The cleansing will change her. It always does."

Shaeleen stopped yelling and thought about TruthSeer Wain. Is that how she would end up? *No. They won't let me live.* How long did she have? An hour? Two? Till the next day? She had put a hasty back-up plan in place with Raimund, but at this point, she didn't know if he had been caught or not. She scooted around until she could lean back into the far corner and closed her eyes. She hadn't slept well in weeks, and it was taking its toll on her. Within a few moments, she succumbed to the drowsiness and fell asleep.

A sound outside the room woke her, and she stood up, wondering how long she had been asleep. She might not have much time. The door opened, and her heartbeat increased. Was it time already? Expecting Garyth or Cailu, she was relieved to see a young girl about Abby's age come in carrying a small bowl of food. She walked across the room and handed it to her. As she placed the bowl in Shaeleen's hand, she passed along a small note. As soon as the girl left, Shaeleen scooted on the floor toward the door and held the paper down by the faint light underneath. She squinted her eyes and read, *Help is coming. Listen carefully.*

Moving back to the wall, Shaeleen took the bowl and took out a small piece of bread and a slice of cheese.

Listen carefully. Was this a message from Raimund?

Shaeleen sat back down on the floor again. She had escaped a cleansing once before when the compound had blocked her powers. How had she done it? She thought back to lying on the table in the town square with Orin at her side.

They had cut their arms and had begun draining their blood and filling it with new blood—in Orin's case, blood that was tainted with the ShadowStone. But it didn't matter if they drained her blood. Her power wasn't in her blood; it was in her stones that hung at her side in the pouch Basil had given her.

Can I really even be cleansed? She didn't think so. *But I can be killed.*

Whatever spell the shadow keepers used to cut off the source of magic, it worked against inherited magic or stones of power, but when Georrod the shadow keeper had tried to cleanse her, the TruthStone had been impacted by the proximity of a ShadowStone. As Cailu had earlier put it, they were a mirror of one another. When one was used, the other responded to it. That is why Orin felt pain when Shaeleen used the power of the stones on him now. That was how she had gotten away from Georrod.

But that would be the last resort. She really did not want to wait until that point to find out if she could do it again with Cailu. And what about Cole? What if they did to Cole what they had done to Orin? Shaeleen leaned back against the wall again and closed her eyes. There was no chance she would fall asleep now. She was awake and alert.

Shaeleen opened her eyes, pulled her stone out, and cradled it in her hand. She ran her fingers over the surface. It was smooth, but still had edges to it—edges that hadn't been worn by years of being hidden in the pools of water on the island of Verlyn. She tried to sense its power. She knew it was there but felt nothing.

Frustrated, she closed her eyes again and thought about

the note. *Listen carefully*, it had said. She held her breath for a moment. What was that sound? She concentrated harder, trying to block out all the other sounds in the building. Something was coming from below. Was this what she was supposed to be listening for?

Shaeleen moved around the floor and knocked on it with her knuckles. She thought she heard a response. She moved to a different spot and knocked again. This time there was definitely an answer. Moving a few feet closer to the back corner, she knocked on the floor again. This time, it sounded different.

It sounded hollow!

She stood up and lightly stomped on it with her foot. She didn't want to make enough noise to alert the guards. Definitely hollow. She dropped to her knees again and felt along the floor. Finally, her fingernails ran across a small crack in the floor. She tried to pry it up, but her fingers were too big. Suddenly, the floor began to lift beneath her, and she scooted out of the way. Once it was enough off the floor to get her fingers under it, she pulled it up. A light glow filled the room.

"Abby!"

The young girl popped her head through the opening and motioned with her hand for Shaeleen to follow her down. Another pair of hands reached up and helped her down. She jumped down through the small opening and looked into the face of Prince Raimund. He held her in his arms. After an awkward moment, he cleared his throat and moved around her to the hidden door she'd just tumbled through. He quietly put it back in place.

"My brother!" Shaeleen said with a loud whisper. "We can't leave him."

"We don't have a way of getting him out easily." Raimund shook his head. A third person, a man, stood next to him, holding a torch to light the tunnel, making shadows dance across Raimund's face as he spoke.

"Thanks for coming. I'm glad you remembered about the tunnels," Shaeleen said. "And by the way, your sister sold us out."

Raimund gasped then lowered his head in shame. "I am sorry. I didn't know. A team of men and I began riding toward the other side of the back wall. We were going to make a diversion for you as you instructed. But before we got there, a troop of Cailu's men intercepted us. Abby here was able to give us a brief warning so we were ready." He smiled at Abby. "Her hearing is better than mine. Only Taren, Abby, and I escaped being caught."

Shaeleen closed her eyes for a moment and felt the sweet power inside her. The boundary of her power being blocked was only inside the house. Cailu hadn't thought about anyone being underneath.

"We don't have much time," Raimund said.

Shaeleen thought for a moment. She remembered her brother's lesson on how important she was to everyone. She hated leaving people here to be cleansed, but Raimund was right. A lot more was at stake.

"Where do these tunnels go?" Shaeleen asked.

Raimund smiled. "We came from the castle. A door in the kitchen leads here. This place use to be used for extra storage."

"And are there more tunnels from the castle to other places?" Shaeleen asked. Based on what she had seen in other castles, she was sure there were.

"Of course!" Raimund slapped his palm against his head. "There are tunnels that go to the harbor, as well as out to the old family home—where my mother is supposedly being kept. I should have thought about that. Not many people know about them or use them anymore."

"Well, let's hope Cailu doesn't," Shaeleen said. She then took a moment to find Cole. She could sense him now. He wasn't far away in the house. The tunnel continued past them a bit, and Shaeleen walked that way. Tall wooden beams rose from the tunnel to support the building. She stopped and turned back. The other three followed her.

"What do you hear in the room?" she turned to Raimund and Abby.

"Heartbeats," Abby said.

"Three of them," Raimund added.

Shaeleen nodded. There were two others besides Cole in his room. She tried to reach her mind out to Cole, but even though she had use of her powers now, he did not, and she couldn't communicate with him. Without warning, Shaeleen staggered and put her arm out. Raimund caught and steadied her.

"What's wrong?" Abby moved to her other side.

"The shadow keeper is back." Shaeleen could feel his presence in the house, which meant if she used her powers, he would feel her also. Shaeleen ground her teeth in frustration. She had been planning on using her powers to break Cole free, but then Cailu would be on their tail immediately. As it was, he would surely find her missing any minute now.

As if on cue, they heard the shouting of muted voices above them.

"They know you're gone," Abby said after a moment.

Raimund pointed down the tunnel away from the building. "We have to go now, TruthSeer. It's the only way. While Cailu is out of the castle, we can get to the other tunnels."

Shaeleen growled but agreed with his assessment. While they were looking for her, they wouldn't do anything to Cole— at least, she hoped so. She would come back for him soon and take the rest of the prisoners at the same time.

"Lead the way," she said to Raimund.

He motioned Taren to go in front of him with the torch, and they jogged along under the ground. It was a fairly straight tunnel and stayed tall enough to stand up in the entire journey. After only a few minutes, the tunnel stopped in a widened out room. There was a ladder in place leading to the floor of the castle.

Raimund climbed up first, lifted the trap door carefully, and peered around. Then he stuck his head back down. "It's clear. Hurry." He motioned his hand forward.

Soon, all four of them stood in a storage room in the back of the kitchen. Shaeleen took a deep breath. The last castle; the last stop. The HearingStone called to her already, but it felt different than the other stones. She tilted her head and tried to figure it out. "The HearingStone isn't here," Shaeleen quickly deduced.

Raimund turned his head back toward her. "What do you

mean?"

"It's gone," Shaeleen stated, worry beginning to seize her. *It can't be gone. I need it!*

"Who took it? My sister? Cailu?" Raimund asked, fear in his voice.

Shaeleen shook her head. "I don't know."

A sound was heard outside the door. Raimund moved closer and opened the door slightly. Through the small crack, they could see the cook and a small kitchen staff rushing around, preparing the evening meal.

"Are they loyal to your mother or Cailu?" Shaeleen asked.

"My mother," Raimund said. "They have all served here a long time."

Shaeleen opened the door and stepped out. One older woman dropped a spoon in a pot she was stirring, and a young woman barely caught a plate she was carrying from tumbling to the floor.

"Prince Raimund," the cook said, rushing over and giving him a big hug. "We've missed you. Are you and your sister well?"

"Well enough," was all Raimund would say. He put a finger to his lips to signal that they needed to be quiet about his appearance.

The cook gave Taren, Abby, and Shaeleen a look, lingering a bit longer on Shaeleen, but then turned back to Raimund. "And the queen?"

"We are going to rescue her," Raimund said. "Shaeleen here—"

Shaeleen jumped in to stop Raimund from saying too

much. Castles had ears all over the place, especially in a kingdom with the HearingStone. "We need to go, Raimund."

The cook gasped at her common way of referring to him.

Raimund nodded. Before leaving the room, he turned and whispered, "You never saw us here."

All in the room nodded and smiled, their eyes full of excitement.

CHAPTER TWENTY-SIX

Running down a wide hallway, the group received their share of stares. A few called out to the prince, and he just waved and continued to run. At one point, they passed a large window that faced out toward the back of the castle. Shaeleen stopped and looked out. Off in the distance, she could see Cailu's men at the building she had been held in. The shadow keeper came stomping out, waving his arms as if yelling at everyone.

"Hurry. He's coming back," Shaeleen said as they moved around a corner. "He obviously doesn't know about the tunnels."

Raimund skidded to a stop. Shaeleen and Abby almost ran into him. Taren moved to the side and tried not to trip.

"Who's coming back?" said a voice ahead of Raimund.

Noelle!

"Get going, Raimund," Shaeleen shouted at him while pushing forward.

"Guards!" Noelle yelled.

Shaeleen stopped in front of Noelle. She drew upon her powers and pushed Noelle back against a wall. She grabbed Raimund's hand. "Let's go!"

"How rude!" she heard Noelle yell from behind them. "I'll tell the king you're here."

Shaeleen could feel something strange coming from Noelle—maybe a spell of some sort—but didn't have time to stop and figure it out.

"He is not the king," Raimund shouted. "Mother is the queen, and he is only her husband, and a bad one at that."

"Guards," Noelle repeated her yell from earlier.

Shaeleen couldn't stand her piercing tones any longer. With the IntelligenceStone giving her inspiration, she used a TruthSpell and threw it back down the hallway at Noelle. The greenish glow wrapped around her mouth, and Shaeleen bound it with power from the StrengthStone. With a wave of her hand, she lifted Noelle off the floor and pushed her flat against the wall, six feet in the air. Her head was still a few feet from the tall ceiling. She flapped her arms a moment until Shaeleen tied them with strings of air to the wall.

"I'm tired of her voice," Shaeleen said. *I'll release her later.*

Abby giggled, and the guard looked wide-eyed. Raimund let himself smile briefly, then pulled Shaeleen along. "Come on."

After a few turns, a brief flight of stairs down, another turn, then another flight of stairs, they entered a dark and damp room in the basement of the castle.

"Taren, light, please," Raimund said.

Taren brought the light forward to a wall. Raimund leaned forward and ran his hand over it. Shaeleen heard a click. With dust blowing over them, a portion of the wall swung forward.

Shaeleen wrinkled her nose at the musty smell and stepped forward, Abby following closely on her heels. Going through the doorway, her breath caught, and she wiped a spider web off her face.

"It hasn't been used in a while," Raimund said. "My sister and I used to play down here when we were young, but well . . . we stopped playing together quite a while ago."

They closed the door behind them and walked forward quickly and carefully. Shaeleen jumped as a rat scurried in front of her. Abby reached over and grabbed her hand. The smoke from the torch drifted back toward Shaeleen, and she covered her mouth to keep from breathing it in. The group walked with little talk, following Raimund through a few turns and twists. Shaeleen didn't like the feel of being so closed in and turned her thoughts to other things to distract her from the surroundings.

She felt the presence of her brother in the back of her mind and wondered if it had been a mistake to leave him in the building. She really needed him by her side—not just for his power as a wizard, but for his steadiness as her brother. She knew she could be rash and undisciplined, but her brother's strength of character kept her from making too many mistakes.

After at least a quarter of an hour—maybe more—Raimund signaled them to stop. In front of them stood a wooden door, its brown wood aged and worn.

"This leads to a basement under the building where I suspect my mother is," Raimund said.

Shaeleen felt a tinge of magic through the door. *The HearingStone is here.* She wondered why it wasn't in the castle, but either way, it was now calling to her as the previous stones had.

Shaeleen nodded her head at Raimund to proceed. "I don't

know who might be here," Raimund said, pulling his sword out. Shaeleen moved behind him, with Abby behind her and Taren holding the rear.

Raimund opened the door slowly, and Shaeleen saw a pale glow through the crack in the doorway. Raimund peeked through, then pushed the door open further. Old chairs, crates, and a rolled-up carpet were pushed to the corners. High up above on one of the walls was a small window, only about six inches tall. It sent a soft light across the room.

"Storage," Raimund said and led them in. On the far side was a stairway leading upwards. He motioned them up the stairs, walking with quiet steps. The torch that Taren held from behind sent shadows out in front of them.

Coming to a small landing at the top of the stairs, Raimund put his hand on the doorknob and turned, but nothing happened. He tried again, then looked at Shaeleen, who stood a few stairs lower.

"It's locked," Raimund said.

Shaeleen walked up the stairs, pushing her way around Raimund. "Ready?" she asked.

Raimund gave her a strange look, but Shaeleen just smiled back, and he nodded. Putting her hand on the doorknob, she pulled up the power of the StrengthStone—it wouldn't take much. With a quick turn, the door lock broke; making a noise that she was sure would be heard by anyone inside. She pushed the door open and stood ready to defend herself, but there was no one in the room.

Shaeleen glanced around. It appeared to be the parlor of a nice home. A set of upholstered furniture sat around a tall and wide fireplace. A dark table with six padded chairs filled the rest of the room. Paintings and tapestries lined the walls. A decorative chandelier hung in the middle of the room. It looked comfortable—finely furnished, but not new.

Raimund and Taren walked around the perimeter of the room, the prince's eyes flicking to every corner. After verifying there was no danger, he walked over to the side of a large, covered window. Heavy gold drapes hung over it. Motioning the others away from the window, he pushed the drape to the side a few inches and peered outside.

"Looks like they didn't expect us to come from the inside," Raimund said. He smiled and motioned Shaeleen to see.

Looking out of the crack, she could see the castle looming in the near distance behind its tall rock walls. Between the wall and where they stood was a broad expanse of wild lawn, unpruned fruit trees, and decorative walks winding through a garden that had seen better days. About fifty feet in front of the house and at the edge of the garden stood six men, heavily armed. A sword and knife hung from each waist, and a bow and quiver of arrows was slung across each back.

Abby walked up, but on the way, tripped on a rug and fell into Shaeleen. She grabbed the young girl but not before she let out a small yelp. Raimund, who had been peering out of the window, suddenly backed away. "They heard us," he said and began looking around the room again. "We need to find my mother."

Shaeleen had always thought that the HearingStone had limited uses, but it was hard living in a kingdom in which you didn't know who could or couldn't hear you and from what distance you were safe to talk.

"Upstairs," Shaeleen mouthed and pointed above her. "Your mother is there." She could feel the HearingStone calling to her.

Raimund stood as if listening for a moment, then leaned in close to Shaeleen and whispered, "There are guards here in the house, but not more than two if I would guess, but if the ones from outside come in, we'll be in trouble."

High on a shelf in the room, Shaeleen noticed two bottles of wine. She motioned for Taren to get them down. Taren turned to Raimund for confirmation, and the prince nodded. When he had them in his hand, he gave Shaeleen a questioning look.

"Bring them to the guards out front, Taren," Shaeleen whispered. "Keep them busy."

Raimund didn't look convinced. "He'll be in danger."

"He'll have wine with him," Shaeleen said. "They look bored and will overlook his clothes for the wine."

Taren understood and nodded. "I'll do it, my lord. We must rescue the queen."

Raimund put his hand on Taren's arm. "Be careful, my friend."

Taren nodded and quietly pushed open a door that led to an entryway. The remaining three stayed behind the door, watching.

"Refreshments, my friends," Taren said as he closed the door behind him.

Up a flight of stairs behind them came a voice. "Who are

you?"

Shaeleen turned around. Two guards stood at the top of the stairs, swords in their hands. One noticed Raimund standing with her.

"Prince Raimund?" the guard said. "You are not to be here. If the king found out—"

"He is not the king," Raimund said. "He is only my mother's husband."

The guard raised his shoulders in a shrug and started down the stairs. "Either way, my lord, he has given us orders and . . ."

Before the guard could finish, Shaeleen drew upon the SpeedStone, raced up the stairs, and took the sword from his hand, then moved up to the second guard and did the same. On her way back, she grabbed each man by the hands and pulled them to the bottom of the stairs. Their bodies banged and bounced on the way down.

Raimund jumped back, startled by what had happened in front of him. The two guards now lay unconscious at the bottom of the stairs, swords off to one side.

"I'm tired of waiting," Shaeleen whispered, then turned to Abby. "Stay here and listen for any trouble, Abby."

The young girl nodded, and Shaeleen headed up the stairs, followed quickly by Raimund. There were three doors down the small hallway, and Shaeleen knew exactly where to go. Heading to the last door, she put her hand on the knob. *Of course it's locked!* With the power of the StrengthStone still flowing in her, she turned it and burst into the room.

A woman sat in a chair at the far end. An oversized bed next to her was unmade, and a small table between the bed and the queen held a tray of food and a cup.

"Mother!" Raimund exclaimed as he rushed to the queen's side. He leaned down and put his arm around her shoulders. "Are you all right?"

The queen moved her head slowly, her eyes unfocused. "Raimund?"

"Yes, it's me, Mother." Raimund knelt next to her. "Are you hurt?"

The queen sat still. Her light brown hair looked to have been done up days ago and now stuck out with wispy strands. Her dress was simple but still of higher quality than anything Shaeleen owned back home.

"He's done something to her," Shaeleen said. Glancing around the room, she spotted a cup on a small table by her bed. Lifting it to her nose, she sniffed. Her head reeled, and she quickly pulled back, but the IntelligenceStone settled in, and she knew what it was. "Poppy," Shaeleen said. "She's been given high doses, I would guess."

The queen turned glassy eyes up at Shaeleen, as if seeing her for the first time. "Who are you?"

"I am Shaeleen, Queen Emmony. I need something from you."

"From me?" Emmony said. "I don't have anything of yours." She turned to her son. "Raimund, who is this? I haven't taken anything of hers. I don't even know who she is." Her voice slurred, and her eyes showed her confusion.

Shaeleen heard a noise outside the room and turned. Abby stuck her head in. "They are done with the wine, Shaeleen. It won't be long until someone comes back to the house and finds the guards you knocked out."

Shaeleen nodded and turned back to the queen. She reached her hand out and touched her arm. Thinking of Orin and Cole, she hesitated a moment. But after taking a deep breath, she pushed forward. It was all she could do in the time they had.

Drawing upon the TruthStone and a TruthSpell, she pushed her power into the queen and felt around for the effects of the poppy flooding her system. Shaeleen had to pull back once so as not to be affected herself. "I need you to listen, Emmony." Shaeleen stared into the queen's eyes. "Do you understand me?"

"Shaeleen, what are you doing to her?" Raimund moved closer to his mother.

"What I have to." Shaeleen said. "I need to get past the poison."

Suddenly, Abby came running back up the stairs again. "The guards are coming to the house."

Shaeleen turned to Raimund. "Go and keep them away from here."

His eyes grew hard. "I can't leave her."

"You must," Shaeleen said. "I have to get the last stone!"

"You mean she has it?" Raimund's eyes went wide. "Where?"

Shaeleen pointed to the necklace hanging around the queen's neck. "But she has to give it to me."

They heard the door downstairs open, followed by yelling. Shaeleen pushed Raimund toward the door. "Fight with all you have, Rai. Buy me a few minutes."

Raimund moved reluctantly away from his mother but did as Shaeleen commanded. She turned back to the queen. Pulling on the small power of the HealingStone she held, she pushed it deeper inside the queen to rid her of the rest of the sedative effects of the poppy extract.

With a jolt, the queen sat up straighter and gazed around her, eyes wild, but then she settled down. "Raimund?" she asked.

"Buying us some time," Shaeleen said. "We don't have much of it, so I'll get to the point. I am the prophesied one. I am the TruthSeer, and I need your stone of power."

The queen opened her mouth to speak, but as she did so, the sound of fighting intensified on the stairs. The door burst open, and Abby came running in and looked around in a panic.

"Hide in there." Shaeleen said to Abby while pointing to another door in the room; one she supposed was a closet.

Shaeleen turned her attention back to the queen. She hoped Raimund and Taren could hold on for a moment longer. The queen appeared to have all her faculties back but was still trying to process what was happening. Shaeleen didn't have time to explain further.

She reached to her side and pulled the large Moldavite TruthStone from her pouch and held it up in front of Queen Emmony.

The queen gasped. "It's so large."

Green power flared from the stone as it raised up slightly out of her hand. The queen reached to her neck and held the pendant from her necklace in her hand. From her fingers, white light streaked out toward Shaeleen.

The queen pulled the chain from her neck, and the stone fell out of the pendant and into her hand. Shaeleen could feel its call pulsing through her. The white Celestite HearingStone rose up out of the queen's palm and flew through the air. It was the size of a very small pebble. As with the other stones, it embedded itself into the TruthStone.

Power rumbled through Shaeleen's mind and body, accentuating every emotion and sense, and she let out a thundering roar that shook the house.

CHAPTER TWENTY-SEVEN

Shaeleen felt her feet leave the floor for a few moments, then she dropped back down. All five stones of power, along with the TruthStone, raced through her body. She felt like she would burst with euphoria. Truth, strength, intelligence, hearing, healing, and speed raced through her veins with such fury that she gritted her teeth as she tried to control it. *I'm going to explode!*

"Shaeleen?" Abby stuck her head out of the closet. Her eyes were wide but held compassion for Shaeleen's well-being. "Are you all right?"

"Am I all right?" Shaeleen wondered if she would ever be all right. Soft laughter dribbled from her lips, then grew louder and louder until it filled the whole room. She couldn't contain it. *How could the universe see fit to give me so much power?* It was almost comical. Her, a mere fifteen-year-old daughter of a carpenter—now the most powerful person on the continent. She laughed again, and windows cracked, the foundation of the home shuddered, and she heard yelling down the stairs so loud it almost burst her eardrums.

The queen stared at her, mouth open, but no sound came out. Since giving up the power of her HearingStone, she had slumped back over, barely staying in the chair. Her breathing slowed. Shaeleen heard a noise outside and moved, without even realizing it, to the window.

"What is it?" the queen asked, her voice barely a whisper.

"Cailu!"

A company of soldiers rode from the back gate of the castle toward the house. In its lead stood Cailu—the pretender king of Althea, a shadow keeper.

"What have I done?" Queen Emmony whispered lifting her head up

"And your daughter rides at his right-hand side." Shaeleen added.

Queen Emmony grabbed her chest and winced. "Noelle!"

"She has sided with your husband," Shaeleen said.

"No, no." Emmony stood up and tried to regain her balance but quickly had to sit back down. "He's tricked and poisoned her, like he did me. He can be very persuasive. Please protect her."

Shaeleen didn't know about being tricked. The princess surely hadn't seem to need much coercion. She was spoiled and obviously wanted power. *But could that just be Cailu's doing?*

"TruthSeer!" Raimund ran into the room. He closed the thick door behind him, but it shook from the other side with guards trying to get through. "We can't hold them off."

Shaeleen needed her brother. His powers were blocked behind the walls that the shadow keeper had set up, but she was more powerful than a shadow keeper's spells, wasn't she?

She turned to the window and looked toward the castle. She couldn't see the small house that her brother was in behind the walls around the castle compound, but she knew where it was. She reached out into the light and rode its rays. She stood in the air over the house. With the power of the StrengthStone and SpeedStone, she threw a bolt of power down at the ground in front of the house. It shook its foundation, and walls began to collapse.

Moving her hands in the air, she flung pieces of the house out and away. Guards and prisoners alike came running out, looking around. Toward the back of the house, Cole stood and glanced around, then took a few steps and left the confines of the ShadowSpell.

"Cole!" Shaeleen yelled at him through their bond. "Come to me now. I need you!"

Without hesitation, he drew upon his wizard powers to protect his sister. He used the power of the SpeedStone and raced to where she stood.

Shaeleen came back out of the light just as the door behind Raimund burst open. She raced over to it and flung each man aside as if they were nothing. Racing down the stairs, she stopped for a brief moment when she saw Taren on the ground, a pool of blood around his stomach. She knew he was dead and groaned, using the anger to firm her resolve. She stepped outside, and Cole joined her just as Cailu and his men arrived.

"You are done, Shadow Keeper!" Shaeleen yelled in the clear air.

"I am the king here," Cailu bellowed. "Attack," he ordered his men.

Over thirty men rode forward on horseback, swords extended, racing toward Cole, Shaeleen, and Raimund. Cole moved in front, raising his sword that he had brought back with him. Fire crackled down its length and he met the first horseman's own sword and cracked it in half; the next man he flung to the side. Raimund joined him, and together they defended themselves, until two men bore down on the prince at once, and he was stuck fighting them off.

Shaeleen took a few steps back and looked out over the men toward Cailu and Noelle, who sat on their horses at the rear. Shaeleen gathered her strength and threw a bolt of lightning at the shadow keeper. Moments before hitting him, he brought up his own hand and, with a black mist, dispelled her lightning bolt, leaving it to waver and dissipate in the air.

The ShadowStone cannot be more powerful than all my stones together, Shaeleen thought. She prepared another attack, when Raimund yelled out from behind her.

"Mother!"

Shaeleen whipped her head around and saw a soldier leading the queen of Althea out of the house. The man held a knife at Emmony's throat. Shaeleen guessed she could get there in time using the SpeedStone, but what if she miscalculated?

Cailu's voice bellowed over the fighting. "Stop or the queen dies."

Cole glanced at Shaeleen, and she nodded for him to stop. Raimund was on the ground, injured, the queen was being held at knifepoint, and Noelle sat next to Cailu, a smug smile on her pretty face.

"We could just leave them all to fend for themselves," Shaeleen said to Cole.

"That wouldn't be right, Shae," Cole said, shaking his head firmly.

"But my job is to save the stones," Shaeleen said. "I have them now. I must get to Verlyn."

"But you also serve truth and justice," Cole said, surveying those around him. "And these people deserve our help. They will die under the shadow keeper's hand."

That they would.

Cailu and Noelle rode forward, then dismounted. Many of Cailu's men were on the ground, dead or injured, but at least twenty still stood, either on horseback or their feet. Shaeleen breathed hard and tried to think of what to do. She had already expended a lot of her power in retrieving the HearingStone and freeing Cole, but there had to be something she could do. Using the IntelligenceStone, she reviewed all she had learned and heard about the power of the stones and the ShadowStone.

"Noelle," Raimund said, standing back up. He winced and barely stayed standing. "Why are you with Cailu? You know what he is."

"He is a king," Noelle said, walking closer to Raimund. "And I will be queen when he leaves."

"Leaves?" Emmony spoke up.

Shaeleen turned to the queen. "He is a shadow keeper. One of many sent to sow discord in Wayland. Their goal is to take magic away from Wayland, then he will return and, with the other shadow keepers, rule in Verlyn."

Cailu clapped his hands a half dozen times. A smile spread across his thin face. "Very good, TruthSeer. But you missed one thing. When we rule Verlyn, we will also rule Wayland. With all the power restored to us, we will rule as gods, and Wayland will be our subject, doing our bidding."

Noelle turned with a frown. "You said I would be a queen."

Cailu smiled and patted her arm. "And you will, my dear. We won't have time to lower ourselves to your daily doings. There are more lands for our taking."

More lands? Alarms went off inside of Shaeleen's head. That was their ultimate goal: to find other kingdoms and countries to put under their control.

Noelle smiled smugly at Shaeleen.

Oh, how I wish I could wipe that smile off her face.

"What about my mother?" asked Raimund.

"I'm afraid she will have to die." Cailu smiled, and black tendrils of power trickled off his skin. He signaled to the soldier holding her.

"No!" Cole yelled, and in a flash, the soldier went flying, but his blade had already begun to slice the queen's throat.

Emmony dropped to the ground in silence and held her throat; blood flowing through her fingers. Shaeleen moved toward her with thoughts of healing her. Before she could get there, a blast hit her from behind, and she was thrown to the ground. She turned and saw the mirthful eyes of Cailu. In her thoughts for the queen, she had forgotten to be careful.

Shaeleen shook her head to clear her mind. She slowly stood up. Cole was fighting Cailu's soldiers off to the side, protecting Raimund from any more harm. She stood and pulled upon all the strength she had . . . and remembered something. The ShadowStones were a reflection of the true stones of power—stones that she held. Shae watched as Cailu prepared to draw upon his power. Black smoke swirled around him until his eyes grew dark.

Noelle stood by his side, smiling. "Now we will see who is more powerful."

Raimund limped closer to Noelle and reached for her arm. "Come with me, Noelle. You're not yourself."

Noelle pushed her brother away. He stumbled a bit but caught himself.

"Please, remember who you are, Noelle," Raimund continued. "Remember all that Father and Mother taught you about ruling. You're a good person. I know you are."

Cailu raised his hands in front of him, and Shaeleen prepared herself. She drew upon all the powers at her disposal and wrapped them in the light to form a defensive shield—not just a barrier to absorb the power of the ShadowStone, but a shield of reflection.

Cailu threw all he had at her. Blackness flew from his fingertips and raced in a swirl of fog toward her. Harm, evil, death echoed in the air around them. Then it struck Shaeleen's defensive shield, almost throwing her from her feet. She stumbled, but stayed standing as a loud boom filled the air.

And in that boom, Shaeleen heard another sound—horse hooves racing over soft grass, coming from behind Cailu. Shaeleen held strong against the power of the ShadowStone and set her powers as a reflective surface that did not destroy but repelled everything that Cailu had thrown at her. Cailu's eyes opened wide as he realized what she had done. The power bounced off her shield and sped back toward Cailu himself.

With only thoughts for himself, Cailu grabbed Noelle, propelling her in front of him to take the brunt of the reflective rebound. Noelle screamed and tried to pull away. At the same time, Raimund realized what was happening and jumped between Shaeleen and his sister just as the backlash of power struck.

An otherworldly scream came from Raimund's lips as he absorbed all the power that Cailu had originally intended for Shaeleen. He fell to the ground with a look of extreme pain.

"Raimund!" Noelle cried, kneeling by her brother. "No. No. Raimund. I didn't mean for this to happen."

The hoofbeats came closer. No one but Shaeleen noticed a lone man, riding as fast as he could.

Cailu glared triumphantly at Shaeleen. "Looks like things still might turn out as we intended."

Noelle stood up and stared at her mother lying lifeless on the ground, then back down at her brother, who was struggling to breathe. She turned to Cailu. "You never said they would die."

"Being a leader has a price," Cailu said. "You wanted to be queen."

Tears dripped down Noelle's face, and Shaeleen felt a glimmer of compassion for the princess. But she couldn't stop and worry about that now. Cole still fought behind her with a few remaining soldiers. His sword spun with fire as he defended himself and took down one soldier after another. The horse and rider were almost there. Shaeleen smiled as Archer appeared. With knees steady on the horse, he used his arms to nock an arrow into a large bow. No one else seemed to notice.

Cailu pushed Noelle away from him. "Maybe you're not fit to be a queen, then."

Archer pulled back on the bow, and Cailu must have heard it. He turned his head slightly. Suddenly, Noelle came running for him from the side. The distraction caused him to turn back.

Archer let the arrow go.

Noelle's momentum carried her toward Cailu and right in the line of the arrow's flight. Shaeleen instantly pulled on the power of the SpeedStone and flew to Noelle. She knocked into Noelle, and twisted her own body in the air as the arrow flew between her outstretched arm and into Cailu's chest.

Shaeleen fell to the ground with Noelle, then quickly untangled herself and stood. Cailu's eyes went wide as the arrow stuck out from the middle of his chest. With one last breath and gurgle, the shadow keeper fell back on the ground, his head bouncing once before his body settled lifelessly on the unkept grass.

"Not all fights are won by magic, TruthSeer," Archer said as he brought his horse to a stop.

CHAPTER TWENTY-EIGHT

The next morning, Shaeleen stood with Cole at the docks in South Bay. The air was hot, but the sky was overcast, and it appeared a storm might be coming their way.

Abby came running up to them. "My father said the ship will be ready to leave in two hours."

Shaeleen nodded. "Thank you, Abby. Tell him we will be there soon."

The young girl went running back toward a brand-new ship anchored at the end of the dock. Hearing sounds from behind them, Shaeleen turned. She couldn't see anything yet but knew what was coming.

"A carriage," Shaeleen said, the power of the HearingStone working in her. Out of all the stones, the HearingStone was the most natural and worked without any thought or much effort.

A few moments later, a six-horse carriage came up next to the docks. The driver motioned Shaeleen and Cole over. A door was opened for them, and they climbed inside. Noelle and Raimund sat on one side. Noelle waved her hand for Shaeleen and Cole to sit on the other.

Noelle then called out, "Driver, take us away from the docks. It stinks here."

Shaeleen rolled her eyes. She had grown up in a port her entire life. South Bay was clean and nice-smelling for a city and port of its size. Soon, they came to a stretch of road that overlooked the sea, and the carriage slowed, allowing for an easier conversation.

"Thank you, TruthSeer Shaeleen," said Raimund. "I hear that I wouldn't have survived without your healing."

Shaeleen smiled. It had been difficult. His wound was deep. But with the help of General Archer's small healing ability and her other powers, she had repaired his insides and closed the wound. "How are you feeling?"

"Tired," Raimund said.

"Shaeleen . . . uh, TruthSeer . . ." Noelle seemed to struggle to find the words she wanted to speak. Since the battle, the princess had been much more subdued.

"Shaeleen is fine."

"Shaeleen, then." The princess paused to gather her thoughts. "I too want to thank you. You saved my life. After how I treated you, why would you do that?"

Shaeleen looked at Cole, then back at the princess. "Because it was the right thing to do. You were under a shadow keeper's influence. You should not be held responsible for that. I also saw how much you meant to your brother when he put his life in front of yours. I figured if he saw something of value there, then I could too."

Noelle's face soured for a moment. "So, what now? Will you take the throne from me for what I have done? Intentional or not, I turned against my kingdom."

"Actually," Shaeleen said, "from what I see, you were only following orders from your king—rightful king or not, he was acting in your mother's stead. With the queen's passing and

Cailu's death, the only other person to assume the throne would be Raimund."

Everyone's eyes were on Raimund. He took his time answering, then placed his hand on Noelle's before speaking. "I will not take the throne from the rightful heir."

The words echoed inside Shaeleen's head. *Basil!* They were very similar to what he had said about his brother, Calix. A situation that still had to be dealt with before this was all over.

"But you will need a regent until you are seventeen," Cole said. "Have you thought about that?"

Noelle nodded and smiled. "Uncle Archer would be a fine regent. I think the people will accept him. It's only for nine months, then we will be seventeen."

Shaeleen clapped her hands in delight. "A great idea." Maybe there was hope for the princess. "With him and your brother, I think you might just make a good queen, Noelle."

Noelle beamed at the praise. "I'm sorry for the way we started off, Shaeleen. You are welcome in our kingdom anytime. You have shown your loyalty to us, TruthSeer. Be it known that I willingly accept you."

Shaeleen was touched by the words. Noelle had been through a difficult time, but was showing decorum equal to her brother.

"But what will happen to the stones of power?" Noelle asked after she advised the driver to turn back to the docks.

Shaeleen shook her head. "I'm not sure what happens next. I need to face the rest of the shadow keepers first, then somehow restore the stones back to Wayland." A task she still wasn't sure how to accomplish. Soon, they were back at the docks, where Shaeleen and Cole climbed out.

Noelle called their attention back. "There is one more thing," she said with a look of concern on her face. "There is news from Galena."

Cole and Shaeleen perked up.

"Prince Calix has married Princess Diamonique," Noelle said.

Shaeleen glanced at Cole. His mouth went tight, and his eyes grew hard, but he stayed silent.

"That was quick," was all Shaeleen said.

Noelle nodded. "Also, it is said that Commander Kerr of Gabor has gone to North Bay, but two armies are at a standoff at the peninsula. Calix holds Stronghaven and North Bay, while Basil's men hold the rest of Galena."

"Where is their TruthSeer?"

Noelle shook her head. "I have not heard."

"Shadow keepers," Shaeleen said and shivered. They had their hands in everything. "Prince Raimund and Princess Noelle, I am sorry about your mother."

They both bowed their heads in respect.

"Thank you, TruthSeer," Raimund said, then turned to Cole. "And Wizard. You both did a great service ridding our land of Cailu and did so at your own peril. You will be remembered always in Althea."

Cole was obviously still thinking about Diamonique but regained his composure and extended his hand to shake Raimund's. "Thank you, Prince Raimund," Cole said, then turned to Noelle. "Princess, may your reign be peaceful."

With those goodbyes, Shaeleen and Cole headed down the

docks to take a ship to Verlyn.

Shaeleen laid her hand on Cole's arm. She felt his muscles twitch, but he left her hand there. She knew his heart still pined for Diamonique. Right before they got to the ship, she felt a few droplets of rain on her head.

"Not another storm," Shaeleen groaned, thinking about their first ship to Verlyn. That had not ended well.

* * *

Shortly after the ship left the dock, a steady rain began. It continued to rain all that day, into the night, and continued as they came around the Hightower peninsula in the southern tip of Althea. Shaeleen and Cole mostly stayed off the deck in one of the rooms in the hull. The ship held steadier than the cargo ship they had taken to Verlyn last time. Shaeleen felt safe but could only sit around so long.

She put a hood over her head and took the stairs up to the deck to get a breath of fresh air. Pushing hard on the door, a spray of water hit her face, and she wondered if this was a good idea. Grabbing hold of a pole, she stopped to look around. Gray clouds billowed above them, and the water churned mercilessly. They hadn't hit the straits yet, and aside from the driving rain, the air between sea and clouds had more visibility than she expected. Moving around to the port side, Shaeleen hung on to the railing and stared out toward the land. Above the rocks stood the city of Hightower, its flag flapping dramatically in the wind high above the city.

"Miss Shaeleen," came a voice from behind her.

Shaeleen had heard him coming. "Captain?"

"You shouldn't be up here. It's dangerous."

"I remember our last trip." Shaeleen smiled, a gleam in her eye. "You needed my help."

The captain rolled his eyes. "I also remember losing a ship each time you were a passenger."

Shaeleen laughed and wiped the rain out of her face. "You should be more careful who you pick up."

"You always had a quick tongue," the captain said. Then his eyes grew soft. "Thank you for what you did for Abby. I don't know what my wife and I would do without her."

Shaeleen nodded. "She is quite a girl."

They began to round the peninsula, and the ship tried to turn north through the Straits of Mist, but the wind pushed back at them.

"Captain," called out his first mate that tended the wheel. "She's not turning. Headwind is too strong coming down the straits."

The captain turned back to Shaeleen. "I have to do everything around here. This is going to get rough. You really should get back down below."

Shaeleen nodded and headed to the door. She was soaked. Being the only passengers did have its advantages; she had her own room. It was something the captain had not been too happy about until he had seen the money they would pay him. She took time to dry off and change into dry clothes. Pulling on black pants, a white shirt and a dark blue cloak, she made sure, as always, that the pouch with the TruthStone hung at her side.

Just thinking about the stones brought up the powers

inside her now. The stones worked instinctively together. Each stone helped support the other stones, the strength of one lending itself to strengthen another. That had been King Wayland's original intention, she was sure: each kingdom having a stone of power, ensuring all of Wayland worked together. However, through the years, they stopped working together—whether it was from sharing too much of the stone or not working together enough or both.

The ship lurched to the side, and Shaeleen put her hand out to catch herself against the door. A knock sounded on the other side of the door, and Shaeleen opened it.

"My father would like to see you and Cole in his cabin," Abby said. She cocked her head to the side, and before she could speak, Shaeleen jumped in.

"Cole's coming right now," Shaeleen said. "I hear his heavy boots."

"Hey," Abby said. "That's what I was going to say. It's not fair now that you have the powers of the HearingStone too."

Shaeleen laughed as Cole walked up.

"What?" he said.

Both girls laughed, and Cole just shrugged while they followed Abby to her father's cabin. Once inside, they were directed to a set of chairs around a small table. The table held a map of Wayland and Verlyn on it.

"We are right here," the captain said without preamble. He pointed to a spot in the water just east of Hightower, between there and the island of Verlyn. Then he moved his finger up the Straits of Mist and farther east to Sylvermoor. "That's where we are supposed to go." He paused. "But the headwind is too strong. We can't get the ship to turn that way; the storm's too hard to sail against."

"Then where do we go?"

The captain pointed farther east, to the southern shoreline of Verlyn. "The storm is taking us this way. We could land somewhere here and wait it out."

Shaeleen and Cole studied the map for a moment. "And then what?" Cole asked.

"Then we could make our way back around, either through the straits or up the east coast and back around the north part by the jungle. Either way is a long trek."

Shaeleen felt a lurch in both the TruthStone and the IntelligenceStone. Her demeanor grew serious. "We don't have that much time, Captain."

He bit his lip and continued to look at the map. "There is one other way—not easy, but possible."

"Go ahead," Shaeleen said.

"There are a few villages on the southern shores, and they have crude roads—well, barely paths,—leading to Mt. Eyvindr, then west to Sylvermoor. The desert there is mighty hot, but it could be faster than sailing around the island."

Shaeleen gave a sly smile to Cole. "We could run it, using the SpeedStone."

Cole grinned. "That we could."

Abby spoke up. "Father, they need you up top."

Her father looked at her, but before he could say anything, there was a knock on the door. "Captain!" a voice called out.

The captain ruffled his daughter's hair and opened the door. They all followed him out.

CHAPTER TWENTY-NINE

As soon as the ship passed by the mouth of the narrow Straits of Mist, the wind died down, and the rain began to dissipate. The island of Verlyn appeared on their port side, while a few smaller islands dotted the sea on their starboard. By the time night fell, all storm clouds were gone, and the stars brightened the sky above them. Cole and Shaeleen stood out on the deck, taking in the surroundings. Stars filled the sky from horizon to horizon, almost seeming to drop into the sea itself.

"On nights like this, it's hard to believe the mess we're all in," Shaeleen said.

Cole leaned against the railing at the front of the ship, staring straight ahead. He didn't say anything for a moment. "Do you think he is treating her well?"

Shaeleen's heart went out to her brother. She knew who he was thinking about—Diamonique. She didn't know if Cole was looking for an answer from her or not.

Cole turned his head to her. "Sometimes I wish I were more like you."

Shaeleen barked out a small laugh. "What do you mean?"

"Sometimes it really hurts to follow the rules and be honorable," he said, his eyes full of pain. "If it were you, you would just barge in, using whatever power was at your disposal and take back what you wanted, stepping on whoever's toes you could to get it."

Shaeleen nodded, smiled, and punched her brother softly in the arm. "I don't know whether to be angry or proud of how you see me. I am trying to be more careful and respectful."

Cole smiled back. "Oh, I'm not saying anything bad about you. You are who you are, and I'm proud of everything you've done. It can't be easy having a destiny to live up to."

"You have no idea." Shaeleen waved her hand out in front of her. "But at times like this, it's hard to think much of myself. I'm just one small speck in all of this. One small person on a small ship in the middle of an endless sea."

"Ever wonder what else is out there?" Cole asked.

"Up there?" Shaeleen pointed to the stars. "Or out there?" She waved her hands over the sea.

"Both, I guess," Cole said. "But I was speaking more of our world. I've heard of massive continents of kingdoms to the east and west, but it's hard to imagine such a large world. "

"I have a hard enough time trying to fix the kingdoms I do know about," Shaeleen said.

Before Cole could say anything more, the captain came up to them. "Quite a sight, isn't it? I've always relished moments like this. Sailing on a clear night is an experience you will never forget—one that can make you think about things."

Shaeleen and Cole both nodded.

"But I didn't come out here to talk philosophy with you two. I wanted to check on your plans." The captain waved his hand toward the dark outlines of Verlyn. "You still want to land here and make the trek over land?"

"Yes," Shaeleen said without hesitation. Something important to vanquishing the shadow keepers was drawing her this way.

"Tomorrow morning, we'll come to a small bay. It's not a big enough port to bring this ship into, but I'll have rowers take you in the smaller boat. There are a few villages there that should be able to provide you what you need."

"Thank you, Captain," Cole said. "You've been very accommodating to us."

The captain laughed. "Your sister has a way of getting things done."

Cole joined in the laugh. "That she does. And I'm here to protect her when it happens."

"I'm glad someone is watching over her." The captain patted Shaeleen on the back. "Someone needs to keep her in line."

"Hey." Shaeleen put her hands on her hips in mock anger. "I didn't do anything."

"Not this time," the captain said, and they all had a good laugh.

* * *

Shaeleen woke early the next morning, the sun shining brightly through the small window in her room. The air was warm, but she noticed a lessoning of humidity on the south side of the island. Grabbing her bag, she headed up to the deck. Cole was already there, waiting for her.

Abby came running up and gave her a big hug. "I'll miss

you, Shae."

Shaeleen moved her arm around Abby's shoulder. "And I'll miss you, too. You are an amazing young woman. I have a feeling we'll see each other again."

Abby's eyes grew wide. "You think so? I sure hope so."

Shaeleen looked over at Verlyn a few hundred yards away. This side of the island was drier than the jungles to the north. A few trees dotted the shore, but farther off, only brown hills and sand met her vision. The faint outline of Mt. Eyvindr rose in the distance.

The captain motioned Cole and Shaeleen to the side of the ship, where a smaller boat had been lowered into the water. Two rowers sat ready to take them to shore.

"Ready to save the world, little sister?" Cole smiled, his blue eyes dancing merrily in the bright sunlight.

Shaeleen glared at him, then laughed. She patted the pouch at her side, hiding beneath a lightweight cloak. "Let's go."

The small rowboat moved swiftly through the water. The closer they got to land, the more apprehension filled Shaeleen. This was it. The last time she left Verlyn, the shadow keepers had vowed to meet her again. Her thoughts turned to Taegen. She wondered how he was doing. She would hate to have to destroy him along with the others—she wasn't sure she could do it.

"So, are we going concealed or in full glory?" Cole turned to Shaeleen.

She thought for a moment, then smiled. A giddiness filled her soul, and she felt the power of the stones rise within her. They gave her strength, resolve, and peace all at once. "It's time, Cole. It's time to defeat the shadow keepers and restore the stones. It's time to be the TruthSeer I was named."

Cole nodded his head, his own face mirroring hers. "Just be careful, Shae."

"Always."

Cole laughed, and she could see the smiles on the two rowers.

"Hey," she said to them. "What are you sailors smiling about?"

They tried to hide their smiles but didn't succeed, and everyone burst into laughter. The release felt good. They approached the shore, and a group of people stood there, wondering who their visitors were. Their long hair—brown, black, and blond—moved slightly with the morning breeze blowing off the water. A few children ran up closer to the water as the boat coasted in.

Cole stood up first and stepped off the boat onto dry land. With a flourish of his hand, he pointed back to Shaeleen, who now stood up in the middle of the boat. A hush fell over the crowd as he announced her. "TruthSeer Shaeleen." Cole's voice carried deep and loud. "The prophesied one!"

Shaeleen drew upon her powers, letting a swirl of colors fly around her body. Using the opposing power of the SpeedStone and StrengthStone, she rose in the air a few inches above the boat. Her brown hair and light blue cloak blew around her in the breeze as she floated forward to the dry land. She held her hands out at her sides, palms opened and relished in the power that filled her. The Verlynians didn't know what to make of it, but they knew she was someone important. Some of the older ones knelt on the sand and bowed their heads. The younger children stood in awe.

Shaeleen brought herself down on the ground. She could feel the soft crunch of sand under her boots. "I hold all the stones of power. Be it known that I am here to vanquish the shadow keepers and restore the stones of power. I am the TruthSeer."

With a swirl of her hands, the colors raced around her then shot off into the small village before dissipating. Cole came and stood at her side, and they walked toward the stunned villagers.

"Is there a keeper of stones here in your village?" Shaeleen asked as she came to the group.

From the back, a man came forward. His face was tan and wrinkled, his long hair gray. He bowed deeply to Shaeleen and Cole. "Welcome, TruthSeer Shaeleen. I have heard about you. I am Keeper Orion."

Shaeleen lifted her brows at his words.

The man smiled. "I met with Keepers Lorelei and Melindra at the gathering. Heard quite a bit of your exploits." The man's light blue eyes sparkled in the sunlight, holding intelligence and humor in them. "Come with me."

They followed the older man into the village. It was small—no more than a few dozen homes set close to the shore. Shaeleen saw fishing poles and small boats. They passed a few homes and came to one at the edge of town. Shaeleen stopped and turned her head around, as if searching for something.

"What is it, Shae?" Cole's hand went to his sword hilt.

"What is that wonderful smell?" Shaeleen asked.

Cole relaxed and laughed. "Shae!"

"What?" She turned to her brother. "I can't help it. It smells so good."

"That is my wife's cooking," Orion said, motioning them to the doorway. "Early morning breakfast rolls, if I'm not mistaken."

"Oh, how wonderful!" Shaeleen felt her stomach rumble. "Please lead the way."

CHAPTER THIRTY

Shaeleen thoroughly enjoyed the morning sweet rolls. It was a wonderful way to start their journey. Orion hadn't heard anything else from Sylvermoor since the gathering. Their small village was quite remote from the rest of the population. He told Shaeleen and Cole about a rough and rarely used road that ran from their village to the southern slopes of Mt. Eyvindr. From there, they could find many larger roads leading to Sylvermoor. An hour later, having gathered a few provisions of food, water, and a small tent, Shaeleen and Cole stood at the beginnings of the road.

"Not much more than a trail," Shaeleen mumbled to her brother.

It seemed that everyone in town was gathered around to wish them well. Shaeleen thanked Orion and the others for their hospitality. Turning from the townspeople to the trail in front of them, Shaeleen frowned and wiped her brow. *It's a hot and dry day to be running.*

"Ready for a run?" Shaeleen said to Cole.

"Let's go!"

Shaeleen pulled on the power of the SpeedStone, coming strongly now with barely a thought for what she was doing. She took off running, her brother farther behind, taking a bit longer to get his power ready. A few moments later, he caught up to her, a blur by her side. They flew by tan and weathered grass, sand, and rocks, a few stray scrub brush scattered around. Up ahead, Mt. Eyvindr grew larger by the minute.

It was exhilarating to run like that, but soon, Cole called for them to stop. "In this heat, we need to make sure we stay hydrated." Cole brought a waterskin to his lips.

Shaeleen followed suit. The cool water tasted good going down her dry throat. She needed to remember to keep her mouth closed as she ran. After a brief break, they started running again. This pattern continued for most of the day, though as the day wore on, they took more time to walk in between, conserving their powers and energy for whatever lay in front of them. By evening, Shaeleen figured they had made it about three-fourths of the way to the mountain—a good two or three days' journey for normal travelers. The road began to bend to the east.

They stopped for the night by a great outcropping of rock and set up their tent. Sleep came quickly, and Shaeleen and Cole rested well that night. Gathering their things in the morning, Shaeleen noticed that the weather was less dry as they got closer to the mountain—though more humidity meant more sweat. She would need a good bath after all this was over.

"Do you know how you are going to beat the shadow keepers?" Cole asked as they gathered their few belongings.

Shaeleen had been asking herself that same question. "I'm not sure. I don't even know how many ShadowStones there are or who holds them."

"But how are you going to destroy them? We have to have a plan, Shae. You can't just go into Sylvermoor blindly and shoot off your power."

Shaeleen smiled at him, then took a swig of water from her waterskin. "I can't?"

"Shae!" Cole said, his face growing stern.

"I'm joking. But . . ." Shaeleen paused a moment. "In one way, I'm not. My powers come to me instinctively now. Sometimes I don't know a TruthSpell or how to do something until the moment it's needed. The IntelligenceStone tells me what to do."

"That's a hard way to go about things," Cole mumbled.

"Tell me about it." Shaeleen folded a cloth and tied it around her head like a headband to stop the sweat. "I do have a few ideas. I know the ShadowStones are a reflection of the stones of power. I know I can cause pain by touching one that has been infected by the shadow." Shaeleen thought about Orin and hoped he and his father had returned to Mistport safely. "And I know the shadow and the light cannot exist together at the same time. I just need to figure out how to tell who has a ShadowStone and then put all of what I know together. I can do it, Cole."

Cole nodded, and his eyes softened. "I know you can, Shae. Just try to keep me in the loop of your plans. I can't help protect you if I don't know what you're doing."

"I'll tell you as soon as I know," Shaeleen said with a smile. "Ready to run again?"

"Let's go."

They both drew upon the SpeedStone and raced down the dirt path, heading northeast around the slope of Mt. Eyvindr. Shaeleen continued to think about what she had to do.

Destroying the shadow keepers was one thing; that was brute magical force. But how was she going to restore the stones of power to Wayland? None of the kingdoms had their stones now. Shaeleen held them all.

As the sun rose, the day grew hotter, and they found themselves stopping more often to drink and rest. Mt. Eyvindr loomed in front of them, blocking out half the sky. Even in the middle of summer, the peak was snowcapped. As they grew closer to it, the ground became more green, rocky, and uneven. Taller trees appeared more often, and the path grew steeper and more irregular.

"We should walk more," Cole said during one of their breaks. "It's getting harder to navigate while running so fast. We need to slow down."

Shaeleen shook her head. "I need to get around the mountain, Cole." She glanced up at the sky. The afternoon was going quick. "One more jaunt with the SpeedStone, and we should be in a good position to reach Sylvermoor by tomorrow."

Cole clearly didn't agree but nodded anyway. "Once more."

Shaeleen took off first, but moments later, Cole passed her up. For about thirty minutes, they ran, weaving between taller trees, leaping over large rocks and narrow ravines. Without warning, Cole yelled out and disappeared in front of Shaeleen. She skidded to a stop so fast that she fell to her knees and banged a leg against a rock.

"Cole!" Shaeleen screamed for her brother. She crawled to the edge of a deep ravine that they hadn't seen. About thirty feet down, next to a small stream, Cole lay, his arms and legs spread out and not moving. "Cole!" Shaeleen yelled again, trying to find a way down. She looked back and forth up and down the ravine but couldn't see any way to get down easily. The rocks along it were loose and wouldn't hold her weight. Her brother still didn't move.

No, no, no. This can't happen! He's my protector!

Shaeleen winced with every step she took. Her pants were ripped and a long red gash ran down the length of her right leg. It didn't feel broken, but it hurt every time she took a step.

"Cole, get up!" she yelled down at him again. There was no movement. His body stayed sprawled out on the hard ground. Standing at the edge of the ravine, she pulled upon her powers—the HealingStone to help her leg, then the StrengthStone. She took a few steps back and jumped out into the ravine. She began to drop down fast, but she took power from the SpeedStone like she had done before and used it as an opposing force to slow her descent, while pushing hard on the air below her. A few feet before crashing into the ground at the bottom of the ravine, she slowed and dropped to the ground in a light crouch.

She moved over to Cole and kneeled next to him. "Cole!" She rubbed her hand on his face, then leaned down and used the HearingStone to listen for his heartbeat. She breathed a sigh of relief. *He's not dead.* Taking her waterskin from her side, Shaeleen splashed a bit of water on his face. She could see his eyeballs fluttering under his lids. "Cole, wake up!"

Looking around, Shaeleen knew she wouldn't find any help. She closed her eyes for a moment and ran her hand over

Cole's body, using the HealingStone to feel for injuries. She cringed when she found his arm and two ribs broken. The ligaments in his ankle were twisted, but not broken. As her hand came to his head, she flinched, then using the StrengthStone to give her strength, she moved her hand around to the back of his head. A significant bump the size of a small egg protruded. There was a trickle of blood. She was surprised there wasn't more.

Using the SpeedStone for two days had depleted her reserves somewhat, and the heat of the day made her weary, but none of that mattered right now. She drew upon all she had and poured it into the tiny HealingStone. Then she pushed the healing into Cole's body.

At one point, Shaeleen heard a sound of faint footsteps behind her but didn't dare turn to see what it was. She used the power to meld his broken bones back together, strengthened his ankle, and healed as many cuts and scrapes as she could. Finally, reaching a point of exhaustion, she pulled away her hands and let her powers recede. She heard the stepping of feet on stone again and jumped up, hand in front of her, a ball of light ready to defend herself.

"Hey!" a boy, not much younger than her, yelped. "Don't hurt me."

Shaeleen glanced around to make sure there wasn't anyone else hiding among the rocks. She lowered her hand, then turned her attention to the young man in front of her. He had long, black hair and smooth skin. He was beautiful in the way that all from Verlyn were but still had the face of one who was young. His eyes were wide, and his hands raised out in front of him.

"I won't hurt you," Shaeleen said. "My brother fell from the ravine. I was trying to help him."

The boy's eyes were round as saucers, and he took a hesitant step forward. "I saw you."

"You saw me what?" Shaeleen was getting impatient. She needed to get back to helping Cole. She bent down and ran a hand over his forehead. There didn't seem to be a fever.

"I saw you fly down here and heal him."

"Oh," Shaeleen mumbled under her breath. *Well, I am not hiding my powers anymore.* Still, she felt strange that someone had watched her.

"You have the power of the SpeedStone and HealingStone." The young man walked closer and stood by Shaeleen's side. A small gasp ensued from his lips as he spoke more quietly. "And the StrengthStone, HearingStone, IntelligenceStone . . ." The young man's breathing grew more ragged.

Shaeleen gazed up at him. His eyes darted around, as if nervous. "You missed one." Shaeleen smiled at him.

A low moan from Cole turned Shaeleen's attention back around before the young man could say anything more. Moving to her brother, she knelt down and put her hand on his shoulder over his leather vest.

"Shae." Cole's eyes fluttered open. "What happened?"

Relief brought tears to Shaeleen's eyes. "Oh, Cole. You fell all the way down the ravine. I'm so sorry. It's my fault."

Cole blinked a few times. "How's that?"

"I made us run farther." Shaeleen wiped her eyes. "You were right . . . as always. We should have stopped."

Cole raised his eyebrows at her and smiled.

"Well, you're not always right." Shaeleen laughed. "Just most of the time."

"Help me up," Cole said, putting his hands against the ground. Shaeleen put a hand behind his head, and the young man rushed up to help. "Ouch!" Cole said. "Be careful."

In a few moments, they had him sitting up.

"Who are you?" Cole said to the young man.

"Feyn," the young man said. "My name is Feyn."

"What are you doing out here, Feyn?" Shaeleen asked.

"I live out here."

"Where are your parents?" Cole asked.

Feyn frowned and took another step back. "In Sylvermoor. I . . ."

Shaeleen stood up. "You don't need to be afraid of us, Feyn."

"I'm not afraid of you. I just don't like people."

"That's a strange thing not to like," Shaeleen said.

"I mean I don't like being around a lot of people—makes me nervous and sick."

Cole stood up and took a step, testing his ankle. "I am Cole, and this is Shaeleen—"

Feyn interrupted, staring hard at Shaeleen. "You are the TruthSeer I have been waiting for."

Shaeleen opened her mouth with surprise. "How?"

"I can sense the power of the stones in anyone," Feyn admitted.

Shaeleen marveled that he could know about the stones through the pouch that had always protected them. Then her mind raced with excitement. "Even . . ." She paused. Shaeleen didn't want to scare Feyn away.

Feyn nodded as if he knew what she'd been about to ask. "Even holders of a ShadowStone. I know who is a shadow keeper."

Shaeleen glanced over at Cole. Surprise spread across his face, then he smiled and nodded.

CHAPTER THIRTY-ONE

Shaeleen and Cole followed Feyn out of the ravine. Then he took them about a mile north to a river. They walked next to it upriver until they came to a beautiful pool of water, a waterfall cascading down behind it. It brought memories to Shaeleen of when she was with Taegen and had faced off against his uncle, Dunstan. She stopped at the pool and peered down. Sparkles of color fluttered to the surface.

"Stones of power," Shaeleen whispered, dazzled by its beauty.

Feyn nodded, not saying much, then led them up behind the waterfall to a cave. Stepping inside, Shaeleen was impressed. Obviously, much care had gone into Feyn's abode. Shelves lined the walls with decorative items and useful tools. A pile of skins sat in one corner. Other crude furnishings spread around the small cave.

"Are you a keeper?" Shaeleen asked.

Feyn shook his head and offered them a place to sit. He went over to where the coals of a former fire still glowed hot. A small pot sat on a makeshift pot holder above the coals. He went to a shelf and took two crudely made cups and went back to the pot. He spooned out something into each cup, then handed it to each of them with a small metal spoon.

"I found the spoons in a village," Feyn said. "I didn't steal them. Just found them."

Shaeleen nodded. "I wasn't accusing you of anything, Feyn. You're a bit jumpy." She took a spoonful of liquid and brought it to her lips. She blew on it a few times, then took a bite. "Rabbit stew."

Feyn nodded.

"You don't talk much, do you?" Shaeleen said.

"Don't tease him, Shae," Cole said. "He's obviously been living here awhile and not used to visitors."

They ate their stew in silence, Feyn getting up a few times and walking to the mouth of the cave and back again. The last time he walked back, he began gathering a few items and placing them in a bag.

"We are grateful for your help, Feyn," Shaeleen said. "But . . ."

"I'm going with you," Feyn said, though his eyes didn't look convinced.

Shaeleen remembered what he had said. "You've been waiting for me?"

Feyn nodded his head. "I thought you would be older."

Shaeleen laughed. "I get that a lot."

"You are here to destroy the shadow keepers?" Feyn asked.

"Yes," Shaeleen said. "And restore the stones of power to Wayland. The council of Verlyn and the gathering of keepers have outlawed magic in Wayland, and I am here to stop that from happening."

Feyn held his lips tight for a moment before speaking. "So, they finally did it."

"Who did what?" Cole asked.

"The shadow keepers," Feyn said. "Last year, they tried to vote on it, but it failed. I've been here ever since."

"Sounds like you have a story, Feyn, but we really need to get going," Shaeleen said.

Feyn's shoulders fell. "Like I said, I'm coming with you."

"You don't seem too happy," Shaeleen said.

"I don't like crowds much," Feyn said.

In short order, Feyn had gathered a few items, doused the coals, and covered a few other belongings. He led Shaeleen and Cole out of the cave, across to the north side of the river. They walked north for a bit before heading west through the thickening trees.

As they walked, young Feyn's story came out slowly. "About a year ago, I found out about the shadow keepers," he began. "Evil men and women wanting the power of the stones all to themselves."

Shaeleen nodded. "I've met them—many of them. Prince Brevin is their head."

"You know?"

"Yes. I am here to take them down."

After walking a bit farther, Feyn said, "I fought them."

"You fought them?" Cole asked in disbelief.

Feyn turned his head. "It's hard to believe. I have the ability to know what stones of power someone holds. I sensed the ShadowStones and tried to tell the queen, her council, and the keepers about it. Some of them believed, but many did not. Prince Brevin took me away from the queen and met up with some of his other shadow keepers."

"Feyn, I can barely defeat one shadow keeper at a time, and even that was difficult, and I have six stones now at my disposal." Shaeleen knew Feyn wasn't lying—the TruthStone told her that—but it was hard to believe. "How did you get away?"

Feyn appeared embarrassed by the attention. "When I sensed the stones, I discovered I could also use their power. All of them."

Shaeleen suddenly understood. "Even the ShadowStones?"

"Yes. I fought them using their own stones against them and some of the other stones in the vicinity. But the shadow keepers were too strong for me. We were at an impasse."

An impasse? Shaeleen was indeed impressed if Feyn had held out against Brevin and the other shadow keepers.

"I needed a TruthStone to destroy them, but the only TruthStone in the vicinity was held by Keeper Melindra and wasn't meant to be used yet." Feyn directed the two of them down the mountain now, winding his way through game trails as if he knew exactly where he was going.

Shaeleen put her hand on the pouch holding her TruthStone. "Melindra gave me the stone a few months ago."

"She left over a year ago to find one worthy of it," Feyn said.

Shaeleen turned her head to Cole. He shrugged his shoulders and followed Feyn down the mountain. It was growing dark, the thick canopy blocking the late afternoon sun. The jungle grew thicker, and large leaves began to block their way more often.

"Where are we going?" Shaeleen asked.

"To find my sister," Feyn said. "Orissa is a keeper. She can help us. We need to draw all the shadow keepers out."

Cole stopped for a moment. "Shae can't destroy all of them at once."

Feyn stopped in front of them and looked back at the two. He sounded older than his years when he spoke. "She will have help, Cole. You and I will be there."

* * *

A few hours later, they emerged from the edge of the trees. Night had fallen, and only candles shining out through windows of homes lit the area around them. The three stood looking down the main street of a small village.

"You will have to stay here tonight," Feyn said. "Tomorrow morning, we will reach the outskirts of Sylvermoor." Feyn pointed to an inn down the street. "You can stay there. I will meet you in the morning." He turned to walk away.

"Hey, where are you going?" Shaeleen grabbed his arm. Feyn stiffened at her touch, and she pulled her arm away. "Why aren't you staying with us?"

"I . . . I can't," Feyn said.

"Maybe it's a trap, Shae," Cole spoke up.

Shaeleen stared at Feyn.

"No. It's not a trap," Feyn said. "Just go without me."

Shaeleen grabbed his arm again. "I don't think so. I know you're telling me the truth, but something is going on that you are not telling us."

Shaeleen and Cole walked with Feyn in tow toward the inn. As they went through the door, Shaeleen felt Feyn stiffen. He stopped walking, his eyes darting around the room.

"Come on." Shaeleen pulled him along. They met the innkeeper and payed for two rooms—one for Shaeleen, one for Feyn and Cole.

"Is he all right?" the innkeeper asked Shaeleen, pointing at Feyn. His face was flushed, his breathing quick and shallow.

"Just not used to being around people," Shaeleen said. After being told rooms would be made up for them, Shae pulled Feyn into the common room, with Cole following behind. They received strange looks—for though their eyes were light and they had slightly upswept brows, their hair was short and their ears not pointed. Mumbling began around the room, and Shaeleen could pick out bits of conversations.

"Not from around here."

"Looks like trouble."

"What are they doing to that poor boy?"

"Maybe they have magic."

Cole motioned Shaeleen and Feyn to an empty table at a far corner of the room. They sat down and ordered some food. The long walk had made Shaeleen famished.

"I'm not hungry," Feyn said, beginning to stand up.

"You're not running out on us, are you?" Shaeleen asked, pulling him back down in his seat.

Feyn put his head in his hands and began to shake. His breathing quickened even more. Finally, he jumped up and screamed, "I can't do this!" He turned to leave but tripped over a chair and fell to the ground. Cole reached down to help Feyn back up. Everyone in the room had stopped to look at them. Feyn looked like he was going to throw up. His face was flushed past the point of normal, and he staggered on his feet.

"What are you doing to him?" asked a Verlynian man at a neighboring table. He stood at least a foot taller than her. Cole moved over next to her and faced the man.

"He's our friend," Cole said.

"Doesn't look like he wants to be here," said the Verlynian.

Cole put his hand on the hilt of his sword. A few other Verlynians stood up and walked over to join the first. Another man with long, brown hair spoke up from the back.

"You don't look like you are from around here," he accused them.

"We are from Wayland," Cole said. "Is there a crime in that?"

"Might be, depending on who you are," said the first man.

Cole inched his sword out of his scabbard.

"You can't take us all on," the second man said.

Shae felt the pain of the lie as it fell from the man's lips. She staggered under its weight. It had been a while since she had felt a lie.

"I assure you, he can take you all on," Shaeleen said, leaning back up. "But I will be here to help. Now go back to your eating and drinking and leave us alone."

"Sit down, little girl," said another man from the back. "This is men's business."

That's it!

Shaeleen jumped from the floor to the table with little

effort. The room fell quiet, and the first man backed up a bit, the second one still holding his place up front. Cole glanced up at her with a look that said, *Are you sure you want to do this?*

Shaeleen nodded her head and drew upon her power. Green waves of iridescent colors wrapped around her body. "Since when did Verlyn become such an inhospitable place?" Shaeleen let her voice carry over the room in an echoing boom. "We on Wayland have always looked to Verlyn as a place of refinement, decorum, honor, and as the great protectors of the stones of power."

A few of those present hung their heads in shame and headed back to their seats. Others stared defiantly but took a few steps away from her show of power.

"You stole our power," came a voice from the back of the room. A man strode forward, and Shaeleen winced inside. She glanced down at Feyn, who was still shaking and sweating but had the good sense to stay where he was. He shook his head at her.

Good. The man wasn't a holder of a ShadowStone, just under its influence.

"Magic belongs in Verlyn," the man yelled. A few others joined in.

"Magic belongs in the hands of those who appreciate it and use it wisely," Shaeleen said. "It was given to us freely by your kingdom many years ago."

"But times change," said the man. "And now you break the law by using it."

"You are under the influence of the ShadowStone," Shaeleen yelled and pointed her hand toward the man. Before she could release a spell, a group of men walked in the front door. They wore official uniforms.

"The local constable and his men," Cole said to Shaeleen. "We need to go, Shae."

The constable and his men walked toward them, hands on swords and grim looks on their faces.

Shaeleen raised her hands in the air. "I hold the power of the stones and am here to rid your land of the shadow keepers."

People started mumbling around the room. Most did not believe in the shadow keepers; some seemed afraid at their mention.

"I will leave you now, but this won't be the last time you see me." Shaeleen spun her hands in circles, and sparks of color came out from her fingertips. The sparks raced toward the man under the influence of the shadow. She struck him hard with the power of the HealingStone. He arched his back and let out a loud scream. A cloud of shadow rose out of him, and those around him scrambled to get away.

"The shadow," said one.

"She speaks the truth," another spoke as he backed away.

"She is the shadow," another person yelled. "Get her."

The shadow flew from the man and toward a window, smashing the glass on its way out. The man, now down on his knees, glared up at her. At first, anger crossed his face, then fear, then a look of amazement as he realized the power of the shadow was gone from his body.

"You there, get down," the constable cried out. "Who are you to defy the laws of the land?"

The constable's men lurched forward, but Shaeleen jumped down and grabbed Cole with one hand and Feyn with the other. They pushed their way through the crowd in a blaze of speed and light; men went flying right and left, knocking down tables and chairs.

She stopped by the front door and turned around. In a voice that echoed out the doors and down the streets of the small village, Shaeleen announced her arrival for all to hear. "I am Shaeleen, TruthSeer and hunter of the shadow keepers. I am the prophesied one."

CHAPTER THIRTY-TWO

They sped down the street and out through the western end of town. Continuing down a main road a bit farther to make sure they were not followed, Shaeleen finally stopped. Feyn glared at her, then leaned over and threw up.

"Sorry to pull you like that, Feyn," Shaeleen said.

"That wasn't what made me sick," Feyn said, his eyes throwing daggers at her. "I told you I didn't want to go in there." His eyes filled with tears, and he looked away with shame.

Shaeleen took a deep breath and walked over to him. "I'm sorry for the trouble. Did you know that would happen? Can you sense things?"

Feyn stood up straight and looked into her eyes. "For the past year, I knew this day would come. The TruthSeer would show up, and we would defeat the shadow keepers together. But I didn't know the TruthSeer would be as dangerous to me as the shadow keepers themselves. At this point, I don't know who is worse."

Shaeleen took a step back from Feyn's angry eyes. Was she really becoming the monster she dreaded? Feyn wiped tears from his eyes.

"Don't ever make me do that again," Feyn said. "I told you I don't like being around people." He frowned and motioned them forward. "We might as well get to my sister tonight. By morning, all of Sylvermoor will know you are here."

For the next hour, they alternated between speeding and walking down the broad road toward Sylvermoor. They passed few people, and it was after midnight before they came to a group of houses. Feyn took them around the back of the house and up to a window. He tapped on it lightly, then stepped back. When nothing happened, he tapped again, this time louder. White curtains parted, and a young girl peered out.

"Feyn!" she said, and her eyes brightened. "Hold on."

The three moved back from the house by a grouping of thick trees. Soon, his sister came running out. She had long, dark hair, much like Feyn's and stood almost as tall. A spark of life lighted her face as she ran into Feyn's arms. After the brief reunion, she stayed next to Feyn but turned to Shaeleen and Cole.

"My name is Orissa," the girl said. "I am Feyn's sister."

Cole gave her a quick nod. "I am Cole, and this is my sister, Shaeleen."

Orissa looked from them and back to Feyn with questioning eyes.

"She's the one, Orissa," Feyn said, though his eyes held no affection for Shaeleen.

"The one?" Confusion crossed Orissa's face for a moment, then her blue, slanted eyes opened wide. "TruthSeer Shaeleen?"

Shaeleen smiled. "That's me, I'm afraid. Here to destroy the shadow keepers. Your brother said you could help us."

Orissa covered her mouth with surprise, then turned to look at her brother again. "Oh, Feyn, you're back. Mother and

Father and your friends will be so happy to see you."

"Not now," Feyn said.

Orissa nodded her head and took hold of Feyn's hand. Shaeleen noticed she began rubbing a finger over the back of his hand. Feyn's breathing slowed down, and his face lost its flush.

"How is the empress?" Shaeleen asked Orissa.

She shook her head. "Feyn didn't tell you? She passed away two weeks ago. Prince Brevin rules now as emperor of Verlyn."

Shaeleen reeled in shock. It had only been a month since she had seen the empress, but she had been quite sick and weak. No wonder the people at the inn had been so crazy. "Prince Brevin is the master shadow keeper."

Orissa didn't look convinced. "Oh, he's not very nice, but a shadow keeper?" She looked at Feyn.

Feyn nodded. "It's true, Orissa. I fought him and Hutchin and Georrod and others that night at the gathering over a year ago."

"Feyn, why didn't you tell me?" Orissa said, looking almost eye to eye with her brother. She was tall for her age, if she was younger than Feyn.

"I couldn't," Feyn said. "We came to an agreement in order to protect our family—one that I am now breaking."

Cole gave him a stern look, and Shaeleen shook her head at him. Now was not the time to push his honor. An agreement with the devil was breakable at any time. It had no honor in the first place.

"You must warn Mother and Father to leave," Feyn said.

"Get to safety somewhere until this is over. He said he would kill my family if I ever told, but I can't let this go on further. The kingdom will fall if we don't rid Verlyn of the shadow keepers."

"I must get to Melindra," Shaeleen said. "She will know what to do."

"I'll come with you," Orissa said. She dropped Feyn's hand. "Let me grab a few things and leave a note for Mother and Father." She ran back into the house, while the three of them stood quietly in the trees outside.

Shortly, she returned, and they walked out on the road. Orissa led the way. Shaeleen walked up next to her with a look to Cole that told him to hang back with Feyn. She needed to find out something from his sister. When the two men were farther back, Shaeleen turned to Orissa.

"You seem young for a keeper, Orissa," Shaeleen said.

"I'm only fourteen and I've been one for over a year now." Orissa smiled. "It's wonderful. The feel of the stones—their power. I can sit for hours by the pools, soaking up their influence."

"I can understand that," Shaeleen said. "Just so you know, I hold all five stones of power and a TruthStone."

Orissa missed a step, but Shaeleen caught her elbow, and they continued walking and talking. She told Orissa how she had come by each stone, ending by how they had met her brother, Feyn. "Speaking of Feyn." Shaeleen glanced back over Orissa's head. Cole was trying to engage the young man in conversation, but Feyn didn't look too talkative. "Your brother doesn't talk much or like people much, does he?"

Orissa shook her head. "Ever since he was young, Feyn would rather be by himself. Crowds bring on panic attacks, and he literally gets sick."

Shaeleen felt sick herself as she finally realized what she had done to him. "Why didn't he tell me?"

"He's embarrassed. He doesn't like people to know. He's scared to death to talk in big groups or even to walk through crowds of people. He feels like everyone is watching him, judging him. He's afraid he'll make a mistake. That's why he went off by himself—at least that's what we all thought. Now I know it's because of an agreement with Prince Brevin. Poor Feyn."

After a moment of silence, Shaeleen confessed, "I brought him to an inn. He tried to tell me not to, but I dragged him into the common room to eat."

Orissa put a hand to her mouth with a gasp. "Oh no, TruthSeer. That would have almost killed him."

Shaeleen nodded. Sometimes she was so stupid. "I should have listened to him. But he does have the power he says he does—to sense stones?"

Orissa nodded. "That's what he says."

"And he can use their power," Shaeleen added.

Orissa almost jumped with surprise. "I never knew that." She turned to look back at him and smiled. "Feyn is a special person, TruthSeer, but he is fragile."

"Please call me Shaeleen."

Orissa blushed. "I'm not sure I can do that, TruthSeer."

"Your brother has a part to play in all of this," Shaeleen said, growing worried. "I need his abilities. I hope he can do it."

The houses began to get closer together, and even though it was late at night, there were more people out as they moved closer to the actual city of Sylvermoor. Orissa had moved back next to Feyn. They huddled together and talked as they continued to walk. Soon, they came to the city walls, and the four of them moved off the road to strategize.

"Sylvermoor has outlawed outsiders," Orissa said. "I think it's best to bring Melindra out here. I know a place close by that is safe." Orissa led them down a few side streets and back out to the edge of the jungle. Taking a small path, they came to a pool of water; a small stream trickled into and out of it.

Feyn's eyes lit up. "How did you know this was here, Orissa?"

"I can tell where all the pools are. That's one of my talents," Orissa said. "I guess similar to yours, Feyn. I can tell where the pools of stones are, and you can tell when people have them."

"And you can use their power too?" Shaeleen put her hand on Orissa's arm.

The young woman's eyes lit up. "Yes, I am beginning to. Master Keeper Lorelei is my teacher. She says I am learning incredibly fast."

"Interesting," Shaeleen muttered, feeling another part of the plan falling into place.

Orissa excused herself and hurried off, leaving the three of them alone next to the pool of water. Cole wiped off a log, and all three sat on it, looking into the pool. Shaeleen decided to try something. She took a deep breath and brought all her powers to the forefront of her mind. Sitting next to the pool full of stones, the stones in her possession seemed to multiply in her mind. Her muscles bulged, her mind quickened, her pulse raced, her body rejuvenated itself. How much power could she hold?

"Careful, Shaeleen," Feyn whispered beside her. "There are a lot of stones in this pool."

The warning resonated with her, and she pulled back. Surely, after her display at the inn earlier, the shadow keepers would know she was back.

She was counting on it.

CHAPTER THIRTY-THREE

Cole nudged her. "Someone's coming."

She twitched and straightened up. She had fallen asleep against Cole's shoulder. The summer air was warm and comfortable, and the use of her power and the strains of the previous day's running had finally taken its toll on her. She readied her power for any trouble, and the three of them stood and peered through the trees. Three figures emerged from the shadows, one holding a small ball of light in her hand.

"Melindra!" Shaeleen stepped out from behind the tree. Melindra's husband, Aeron, stood next to her, with Orissa on the far side.

The old keeper hugged Shaeleen with one arm. "My dear, I am glad to see you again—and still in one piece."

Shaeleen laughed. "I've had some close calls."

"I felt your powers tonight." Melindra frowned. "I'm sure all the keepers did."

"I hope so."

Melindra shook her head. "You do have unconventional ways." She paused a moment and looked down at the pool of stones next to them. She turned a questioning look to Orissa. "How did you know about this pool?"

Orissa smiled broadly. "I know about them all, Keeper Melindra."

Melindra put a hand to her head. "My goodness. Lorelei had not told me that. We are lucky to have you." Then she turned to Feyn, who had shrunk back farther with the growing crowd of people. "Nice to see you again, Feyn. We could have used your abilities at the gathering this year."

Feyn hung his head low. Orissa stepped over and grabbed his hand. "It's all right. You're here now." She shot a daggered look at Melindra.

Aeron cleared his throat. "Let's take this conversation somewhere else. Morning will be here soon, and prying eyes will be out looking for our young TruthSeer here."

While Aeron motioned the group forward, Feyn stayed where he was. "I can't go into the city," he said quietly, his voice quivering with fear.

Shaeleen gave him a look of compassion. Though taller than her, he seemed so much younger than his age and vulnerable. His slanted eyes looked down at the ground.

"What about Lorelei's home?" Shaeleen offered.

Aeron looked at Melindra, who nodded back to him. "That should work," Aeron said. "If you're all right with a bit more walking. It's about an hour from here."

Shaeleen turned to Feyn. "Lorelei lives out in a small clearing in the jungle north of here."

"Thank you," Feyn said. Shaeleen could see relief flood his eyes.

Shaeleen turned to the others. "But it needn't take an hour," she said with a mischievous smile. "Cole and I have the power of the SpeedStone and can take you there if we all hold hands."

"I have the power also," Feyn said.

Melindra jerked her head in his direction. "What do you mean, Feyn? You are not a keeper."

"I . . . I . . ." Feyn stumbled on the words. "With my ability to sense the stones that people hold, I can access their powers. I can use Shaeleen's SpeedStone, that is, if she doesn't mind. I'm not sure what it does to the holder when I use their power."

Melindra's hand went to her mouth, and she turned to Orissa. "And do you have this ability also?"

Orissa nodded. "Yes, though I am still learning." She took a few steps closer to the pool of water and knelt down at the water's edge. She brought a hand forward and held it over the water. "I can feel the stones here in the pools; Red Jasper, Celestite, and there is a Garnet SpeedStone." Orissa took a deep breath and stood up. There was a blur around her, and she stood instead a few feet away. She put her hand out against a tree to steady herself and laughed with pure joy. "It worked," Orissa said with excitement.

Melindra leaned against her husband. "Oh, Aeron, I'm getting too old for this. The abilities of all these young people."

Aeron patted her back and squeezed her lovingly around the shoulders.

"I'll help you, Orissa," Feyn said.

"I'll take Melindra," Shaeleen said, then looked at Feyn. "It's not far enough to drain my powers." Turning to Cole, she continued, "Cole, you take Aeron. Feyn and Orissa will follow."

Everyone did as Shaeleen outlined, and soon, they were

speeding along roads and trails on their way to Lorelei's home. In no time, they arrived at the edge of the small clearing and came to a stop. A small group of five houses stood in front of them. It was still a few hours until dawn, and all was quiet, except for the chirping of crickets and frogs. A slight breeze blowing off the Straits of Mists rustled large leaves above their heads.

Melindra took the lead, and they all followed. They walked quietly to Lorelei's small home. Seeing the home again brought back memories to Shaeleen—not all good. After a quick rap on the door, they heard movement inside. Lorelei's husband opened the door a few inches and peered out. His eyes opened wide at seeing the group standing there. He glared a moment longer when looking at Shaeleen.

"Please, Ruven, we need to come in," Melindra said.

"Of course, Keeper." Ruven opened the door wide and ushered them inside. He reached over and lit a small lamp, bringing light to the dark room.

Lorelei stood there, wrapping a cloak around her nightclothes. Her long, blond hair appeared flawless, even in the middle of the night. A concerned smile sat on her otherwise calm face.

"Master Keeper." Orissa bowed her head.

Lorelei glanced over the group, her eyes widening when she settled on Feyn. "Ahhh," was all she said as she motioned the group to chairs. There weren't enough, so the men sat on furs on the ground. Cole scooted closer to Shaeleen, who had taken a chair, and looked up at her with concern in his eyes. All were quiet as people settled. A sound behind another door drew their attention, and Lorelei's oldest, Cameron, poked his head out. His eyes went wide at the esteemed company.

"Dear," Lorelei said, "please go back to sleep."

He nodded his head, eyes tired on his teenage face. Once the door was closed, Lorelei pursed her lips for a moment, let out a small sigh, and sat back on the small couch she shared with Melindra.

"I suppose this is your doing," Lorelei said to Shaeleen. "By the look of you—you're almost shining—you have recovered all the stones of power from Wayland?"

Shaeleen nodded and rubbed her eyes. She was exhausted. She and Cole had been up early the prior morning, dealt with the fall into the ravine, found Feyn, sped through the night, went to the inn, met Orissa, Melindra, and now were here with Lorelei.

"I don't have the energy for a long explanation right now, Lorelei," Shaeleen said, barely able to hold her eyes open. "Please call a gathering of keepers."

Lorelei and Melindra both sucked in air.

"We just had a gathering a month ago," Lorelei said through pinched lips. "It did not go so well."

"I heard you let the shadow keepers and others sympathetic to them vote to outlaw magic in Wayland," Shaeleen said, her temper short.

"Please have some respect for the keepers," Aeron said to Shaeleen, his eyes growing hard. Cole glared back at the man, ready to protect Shaeleen.

Shaeleen took a deep breath, pulled upon the powers she had available—as tired as she was, they were still considerable.

An alternating glow of colors surrounded her. The others in the room took in a collective, quick breath. Her powers had grown considerably since collecting the last stone. A breeze picked up outside, and branches scraped against the side of the house, causing Feyn to jump. Orissa reached down from the chair she sat in and put her hand on Feyn's shoulder. He seemed to relax.

"It's my right to call another gathering of keepers," Shaeleen said, her voice devoid of emotion as it echoed around the room. "I am the TruthSeer, the prophesied one, the destroyer of shadow keepers, the hope of Wayland, and the holder of six stones of power."

As she spoke, she turned her head slowly, looking into the eyes of each person in the room. The only one not to turn away was Orissa. There was a strength there that Shaeleen could sense, and the TruthStone revealed to her that she had a special destiny ahead of her—one that would proclaim itself soon. She nodded her head at Orissa before turning back to Lorelei.

"This is not a request," Shaeleen said, voice firm. "I demand a gathering to be held in three days' time. All keepers are required to attend. If they need help getting here quickly, that will be provided." She looked at Cole, Feyn, and Orissa, making it clear what she meant: their use of the SpeedStone would help. "The demise of the shadow keepers will be met there." With those last words, Shaeleen let the power go, leaned her head back, and felt herself fall instantly into a dreamless sleep of pure exhaustion.

CHAPTER THIRTY-FOUR

Shaeleen woke up sometime later lying in a soft bed of skins and blankets in what she supposed was the children's room. She had slept well and could tell the HealingStone had rejuvenated her body. She sat up, brushed her hair with her hands, and prepared for the day. The smell of something good cooking floated through the air, and her stomach growled. She realized she hadn't eaten anything in a while since their meal at the inn had been interrupted.

Standing up, she reached her hand out and opened the door. All eyes in the room turned her way—some held relief at seeing her well, some held worry. Cole was the first one to her side, followed by Orissa.

"What time is it?" Shaeleen asked. Glancing outside, she could see small streams of sunlight through the branches, throwing speckles of light across the ground and into the windows of the small house. A few younger children were outside running around, including Lorelei's two youngest, Amara and Grace.

"It's late in the day, Shae," Cole informed her. "Almost suppertime."

Shaeleen couldn't believe she had slept that long. She glanced around the room. Melindra and Lorelei stood in the kitchen, while Feyn sat alone in a far corner, his eyes still tired.

"Did the rest of you get some sleep?"

"Enough," Cole said.

"We were worried about you, TruthSeer," Orissa said.

"Call me Shaeleen."

Orissa shook her head. "I can't do that. That would not be respectful of one with so much power."

Again, Shaeleen had a flash of truth about Orissa come to her mind as she studied the tall Verlynian young woman—already the height of Shaeleen. She opened her mouth to say something but thought better of it. Events would have to play out as they should. Shaeleen marveled at the insights she received now as a TruthSeer with all the powers of the stones at her disposal. Shaeleen moved closer to the kitchen and opened her mouth to apologize for her behavior the night before. Before she could say anything, Lorelei smiled and waved her hand to the table.

"Have a seat, Shaeleen. Food's almost ready." Lorelei grabbed a plate full of steamed vegetables while Melindra grabbed a loaf of fresh-baked bread. "And don't worry about last night, dear. We were all tired."

Shaeleen let out a deep breath. "You are such good friends." Her outburst had been uncalled for, and Shaeleen felt bad about her words—not the facts of them, but how they had come out. "Did the call go out?"

Melindra laughed, and Orissa giggled from behind. Shaeleen looked at Cole, and even he had a big grin on his face.

"My dear," Lorelei said as she brought over a pitcher of fresh juice, "with all that power gathered around you and the words you spoke, every keeper and magic user on Wayland and

Verlyn heard your call." Her face grew darker, and she looked at Melindra, then back at Shaeleen. "Emperor Brevin has expressed his desire to attend."

Shaeleen knew what that meant. All the shadow keepers would be there, which was just as she had intended. "As well he should. You do know he heads the shadow keepers?"

"Feyn has told us so," Lorelei said. "I do not like the man, but I would have never thought that of him. That's how they were able to get the vote passed. There surely cannot be more shadow keepers than true keepers of the stone."

Shaeleen shook her head. "No, I don't think so either, but Feyn will help us deciphering who had a ShadowStone."

With his name mentioned, the young man glanced up from his seat at the far corner of the room.

"I suspect that many supported the motion only to please Prince Brevin at the time," Shaeleen said as she reached for a piece of bread. Dipping it in a bit of sweet honey, she took a bite and relished in its sweetness. After swallowing, she continued, "The stones have been failing in Wayland, and some keepers with good intentions may have backed the measure. However, now they will have to take sides. There will be no middle ground."

"The shadow has its hooks deep here in Sylvermoor, TruthSeer," Melindra said. "It's not something we are proud of."

Feyn joined them at the table, and as they ate, conversation turned to talk of Lorelei's children, the warm weather, and the delicious food. After they were done eating, they all sat in silence for a moment. Shaeleen's eyes roamed around the kitchen.

"Looking for something, dear?" Lorelei said with a twinkle in her eye.

"Do you have any of those wonderful cream puffs you gave me last time?"

With a laugh, Lorelei stood and took a small tin off the counter. Bringing it to the table, she opened it for all. Everyone took a piece. Shaeleen reveled in the sweet pastry, closing her eyes to concentrate on it as she chewed and swallowed.

"Thank you," Shaeleen said.

* * *

The next few days passed quickly. Shaeleen and Cole were sent out to help some keepers at the edge of the island return for the gathering more quickly. Shaeleen found it easier to deal with what was coming up by doing something. She met a few times with Lorelei, Melindra, and some of the other Master Keepers. Feyn had shared with them the names of the shadow keepers that he knew, most of whom Shaeleen had already met.

Hutchin, Georrod, and Dunstan were still on Verlyn and had been sighted by other keepers going to and from the palace. Cailu had already been taken care of in South Bay. They'd have to wait and see if either Amara or Erwin, two other ShadowStone holders, would be able to return to Verlyn from Wayland in time.

Orissa had taken Feyn to visit their parents. Their mother was a keeper and had heard Shaeleen's call. They were supposed to be back to Lorelei's already, and Shaeleen was getting worried. It was late in the evening, and the gathering was to be held at the base of Mt. Eyvindr the next morning. Most of the keepers had already gathered there. Melindra had gone ahead to try to keep things under control. The keepers didn't like being told what to do and then being kept in the dark. Shaeleen, Lorelei, Cole, Orissa, and Feyn would wait and use the power of the SpeedStone to arrive in the morning.

An hour later, Orissa came bursting through Lorelei's front door. Cole and Ruven were up instantly, and Cole's hand went to his sword. Seeing who it was, they relaxed.

"What happened?" Shaeleen said.

Tears streamed down Orissa's face as she tried to catch her breath. The side of her head was scraped, and her hair was matted with blood. Orissa took a few deep breaths before blurting out, "Feyn is gone!"

Lorelei was instantly at the young woman's side. "Orissa, what are you talking about? You're hurt."

Orissa raised her hand to the side of her head. "I tried using the powers of the SpeedStone, but it was only good when I was close to a pool of stones. Every time I moved farther away, I fell out of the speed. Once, I ran into the side of a tree."

"Oh, you poor thing." Lorelei put her arm around Orissa, who leaned into the Master Keeper. "Tell us what happened."

"We met with our parents for a short time," Orissa began between sniffles. "But my mother had to leave for the gathering. Feyn and I walked out with her. The streets got more crowded, and Feyn just stood there, not moving. I grabbed his hand and pulled him after Mother and Father for a few minutes while we finished a conversation. Before we turned to leave, Feyn whispered to me that riders were coming. Sure enough, thirty seconds later, the rest of us heard the sounds and moved over to the side of the road. I asked him how he knew, and he said someone around us had a HearingStone . . . and he used it."

Lorelei looked at Shaeleen with surprise. She obviously hadn't really believed Feyn could use the power of the stones that others held. Lorelei brought Orissa over to a chair, sat her down, and gave her something to drink.

Orissa nodded her thanks and gave the empty cup back. "As the six riders went past, one looked over at us. It was Feyn's friend, Tanyth. His father, Keeper Hutchin, was with him along with two other women. Leading the group were two other men. One was Cole's age, and the other quite a bit older than the rest. I think it was Keeper Dunstan, though I'm not sure."

With that news, Shaeleen's heart skipped a beat. "Was the other young man's name Taegen?"

Orissa thought for a moment. "Tanyth answered him once—Taegen might have been what he called him." She shook her head. "But I'm not sure."

Shaeleen's heart sped up. She would have to face Taegen one way or another. Had he changed? Would he leave the shadow keepers?

"We tried, Shaeleen," Lorelei said. "We tried to help him, but he went back."

Shaeleen shook her head. She knew he had good in him. She had seen it, and he had told her he wanted to be free. She would have to try again. Turning back to Orissa, she told her to continue.

"Tanyth stopped and dismounted. He and Feyn talked for a moment, but Tanyth's father called to him to get back on his horse. Before they left, Feyn's eyes filled with tears." Orissa turned from one person to the other in the room as she spoke. "I thought he had missed his friend, but then Feyn spoke to him and told him he knew that Tanyth had a ShadowStone and that he needed to get rid of it. Tanyth glared back at Feyn and told him to mind his own business. He said that since Feyn had been gone, he didn't have any idea what was happening."

"What did Feyn do?" Shaeleen asked.

"Well, Taegen, if that was his name, called to Tanyth and told him to hurry." Orissa closed her eyes for a moment, as if reliving the event. "Feyn grabbed Tanyth's arm—I've never seen him be so forceful—and pleaded with him not to go, but Tanyth yanked his arm away, jumped on his horse, and rode off. Feyn was inconsolable. He just stood in the middle of the road in a daze. I tried to pull him, but he wouldn't move. I saw his lips moving, mumbling to himself." New tears came to Orissa's eyes. "It was so scary. Our parents had moved on ahead before the riders had come past. I wanted to find them but couldn't leave Feyn alone there."

"Where is he now, Orissa?" Lorelei asked.

Orissa took a deep breath. "After standing there a moment, he looked around and yelled. He told everyone to stop staring at him. Then with a flash, he was gone. He used a SpeedStone and ran off and . . ." Orissa paused and wiped her eyes again. "And I have no idea where he went."

Cole grabbed Shaeleen's attention and whispered, "You need him, Shae. You don't know who they all are without him."

Shaeleen nodded, then turned to Lorelei, who was comforting Orissa. "We have to find him."

"You need to stay safe, TruthSeer," Lorelei said. "No running off on your own this time. Things are too important for that."

I'm not a child to chide. Shaeleen pouted a moment but kept her thoughts to herself.

"She's right," Cole said. "I will go and find him."

Lorelei shook her head. "No, you need to stay with your sister, Cole. We have other guardian wizards and keepers with significant abilities. I'll have Ruven go and tell others to be on the lookout for him."

"He will stay away from the crowds," Orissa said. "He'll be in a place all alone."

"That should make him easier to find," Lorelei said.

"How is that easier? There is a lot of jungle out there," Shaeleen said. "What if he went back to the mountain where he was living?"

Orissa shook her head. "Feyn wouldn't do that. He knows we need him."

Shaeleen wasn't so sure. "He's not well," she muttered to herself.

Orissa heard. With arms folded in front of her, she walked over to Shaeleen and glared down at her. "My brother is fine. He just sees things differently. I don't care that you are the TruthSeer; I'll not have you talking poorly about him—or any of us for that matter. We are all here to help you, and don't forget it. This is as much our fight as yours."

Shaeleen leaned back in her seat. Her eyes went wide, and she turned her attention from Orissa to Cole. Her brother was trying to hold in a laugh. She scowled at him and shook her head. She turned back to Orissa and stood in front of her, as tall as she could. "Yes, Your Highness." Shaeleen mocked Orissa with a bow, then turned around and walked toward the children's room. "I need some rest if I'm going to save your kingdom tomorrow."

"Shae!" Cole and Lorelei called after her, but she ignored them, only turning around to give one last direction to Lorelei. "Please find Feyn. Cole is right. This will be a lot easier with his abilities."

With that, she walked into the room and closed the door behind her. Lorelei's children had been taken to one of the neighboring houses to allow more room for the visitors. She went to a pile of furs on the floor and laid down. She berated herself for losing her temper again, but there was a lot of strain on her. *How am I supposed to do this?* Her nerves were on a tight string. The next day would tell whether she could succeed or not. She had doubts, but she also knew that the shadow keepers were wrong, and it was up to her to make sure truth won out over the shadow.

CHAPTER THIRTY-FIVE

As the sun rose the next day, Shaeleen, Cole, Orissa, and Lorelei stood outside Lorelei's home. The air was moist, and Shaeleen could tell it would be another hot and humid summer day in Verlyn. How she longed for the cool mornings of autumn. It was her favorite time of year. Memories of running through the apple orchards west of Stronghaven as a young girl came to her mind. And with that memory, she thought about something else west of Stronghaven: Basil. Would she ever see him again?

"Any word of Feyn?" Shaeleen asked Orissa and Lorelei.

Orissa shook her head, not even looking at Shaeleen.

"Well," Shaeleen said with a deep intake of air, "he knows where we'll be. I trust he'll do the right thing and show up." She didn't know what she would do without him. All along, her biggest question had been how she would find all the shadow keepers and ShadowStones at once and destroy them all. Feyn was now the key. His abilities would give Shaeleen the edge she needed. If he didn't, she would do her best and hope that it was enough.

"Let's go," Cole said as he grabbed on to Orissa. Shaeleen grabbed Lorelei's hand.

The trees went by in a blur as they sped along the path leading around the east side of Sylvermoor. The crowds grew thicker as people went about their daily business. They weaved in and out of people without the crowd knowing they were there. Shaeleen accidentally knocked into the side of a cart and skidded around it. Slowing down, she caught the surprised looks of those around her in the street. But in the next moment, she was speeding away again.

The crowds thinned as they made their way toward Mt. Eyvindr. A few last-minute keepers who had stayed close by were on the road. Above the people and the trees, the mountain loomed closer. Coming to a grassy field, the four slowed down and appeared at the edge of a large gathering of people. A few closer by yelled out in surprise at the newcomers and took a step back.

"Master Keeper," a woman said to Lorelei, once she regained her composure. "Where did you come from?"

Lorelei just smiled and led the other three forward.

Shaeleen looked out at the growing crowd, and a small shiver went up her spine. There was a lot of magic here. Keepers, men and women both, were scattered around. Some had their families with them; others stood alone. Some were dressed in their finest, while others appeared ready for battle. Tents had been erected around the field, with a large pavilion sitting next to a tall, colorful tent in the middle.

"Prince Brevin's tent," Lorelei said when she noticed where Shaeleen was looking.

Shaeleen's heart began to race, and she shook her head. Cole put a hand on her shoulder.

"I'm here with you, Shae," Cole said softly, his eyes looking everywhere for trouble.

Shaeleen nodded, not trusting her voice at the moment. Her brother didn't know how much his steady presence meant to her. She knew she could be rash and impossible at times, but his love and care was her rock. She was just worried that before it was all over, he would have to give much more to her cause. She was afraid she would need to take his powers again, especially if Feyn didn't show up.

Melindra walked up and gave Shaeleen a large smile. "Are you ready, my dear?"

Shaeleen took a deep breath and pushed away her fears and worries. "Ready or not. It's time, isn't it? Is this what you envisioned when you gave me this cursed TruthStone, Melindra?"

"Shaeleen!" Melindra gasped. "Don't talk like that. I traveled across the kingdoms of Wayland for almost nine months before I found you. The stone chose you. Of all the people in Wayland, of all the keepers in Verlyn, it passed us all by and found a young woman of little renown, but a young woman of heart and strength."

Shaeleen dabbed tears away from her eyes. "Stop that," she laughed.

"You can do it, Shaeleen!" Melindra closed her words.

"What's the word of things, Melindra?" Lorelei asked.

Melindra pulled the small group off to the side. "At least five known shadow keepers, six if you include Brevin. A few came in last night."

Shaeleen groaned at the news. "Feyn had seen more. Any news of him?"

Melindra shook her head. Orissa let out a small whimper

but otherwise held her composure. Melindra made sure she had Cole and Shaeleen's attention. "There is news from Wayland—whether rumors or true, I do not know. The king of Antioch is said to be very ill and will die soon. His youngest son is at his side, but there is much fighting there with those trying to do away with magic."

Shaeleen breathed a sigh of relief. Marcus and Orin had made it to Mistport.

"Lightfort is still closed off to all, but they have sent an army into Galena. King Haelen and Prince Basil's forces seem to still hold most of Galena, except for Stronghaven." Melindra looked around. "Mind you, I have pieced this together from multiple sources, and it may not be reliable."

"Go on," Shaeleen said.

"Rumors have King Calix traveling to North Bay to secure more of Galena under his control. Next door in Gabor, Queen Victoria is old, and her health is failing rapidly. Commander Kerr was commanded to go back home, but it seems he may actually be helping King Calix still at North Bay. It's hard to tell."

"And what of Princess Diamonique?" Cole asked, his face devoid of the emotion that Shaeleen knew swirled within him.

Melindra's lips grew tight and her eyes fell. She took a moment before answering. "It is said she is pregnant."

Cole swayed on his feet, and Shaeleen reached over to hold him up.

"Excuse us," Shaeleen said to the others and pulled Cole away from the group.

"Is it true, Shae?" Cole asked with a hope that Shaeleen

could not give him.

"Yes, it is." Shaeleen knew everything that Melindra had spoken was true. "Cole, you knew this would happen. That's what happens when kings and queens marry. They secure the throne. But I need you here, Cole." She shook his arm. "I need you here, not back in Stronghaven. Please."

Cole looked down at her. She could see the pain in his eyes. A glint of tears stood in the corners, and he wiped it away. His face grew as hard as steel. "I'm here, TruthSeer. Don't worry about me. I will protect you and keep you from harm like I promised."

"Cole!" Shaeleen pleaded with him. "Don't treat me this way. I am your sister. I need you, Cole—my brother, not just my guardian wizard."

Cole shook his head. His hand rested on the hilt of his sword, and orange flames danced around his hands. "I can't do that right now, Shae. All I have is my duty to fall back on. And that duty is to the TruthSeer, the savior of Wayland. I will guard and protect you in whatever way you need. I repledge to you." With those words, Cole knelt in front of her. Others began gathering around to see what was going on.

"Now look what you've done, Wizard Protector," Shaeleen mumbled under her breath.

Cole turned his eyes back up at her and even though his face was grim, there was still a sparkle in his eyes. "I do what needs to be done. Are you ready to truly be the TruthSeer?"

"Let it be so," Shaeleen whispered, her heart heavy for her brother, but her mind clear and ready for the fight.

Cole stood up and raised his sword high above his head.

Fire raced up the blade and into the air. He wore black leather pants and vest, the muscles in his arms bulging. A dark black cloak floated behind him in the breeze as he moved. He stood with his back to Mt. Eyvindr. A crowd had gathered at the edge of the field, and quiet filled the air.

Shaeleen turned and faced the crowd. Lorelei had provided a new outfit for her also. With black pants and vest like her brother, she wore a red shirt under the vest and a red cloak hung behind her. She drew upon the stones of power in her pouch, and colors swirled around and enveloped her—tendrils of green, blue, white, red, orange, and pink—the colors of all the stones encircling her. Turning away from the small crowd, she motioned for Cole to join her, and they began walking toward the pavilion.

Passing Orissa, Shaeleen nodded to the young woman, and to the surprise of Lorelei and Melindra, the young keeper took a step forward and fell in directly behind Shaeleen. Shaeleen could see the colors of power swirling around Orissa herself— most likely drawing them from the nearby Lake of Eyvindr, where the original stones of Wayland had come from.

Lorelei and Melindra got in line behind Orissa. Whispers, rumors, and voices picked up around them. Shaeleen could hear them all but pushed most of it away.

"It is time for the gathering!" Shaeleen yelled into the air, filling her words with the demands of the TruthStone. People hurried from the edges of the field in unison to join those already there. Soon, everyone headed toward the pavilion.

Off to the right of the pavilion tent stood Emperor Brevin. He was dressed in a colorful blue outfit, layered robes flowing off him. Shaeleen recognized a few of those he spoke with; Georrod, Dunstan, and Hutchin were three of them. She searched the group for signs of Taegen, but he was not there. She remembered that Georrod was Lorelei's father. Shaeleen spared a glance at the Master Keeper and gave her a reassuring look. This had to be hard for her.

The shadow has infiltrated all our lives. The thought grew to steel in her mind as she firmed up her resolve. Under the pavilion, more than a hundred chairs sat empty as the keepers began filling the rows. Shaeleen, Cole, and their party stepped to the side watching as each keeper stood in front of their chair. She tried to look at each one of them to tell whether they were holders of ShadowStones or sympathizers but couldn't tell.

Where is Feyn?

A few gave her looks of encouragement with a nod of their head. For that, Shaeleen was grateful. The front row was left open for the twelve keepers of the council. Lorelei and Melindra stood there, as did Dunstan, Georrod, and Hutchin. Shaeleen spied Amara off to one side of the pavilion and gave a glare to the weasel Erwin, Apprentice TruthSeer for Gabor, who stood a few rows away from her. Orissa stood at the edge of the second row. Her eyes darted around, most likely looking for signs of her brother.

Shaeleen and Cole stood in the back at one corner, while Emperor Brevin stood on the side up front. There were not enough chairs for everyone now, so the remainder crowded in as close as they could get. Shaeleen felt someone brush by her shoulder. When she turned, she gasped.

"Taegen." The word barely came out. His dark blond hair

glowed in the morning sun. He smiled at her, and she found herself blushing in his presence. *How could any man be so beautiful?*

Cole elbowed her, and she regained her composure. Taegen passed her and stood in the back of the gathering. She tried to read his eyes but couldn't. He gave her a short smile and turned his head back up front. What if she had to kill him? She closed her eyes briefly, and an image of Basil surprised her.

When she opened them again, Emperor Brevin was walking forward. He came to a dais, on which an ornate seat had been placed. He took the two steps up and took his time surveying the crowd in front of him.

"Hail Emperor Brevin," came a voice from the crowd.

"Hail Emperor Brevin," echoed the crowd, though Shaeleen was glad it didn't hold much enthusiasm. As one, they bowed their heads, their bodies bending as low as they could without hitting the chairs in front of them.

Only Shaeleen and Cole stayed standing. Over the bowed crowd, the emperor glared right at Shaeleen, and she kept his stare without looking away. His eyes narrowed as he glared at her. She could see his hand in his pocket, fingering something—a ShadowStone, she guessed.

"All may be seated," the emperor said, then he sat down himself in what could only be described as a throne. "Who calls this unsanctioned gathering?"

Shaeleen wondered why a keeper wasn't running the gathering. Brevin was the emperor, but not in the leadership of the keepers.

All was quiet for a moment, then Cole's voice rang out loud and clear. "TruthSeer Shaeleen has called this gathering."

Everyone turned and looked their way. Shaeleen and Cole walked slowly up the side of the rows of chairs and around to the front, standing at the corner of the group.

Here I go!

CHAPTER THIRTY-SIX

Shaeleen turned to the emperor and spoke, her voice loud and clear and full of the power of the stones. "I don't remember inviting you here, Brevin. This is for keepers."

There was a collective gasp at her informal use of the emperor's name. The emperor's cheeks twitched, and his hand gripped the side of the throne. "I am the Emperor of Verlyn, young Shaeleen," the emperor said, also avoiding the use of Shaeleen's title. "This is my kingdom. I am invited everywhere. And last I knew, you are not a keeper either."

Shaeleen smiled and reached inside the pouch at her side. *It's time!* Shaeleen undid the drawstring and pulled out the large TruthStone and held it in the air. Gasps echoed through the gathering, and whispers grew to whines and exclamations of disbelief.

"In that you are mistaken, Brevin." Shaeleen held the stone out in her palm, and it rose, hovering an inch above her hand. It began to spin around, and all the colors of the stones flared out over the gathering. "I hold in my hand the pink Azeztulite HealingStone, the white Celestite HearingStone, the Red Jasper StrengthStone, the orange Garnet SpeedStone, the blue Labradorite IntelligenceStone—and the green Moldavite TruthStone. I am the keeper of all the stones of power given by your ancestors to King Wayland."

Confusion reigned around the meeting as each person tried to see Shaeleen and the stone she was holding.

"I've never seen a stone so large."

"She has all the stones!"

"She's the TruthSeer."

"She's the prophesied one."

The voices grew louder and louder. Emperor Brevin stood up. "Silence." He glared over at Shaeleen. "How dare you show such a display here among the keepers? You should have come to me first. You had no right to call a full gathering."

"Once again, Brevin," Shaeleen said, using his name without the title to emphasize how little she thought of him. "You were not invited, because you are not a keeper." Shaeleen paused to give a moment of quiet before she released the full fury of her words. "Unless you believe that the leader of the shadow keepers, a holder of a ShadowStone, is deemed worthy of being called a keeper."

This time, keepers jumped out of their seats. Georrod, Dunstan, and Hutchin leaped in front of the emperor as a barrier between him and the restless crowd.

"How dare she accuse the emperor," Georrod said.

Shaeleen laughed and brought her hands up in the air, then clapped them together. A loud boom ensued, echoing through the gathering. Lights flashed from her fingers, spreading over the crowd. She took a few steps closer and stopped. Some of the crowd sat back down; others remained standing.

"Georrod," Shaeleen began the interrogation. "Do you deny you are a holder of a ShadowStone?" She knew he was, but without Feyn's help, it would take a long time to find everyone.

"I . . . I . . . Uh . . ." Georrod stumbled over his words. "This is ridiculous. We are not on trial here."

"Actually, you are," Shaeleen said. "I hereby call this gathering to begin. Its purpose is to determine who is a holder of a ShadowStone. Each shadow keeper will voluntarily give up his stone or be punished accordingly."

Shaeleen caught the eyes of the emperor. They were smoldering, but he appeared relieved for the moment that the current accusation wasn't on him. She would get to him eventually. Turning to the leaders of the council of keepers, Shaeleen spoke. "You can see I am a holder of the TruthStone. Are there any who deny the uses and powers of such a stone? Do you deem this trial fair if questions are asked by a TruthSeer?"

Members of the council turned back and forth one to another. Shaeleen was sure there were others in that group besides the ones she knew who were under the influence of the shadow. Would they keep quiet or sell each other out?

Lorelei stood. "I agree by the words of a TruthSeer." She looked at her father, but kept her composure.

"I agree also," Melindra said.

A third stood up. "I also agree. Three in agreement is binding. The trial will proceed according to TruthSeer Shaeleen's words."

Shaeleen looked back at Georrod. His eyes flicked around the group, and she knew he wasn't going to give up the ShadowStone.

"Do you have in your possession a ShadowStone, Keeper

Georrod?" Shaeleen asked.

"Of course not," he said.

Shaeleen yelled and bent over in pain. Cole grabbed her and helped her remain standing.

"He lies," said a keeper from the audience. "The TruthSeer feels the pain."

"I do not lie. I swear as a keeper."

Shaeleen grabbed her stomach again, trying as hard as she could not to throw up from the vehemence of the lie.

"Liar!" shouted a keeper.

Lorelei walked forward with her hand out. "Hand over the ShadowStone, Father."

Most of the crowd was standing now. Half were shouting for him to show the stone, the other half still not believing there was such a thing. From behind Lorelei, Hutchin stood, gathered a ShadowSpell, and threw it at Lorelei. The black fire burned into her left shoulder, throwing her to the ground at her father's feet.

"If you would've just stayed out of the way, Lorelei . . ." Georrod left the remainder of the sentence unsaid as he moved away.

Shaeleen jumped into action with Cole at her side and ran toward Hutchin. Before getting there, a young man stood up to block their way.

"No, Tanyth!" Orissa yelled.

Tanyth hesitated, and Cole knocked him to the ground with his fist as he followed Shaeleen forward. Pandemonium broke loose under the pavilion. Shaeleen looked to the throne and noticed the emperor was gone.

"Cole, Brevin left," Shaeleen shouted.

He turned around and shook his head. "I can't see him anywhere."

Shaeleen ducked as a fireball of darkness came at her. She put the stone safely back in her pouch. She didn't need to hold it to access the power.

"We can't fight in here," Shaeleen said to Cole as he brought his sword down toward Georrod. At the last minute, the shadow keeper twisted out of the way. A sudden thought came to her. "Cole, cut the ropes," she shouted at her brother.

Dunstan came up in front of her. "You've messed with us enough, little girl. My nephew should have killed you when he had the chance. He was weak. But not anymore." He paused, then called out. "Taegen!"

Taegen joined his uncle. There was hardness in his eyes, but Shaeleen caught a flicker of light in them. He turned to his uncle and grabbed his arm. "Let's get out of here. It's collapsing."

Dunstan tried to get back to Shaeleen, but Taegen pulled him away. Was he helping her, or did he just want to get away safely without being killed? Shaeleen ran out the opposite way. Cole had raced around the pavilion, cutting all the ropes. Now it began to fall. Keepers yelled and screamed, trying to get out. In this, all were equal—shadow keeper and true keeper—and forgot their fight with one another.

Cole pulled Shaeleen out to the side and found Orissa standing next to them. She pointed toward the lake, and Shaeleen saw Brevin gathering in his followers. The three of them raced forward using the SpeedStone, and suddenly, they were between the shadow keepers and the lake.

Besides Brevin, there were ten others with him. Dunstan and Taegen were not there yet. Shaeleen shut the yells and screams from the pavilion from her mind, concentrating on what was in front of her. She had never fought so many at once. With the power of the HearingStone, Shaeleen heard a soft voice and turned, looking around for its source.

"TruthSeer, I am here," it said again.

"Feyn!" He had come. She breathed a sigh of relief. She didn't know if she could have found all the ShadowStones in time without him. She turned around, and in a copse of nearby trees about halfway up a tree sat the young man who was afraid of crowds. "I hear you," Shaeleen whispered.

"Four with the prince do not hold ShadowStones," came the faint voice.

That will help even the odds. "Which ones?"

Feyn described them, and Shaeleen strode forward, pulling Cole along with her. Before Brevin and his men could organize themselves, Cole and Shaeleen had separated the shadow keepers from the others. Cole drew his sword and took them on; Shaeleen had full faith in his abilities.

Shaeleen turned back to Brevin. He was the key. "Give up the stone, Brevin, and I will let you live."

Brevin laughed. "Never. I will rule all of Wayland with this stone." He pushed out his hands, and black tendrils flew at her. She put up her hands and formed a green wall that stopped the ShadowSpell from reaching her.

Then from the side, another shadow keeper shot a ball of fire at her. She jumped up in the air, twisted, and with a spell of strength, kicked it back at him. He dodged it but only barely. Before she could land and get her bearings, another barrage of fire came at her. She used the SpeedStone and moved out of the way, knocking down one of the shadow keepers.

More keepers joined them. Small fights broke out all over. It was hard to keep track of the shadow keepers. She saw Cole with a group of men—Brevin's soldiers who had joined in the battle. Other keepers were fighting each other with spells and in hand-to-hand combat.

Where was Brevin?

She cursed being short. She put her hands down, palm toward the ground, and used strength and speed to lift up in the air a few feet. She saw him trying to get away again. She pointed her fingers at him, and a stream of red and green light sped through the air, knocking him to the ground. He jumped up, his sword in one hand and a spell of fire in the other. His now-dark eyes bore into hers. Joining him were other shadow keepers. They began holding hands, something that Shaeleen found quite ridiculous in the middle of it all.

"They all have stones," Feyn whispered to her. He was close above them now, Brevin's group having moved toward the trees. He slipped on a branch, and one of Brevin's keepers looked up and pointed.

"You!" Brevin yelled and thrust his hand toward the tree. It cracked in half and began falling.

Using a SpeedStone, Feyn immediately appeared by Shaeleen's side as she glided back to the ground. "Nice to see you again, Feyn. Where've you been?" She glared at him but was grateful for his presence.

"I don't like crowds," he said. "I couldn't go to the gathering again."

Shaeleen nodded in understanding and softened her voice. "Well, you're here now, but I need to keep you safe." She saw Orissa standing by the lake. Using her speed, she whisked Feyn to his sister. "Watch him for me."

Before she left, Orissa grabbed her arm. "You can't beat them this way, TruthSeer. You can't beat them in battle. You need to use the stones."

Shaeleen smiled at her. "You're right." She had to remember all she knew. She had beat Cailu by using the reflective properties between the ShadowStones and the real stones of power. Could that work here with so many of them? Looking toward the fighting, she saw Brevin and a group of shadow keepers moving toward them. Chaos reigned among the rest of the keepers. She spied Cole zipping through the crowd, trying to protect the keepers he knew were true. He was an army unto himself, swirling his sword around with one hand and spewing forth fire and lightning with the other. Another group of shadow keepers tried to get to him, but it seemed like a stand-off for now—one that Shaeleen knew couldn't continue long. Cole would tire out by himself.

Shaeleen stood at the edge of the lake and took a deep breath. Her stones of power flared to life inside of her. She felt the stones in the lake behind her. They beckoned to her, and she called them forth to merge with hers. It was amazing and beautiful. The power raced through her body, filling her with strength, joy, peace, and rage all at once. And it needed a release.

Then she remembered the power of the light.

Using all she could take in, she brought it all to bear and struck her fist in the air. A white hot pillar of brilliant light rose a thousand feet in the air. Power crackled over the field, and Shaeleen could sense each individual there. She reached over and grabbed Feyn's hand. He resisted at first, but she held it tight.

"I need you, Feyn," she whispered to his mind. "Show me all of the ShadowStones at once. Now!"

Shaeleen rose up in the pillar of light, and Feyn's mind was merged with hers. He pointed out each ShadowStone to her, and she memorized them in her mind. There were twenty in all—far more than she had supposed and far more than she would have discovered on her own. They were mixed among young and old, male and female. Many she had suspected; others she hadn't. She found Taegen and paused for a moment before moving on. Feyn hesitated when she spotted his friend Tanyth, but he pushed on.

After she had marked them all in her mind, she gathered a spell of white fire and threw it toward all of them at once. A simultaneous roar erupted among the crowd, and those not marked backed away. Some she had hit fell to the ground. Some dodged it, while others threw up their own defenses and pushed back at her. Their attack hit her hard, and she barely stayed in control of the pillar of light.

Shaeleen's body stood on the shore, but her spirit rose inside the pillar and looked down on them from above. Her spirit was free to move quickly over the field, assessing the battle.

She saw Brevin and a few other followers running toward her body on the ground. She shot firebolts of varying colors and strength at them, but they put up their own defensive shields of shadow magic. She still couldn't fight so many at one time. It was getting harder to stay focused.

A lone man ran at her body by the lake. She had been distracted from above, and he crashed into her. The pillar of light went out, and she fell back into the water, her spirit and body back together.

"Cole!" she called out to him as she stumbled to get back up. "Help me."

CHAPTER THIRTY-SEVEN

The lake was shallow but walking in the water hampered her movements. The man who had taken her down stood in front of her now; it was not someone she knew. Swirls of shadow spread out from him, then shot forward quicker than Shaeleen thought possible. She twisted to the side, but it caught her on the left arm. Crying out, she crashed into the water.

Splashing through the knee-high water to get back up, she gathered a spell and threw it at the man. Green light encompassed him, and he fought to get away but couldn't. Shaeleen dove at him and grabbed hold of his leg while he struggled to get away. With a quick thought, she pulled on the power of the TruthStone and dove into his mind. Before she could do anything to him, he lurched forward and fell on top of her. Shaeleen struggled under the water until a strong hand pulled her up out of the water.

"Cole!"

He moved to the man who had fallen on her. An arrow stuck out of his back. Shaeleen looked up the hill and spied Hutchin's son, Tanyth, with a bow in his hand. They had shot one of their own rather than let Shaeleen get information from him. Shaeleen shook her head at the waste of lives the ShadowStones caused.

Cole pulled Shaeleen closer to the edge of the water, but

before Shaeleen stepped out, she thought of something else. The combined powers of the stones in the lake had to be tremendous. As long as she stood in the water, she could feel them augmenting her own to an even greater degree.

"Orissa," Shaeleen called out.

The young keeper came to her side. Before they could talk, a blast of shadow power whizzed by them. Cole moved in front of her and began batting away blasts from the shadow keepers.

"You better do something quick, Shaeleen," Cole yelled back at her.

"Feyn!" she called him over. "I think I know how to defeat them, but it will be risky. I'll need your help and Orissa's."

Brother and sister nodded, and Shaeleen smiled at their bravery. With Cole guarding them for the time being, she summoned the power of her stones and formed a canopy of light around her, Feyn, and Orissa.

"Orissa, show me the other pools of power on Verlyn."

Orissa hesitated a moment. "All of them?"

Shaeleen thought a moment. "A few at a time might be better." She closed her eyes to concentrate. Orissa grabbed her left hand, and into Shaeleen's mind came the locations of the pools that contained stones of power. She was surprised there were more than just the five stones of power and the TruthStone. There were other minor stones that contained power also—CompassionStone, SeeingStone, LeadershipStone, WindStone, and the list went on and on. Each attribute of good in humankind and in nature had a stone of power associated with it.

Incredible!

"Orissa, can you access them all?" Shaeleen asked.

"Yes." Orissa's voice was small but firm. "I think so."

Holding Orissa's hand, Shaeleen felt power fill the young keeper. Shaeleen called the power to her, and it came, washing over her like a waterfall. She could barely stand and took a stumbling step forward in the water but stayed upright.

Feyn grabbed on to her other hand and yelled out with the power she held. "It's too much, Shaeleen. I sense too many stones with you and Orissa." He squeezed her hand tighter.

"Hold on, Feyn." Shaeleen took a moment to stabilize herself and relished the amount of power she held in her. The water churned at their knees and lapped at the shore.

So much power!

Through her connection with Feyn, she felt each ShadowStone and shadow keeper. Through her connection with Orissa, she had access to all of Verlyn's stones of power, her own stones feeling insignificant in her pouch. Opening her eyes, she saw everyone else had stopped fighting and stood in the field, staring at the four of them.

"TruthSeer, I need to leave," Feyn said behind her. "I can't do this."

"Yes, you can, Feyn," Shaeleen whispered.

"They're all looking at me. What if I fail?" Feyn tried to pull away. Shaeleen could feel him begin to pull on the SpeedStone to get away.

"No, Feyn!" Shaeleen roared. "I need you and Orissa. I can't do this alone. Now close your eyes and don't look at them."

"Feyn, pretend you are at a pool of stones all by yourself,"

Orissa said softly to him. She moved around in front of Shaeleen and, with her other hand, took Feyn's and began rubbing her fingers on the back of his hand. "Think of the beautiful stones of power, Feyn. They're all yours to do with what you want."

Through their shared magical bond, Shaeleen could feel Feyn's heart rate decrease, and his grip on her hand lightened. The three now stood in a circle holding hands. Cole stood in front of them. He turned his head from them to the crowd where Brevin was walking toward them.

"Light and dark cannot exist at the same time," Shaeleen said out loud, to no one in particular. She knew what she had to do. "Feyn, pull the power of the ShadowStones to you," Shaeleen ordered.

"TruthSeer, there are too many," Orissa said. "It will kill him."

"Feyn?" Shaeleen asked him.

She watched him stand straighter, eyes still closed. "I can do it," he said in a soft voice. "I must."

Shaeleen felt a change in the power she held—a taint. As Feyn pulled on the power of the ShadowStones, she drew it into herself. She breathed in the evil shadow power. It was intoxicating. It was beautiful. She could feel the presence of each ShadowStone.

Brevin stopped a dozen feet in front of them. Hutchin, Georrod, Dunstan, and Amara stood behind him. The rest of the shadow keepers stood farther back, slowly moving together away from the other keepers.

"It's wonderful, isn't it?" Emperor Brevin shouted at her.

Shaeleen nodded. It was amazing. The amount of power in the shadow was breathtaking. A dark black fog began to form around her as she pulled more and more from Feyn.

"Shaeleen," came a faint whisper through the power of the ShadowStone.

Shaeleen glanced over the entire field. Who had spoken to her? Then she saw a lone man leave the rest of the shadow keepers. *Taegen!*

"Fight it, Shaeleen," his whispered voice loud in her ears. "Do it for both of us."

Feyn yelled out—a horrible screeching sound that hurt her ears. He sagged next to her, but she held on. She needed it all—all the power of the shadow. Orissa squeezed her hand on the other side, and Shaeleen was imbued with additional power from the stones. The stones were as much a part of Verlyn as the people and the trees were, and she could feel them all. They were the essence of everything around them—the air, the earth, the water, the sky, the spirit, and the light! She rose up in the light once more, bringing the power of the shadow and the stones of power with her.

"Come to us," Brevin said. "I'll make you the ruler of Wayland. You can rule by my side."

Rule Wayland? Hadn't she thought at one time what she would do when she was all-powerful? She had said she could kill Calix, make Basil the king of Galena, destroy Commander Kerr and TruthSeer Erwin—where was he anyway? She looked around and saw the coward behind a tree, trying to ride out the battle unscathed. Drawing upon the power of the ShadowStone, she struck at him, and he hit the ground, a small stone of black rolling from his fingers.

I can rule Wayland and fix it all!

There was so much power to be had. She had never supposed there was so much. It battled inside of her—light versus the shadow. One had to go, but which one? Were the shadow keepers so wrong to want to remove magic from Wayland? The kings and queens there had squandered it. Were they worth it anymore? Did Wayland deserve another chance?

"Shaeleen, fight it." Taegen now stood a few feet in front of Cole, who blocked his way with his sword. Tears ran down his beautiful face.

"I don't know if I can," Shaeleen mumbled. It seemed there was a standstill in her mind. A moment from tipping one way or another. All the stones were a balance and reflection of one another. She knew she was as much evil as good. She had told lies, treated others badly, forced the truth—maybe she was meant for the shadow. Maybe this was her destiny.

She watched everyone from two perspectives: up above the crowd, sitting in a shadowy light, and down below, in her body. She watched Cole's back. He stood there, waiting to fight the entire crowd for her. Why would he do that? Who was she to warrant such loyalty?

Cole turned now, sensing her thoughts about him, his back to Taegen and the others.

"Shae," he wailed. "What can I do to help you? I can feel your pain. I am here for you. Always."

Shaeleen still held Orissa's and Feyn's hands. Sister and brother. One full of shadow at the moment. One full of light. One full of fear and anxiety. One full of strength and compassion.

Much like her and Cole.

Shaeleen left the light and returned fully to her body, where she almost fell down. Cole reached over and held her up. "It's now or never, little sister. This is what you were born for." He spoke in soft tones. Then his voice grew loud and powerful. Filling the air around them, he turned his head upward and cried out, "This is your time, TruthSeer. Vanquish the shadow!"

The air around Shaeleen shook, and Cole looked back at her, his eyes full of power.

"My guardian protector." Shaeleen sighed. "My wizard, my strength." Tears streamed down her face as she balanced the forces of power raging within her. Cole was the best of both of them—of all of them. Her brother was the rock that gave purpose to all she did. He was true and right and honorable, and now she knew what she had to do. She had to take his strength from him.

And she did. She drew power from her brother, without finesse, in one quick pull.

Cole roared in pain—a devastating sound—but continued to keep his hands on her upper arms. Shaeleen pulled all the power he had as a wizard, as a protector, as a guardian, as an honorable brother. She took it all—all the goodness inside of him. And her mind began to shift. The shadow began to back away.

Cole started to slip away from her toward the ground, but Taegen stepped forward and held him up from behind. Shaeleen felt a shift as he did so; the shadow surged back.

"Taegen!" she screamed at him. "What are you doing?"

"Use my power, Shaeleen," Taegen said. "Use all of it. Restore the balance."

And so she did. She pulled everything from both of them. Cole and Taegen—light and shadow. They were a reflection of one another. The ShadowStones were part of the stones of power. They should have never been separated. Together, they formed balance in all they did, but apart, they were both dangerous. You needed sadness to feel joy, bad to know what was good, sickness to appreciate health, and pain to make you strong.

With the power of the stones from Feyn and Orissa and the power of dark and light from Taegen and Cole, Shaeleen reached out over the field and felt all the power there. She pulled it to her. She yanked the power from Melindra and the other keepers. They screamed as one and fell to the ground. Their life had been guarding the pools where the stones of power sat, and that power had become a part of them to varying degrees.

Then she reached toward the shadow keepers, guided by Feyn, and took their stones from them. One at a time, they came flying through the air toward her. She reached Brevin, and he held on stubbornly.

"You are not meant to have a ShadowStone, Brevin," Shaeleen yelled. "None of you were. It was never meant to be separate. The ShadowStones are an abomination."

"I will never give it up!" Brevin yelled and thrust his hands in the air. A stream of blackness zoomed toward Shaeleen. Without hesitation, Taegen stepped in front of the ShadowSpell and tried to push it back. But in his weakened state, it was too much for him, and he fell to the water, absorbing all of Brevin's power. A small black stone came out from Taegen's pocket and somehow floated to the surface of the water.

"Taegen!" Shaeleen screamed and took her hands from Orissa and Feyn, letting Cole slip to the water beside Taegen. Her brother tried to pick Taegen up, but the shadow keeper's body slumped lifeless in his arms.

What have I done?

She glared at Brevin. Filled with anger, she grabbed the TruthStone from her pouch and held it up with both hands. Still bursting with the power of all the stones—both dark and light— she called the power to the TruthStone. Brevin's stone came, along with the rest of the ShadowStones, and embedded themselves into the TruthStone. Other stones of power raised themselves from the lake around them and attached to the TruthStone. It grew bigger and bigger until Shaeleen could hardly stand under its immense weight.

Shaeleen's arms felt heavy. Someone came to her side and helped her hold it up. It was Orissa. She added the power of all the stones throughout Verlyn.

Brevin yelled and raced toward her. At that same moment, Shaeleen called forth the sunlight, and the TruthStone absorbed the daylight around them, pulling the gathering into twilight. The TruthStone itself filled with the light of day, and Shaeleen had to squint her eyes to keep from being blinded. With her last effort, she pushed at the light of the stone, and it shot out in all directions, a hundred different rays of blinding colors—red, green, white, blue, orange, pink, and black.

Caught in midstride, Brevin was struck down by a shooting

ray of black light—dying instantly and falling to the ground. Then the black shadow light raced across the field taking down each shadow keeper. On the other hand, the other bolts of light raced through the other keepers, sharing with them once again the light of the power of the stones that they were responsible to keep. Death and life—another powerful balance.

The light of day eventually returned, and the power of the TruthStone blinked out. Orissa let go, and Shaeleen took a few steps out of the water and dropped the stone on the ground. It shattered into multiple pieces, and Shaeleen smiled at the pattern she saw.

There were five new stones of power sitting on the ground in front of her. A new StrengthStone, IntelligenceStone, SpeedStone, HearingStone, and HealingStone had been formed. They sat in a circle with a large green TruthStone in the center. Then the TruthStone itself split open, and five new pieces tumbled off of it, still leaving one large TruthStone in the center, embedded itself with multiple stones of power.

Shaeleen heard quiet footsteps and turned her eyes up. Melindra walked slowly over the field toward her. Images flashed through Shaeleen's mind of the first time she had seen the keeper in the marketplace of Stronghaven many months ago. When the TruthStone was given to her that day, she never could have guessed what would lie ahead of her.

"You have done well, my child." Melindra smiled as she came near. "Now we have quite a mess to clean up."

CHAPTER THIRTY-EIGHT

Late that night, Shaeleen sat in a room in the Verlyn palace in Sylvermoor. A small group was assembled with her. They had just eaten a meal and discussed what their next steps were. Brevin and all the shadow keepers had died, including Taegen. Shaeleen brushed a tear away, remembering his final sacrifice to save her from Brevin's assault. He had broken away from the shadow at last and found the light. She hoped his soul would be treated with that in mind. He had given of himself selflessly.

Shaeleen glanced around the table at those she knew. Melindra sat with her husband, Aeron, on one side. Orissa, Feyn, and their parents sat on another, and Cole sat at her side. He had been very quiet since the ordeal at the lake. She had taken a lot from him and didn't know if he would or could truly recover. Physically, he was fine, but she wondered at the depth of hurt she had done to his soul and mind.

Four others sat at the table with them. They had just returned from a four-hour council meeting and had called the current group together. They were members of the Verlynian royal council. It would be their task to choose a new leader of their kingdom. She knew that Brevin hadn't any children and didn't know what other distant relatives there might be to the recently deceased empress.

"I'm sorry we had to meet this late," said Haydyn, the senior council member. "The council meeting went later than expected." He turned to Shaeleen. "First of all, TruthSeer Shaeleen, we thank you for ridding our nation of the shadow keepers. Many of us were blind to what was going on; we should have seen it earlier. What can we do to thank you?"

Shaeleen had already thought about it. "First, rescind the law about magic in Wayland and open your land back up to visitors. Also, I would ask for an embassy from Verlyn in each kingdom of Wayland as an opportunity to learn more from each other, for you to help teach those in the kingdoms of how best to use their stones of power, and to provide a new TruthSeer, if needed."

Haydyn turned and looked at the other three. One of them, a woman, spoke.

"I am Karolyn, TruthSeer Shaeleen. We agree to your request." She spoke directly to Shaeleen with eyes that were intelligent but also held a bit of trepidation. "May I ask, where will you be and what role will you take in the kingdoms going forward?"

Shaeleen put her hand on Cole's arm, and he turned his face to hers but didn't smile. She really hoped he would be all right. "My brother and I will deliver the new stones of power to each kingdom, then return to Galena." *And see Basil again*, was what she wanted to say, but after all of this, she really didn't know what her place would be. "After that, I am not sure."

Karolyn nodded her head. "I understand. You are always welcome here in Verlyn as our friend."

"Thank you," Shaeleen said.

Next, Haydyn turned to Orissa and Feyn. Feyn looked sick again. He'd already tried to leave once. "Both of you have given a great service to your kingdom. Your powers are strong, rare, and frankly," he added with a nervous laugh, "quite fearful to some."

Feyn blushed and flicked his eyes downward, while Orissa opened her mouth to say something, but Haydyn pushed forward before she could. "Orissa, your family is a distant relative of the empress," he continued, taking a moment to glance at Orissa's parents.

Shaeleen smiled, and she felt the power of being a TruthSeer tell her what the next words would be.

Orissa nodded, her face uncertain.

"In the history of Verlyn, we have had many emperors and empresses. Some have been older, some have been younger, but all have been strong in the power of the stones, and outside of our recent problems with Emperor Brevin—who was persuaded by the shadow—all had great compassion for their people and a propensity to use the powers they held for good." Haydyn looked at the other three council members for a moment, and they all nodded at him to proceed. He cleared his throat and continued, "After much debate, the council would ask you, Orissa, to be the next empress of Verlyn."

Feyn's head shot up at that news. Their parents' faces went white, her mother reaching her hand over to Orissa.

"Are you sure?" Orissa's father spoke. "She is so young."

"Not as young as some have been," Karolyn said. "As Haydyn said, a good empress is strong in the power, knows how to use it, and has compassion for her people and the land.

Orissa is all of those. She will be guided by the council at first, but she will grow and learn quickly, I am sure."

Shaeleen looked across the table at Orissa. "Your Highness," she said with a laugh.

"TruthSeer, did you know about this?" Orissa asked.

Shaeleen nodded her head. "I've had a few premonitions—something new to me since I gathered all the stones. If you care for your kingdom as much as you care for Feyn, the people will be blessed to have you."

"Empress." Cole nodded his head to her. "May you find happiness as you serve your people honorably."

Soon, everyone was out of their seats, congratulating Orissa. Shaeleen took a moment to go over and talk to Feyn.

"What will you do now?"

Feyn shrugged his shoulders. "I was going to go back to my mountain home, but now that Orissa is empress, I'm not sure." He looked Shaeleen in her eyes. "She might need me."

Shaeleen grinned as she reached over and gave Feyn a hug. He was stiff and tried to get away, but Shaeleen held him for a moment anyway. "At the lake," she whispered in his ear, "that was the bravest thing I have ever seen anyone do. Taking in all the power of the ShadowStones was so courageous." She pulled back and looked at him seriously. "I know you worry about things, but Feyn, you are a hero. Without you, I couldn't have done it. I think you still have great things to do."

Feyn blushed at her words. "Thank you, TruthSeer. I don't know if I'm cut out to be a hero or not."

Shaeleen laughed and slapped him on the back. "None of us are ready for that, Feyn. None of us."

The group continued to visit for a few more minutes. Then Shaeleen and Cole excused themselves and went to rooms in the palace that had been prepared for them. Before going into their separate rooms, Cole turned to her. "Any more word from Galena?" he asked.

Shaeleen shook her head. "No word. Maybe when we get back to Wayland, we will find out more." She patted his arm. "Get some sleep. We leave in the morning. I saw Abby today. Her father is in port. He is waiting for us at the docks."

Cole raised his eyebrows but didn't say anything before opening the door to his room. After he went inside, Shaeleen headed toward her own room a few doors down. She worried about her brother. He needed to find a purpose again—something to live for.

She put her hand on the doorknob but stopped. Something wonderful wafted up through the air, and she breathed in deeply. Instead of going to her room, she made her way to the kitchen. *Nothing wrong with a little late-night sweet!*

CHAPTER THIRTY-NINE

A few days later, Shaeleen and Cole disembarked in South Bay, Althea. The captain had insisted on going into town first to announce their arrival. A few hours later, Prince Raimund met them at the docks with a crowd of people. As Shaeleen walked off the ship, the people cheered and yelled for her. She wondered what the captain had said about them.

People bowed low to Shaeleen and Cole as they made their way to a carriage pulled by six white horses. Footmen helped them inside where Prince Raimund sat with them.

"What did the captain tell you?" Shaeleen laughed. "This wasn't the reception I had envisioned."

Raimund laughed. "He said you saved the world."

"Hmmm," Shaeleen said. "What do you think about that?" She elbowed Cole in the ribs.

"We did what you were supposed to do," Cole said.

Shaeleen rolled her eyes at him. "Come on. Enjoy it a bit. Not every day we get to ride in a fancy carriage."

Upon arriving at the castle, Princess Noelle and General Archer met them at the doorstep. They were taken inside and brought to a reception room. After a bit of small talk, Shaeleen took out a pouch and handed it to Noelle. She slowly opened it up, then a broad grin spread across her face.

"Oh my," she said. "It's so much bigger than the last

HearingStone." In her hand sat a large, egg-shaped, white Celestite HearingStone. "Thank you."

Shaeleen walked over to TruthSeer Wain and Wizard Cara, who stood in the corner of the room. "I have something for you also."

They looked at her hands, but there was nothing there. Instead, she took the TruthSeer's hands in her own and called upon the power of the stones she still commanded. Inside the TruthSeer's mind, she found the shadow that had replaced his powers during the cleansing and infused the spot with power from the HealingStone and strength from the StrengthStone. In a matter of moments, TruthSeer Wain stood up straighter and smiled.

He bowed low to Shaeleen. "TruthSeer, how can I ever repay you?"

"Watch over these two," Shaeleen said with a nod of her head toward Noelle and Raimund. "An embassy from Verlyn will be here soon to help you also. We want more cooperation between them and us."

Wain and Cara thanked her again, and she moved back by Cole and Raimund, who stood talking. After a short visit, they were escorted back to the ship.

"Where to now, esteemed one?" the captain said to Shaeleen.

"Father!" Abby said. "Have some respect for the TruthSeer."

Shaeleen laughed and winked at the captain. "It's fine. We go north to West Bay. Please have a quicker boat go ahead of us and tell King Haelen to meet us there, so we don't have to go all the way to the castle."

The captain nodded, and soon they set off.

* * *

The crowds in West Bay were not as big or friendly as in South Bay. This didn't bother Shaeleen in the least. It had taken them four days to get there, and she was tired and looking forward to a night's sleep off the ship. They had to wait another day until the king arrived.

The next morning, King Haelen, along with his TruthSeer and wizard, met them at the governor's mansion in West Bay. They did not look too happy to have been summoned there.

"How was the trip from Lightfort?" Shaeleen asked.

King Haelen had on a sour face. "You knew of our desire to stay in Lightfort. Why did you, uh, what were the words that were used to get me here? Ah, yes, why did you *command* me to meet with you here?"

"You're lucky we came," TruthSeer Julianna said.

Shaeleen put out her hand to offer them a seat. "I think you might want to hear a little story of what has happened since we left you."

"If we must," Martin said.

"Please treat TruthSeer Shaeleen with respect, Wizard," Cole said, his first words since they had met with the king and his two advisors. "I don't think you want us to leave yet."

Shaeleen smiled at Cole, relieved to see a little bit of fire back in his eyes. Maybe he would be all right after all.

Shaeleen then proceeded to tell them about all that had

transpired. They were generally surprised, but happy that General Archer would be the regent in Althea. As she neared the end of her story about vanquishing the shadow keepers and the subsequent splitting of the TruthStone, the king was suddenly sitting anxiously on the edge of his seat.

"Quite a story, young lady," Julianna said, but then let out a great sigh and turned to Martin and the king. "But I can assure you it is all true."

Martin was surprised. The king looked at Shaeleen expectantly. Shaeleen smiled at him and reached into a bag she had carried in. She took out a small pouch and gave it to him. When he opened it, his eyes widened. A pink Azeztulite HealingStone fell into his hands. Tears ran down his face.

"How can I ever thank you for bringing this to us, TruthSeer?"

Martin and Julianna gasped and examined Shaeleen with new eyes. They too expressed their profound thanks.

"You have given hope to our kingdom and to me," King Haelen said.

Shaeleen smiled. "Use it wisely this time, Haelen. It will do you good, and I feel that you will live a long time. Don't keep your kingdom so closed off from others. The power of the stones are at their greatest when they are used together. I will be leading a council of leaders on Wayland to meet every so often to discuss magic and how best we can serve one another."

Martin stood and came over to Shaeleen. He went down on one knee and looked at her seriously. "Please forgive my rudeness, TruthSeer—for things I said before and now. You truly have given us a gift that can never be repaid."

Shaeleen put her hand on the man's shoulder. "No need for this, Martin. We've all said things we regret—surely me more than most."

Martin turned to Cole. "You will be honored above all other wizards, Cole, for your service to the TruthSeer and to all of Wayland."

Cole nodded. "Thank you, Wizard Martin. It was my duty to serve the TruthSeer." He turned to Shaeleen and gave a bit of a smile. "And my sister."

Another hour of visiting, then Cole and Shaeleen bid their goodbyes and went back to the ship.

"Where now?" the captain asked.

Shaeleen thought about it. She wanted to get back to Galena and find out what was happening, but they had two more stops still, and they were at opposite ends of the continent. "First to Gabor, then to Antioch."

The captain nodded, turned, and yelled to his crew, "We sail to Riverton in Gabor. Now get going. The TruthSeer needs to hurry."

* * *

The weather held as they sailed around the northern end of Wayland, stopping once in Fisher's Landing for supplies. Shaeleen had been mesmerized by the white salt cliffs there and learned that most of the salt for Wayland came from there, making the region very prosperous. Five days later, they arrived at Gabor's capital of Riverton.

Word from Verlyn had already spread north by the time Shaeleen and Cole landed there, but the reception was more hostile than the previous meetings. Crowds booed as much as cheered, and Cole had to walk Shaeleen to the castle as there had not been a carriage to meet them. It seemed many of the soldiers still held loyalty to Commander Kerr's ideals.

At the castle, they were met by TruthSeer Justyn. His stoop was lower and his eyes troubled. He motioned them to follow him but didn't say anything until they neared the queen's room. A woman joined them in front of the room. She was barely older than Shaeleen herself.

"TruthSeer Shaeleen." She bowed. "I have heard much about you. I am Wizard Tessalaine—Tess for short. I was on the northern coast taking care of some business for the queen the last time you came."

The woman had blue eyes—though not as light as Shaeleen's—set in a tanned face framed by light brown hair. Her youthful face was filled with an excited smile. Shaeleen turned a questioning look to Justyn.

"She is my third wizard," he said with a frown, then a sparkle filled his eyes. "I'm getting too old for this, though. She runs circles around me with her limitless energy."

Tess touched Justyn's arm in a friendly manner and smiled at him. Shaeleen could feel the strength of her powers.

"It's nice to meet you," Shaeleen said.

Tess turned and seemed to size up Cole for a moment. "Wizard," she said to him with a slight bow of her head, but Shaeleen noticed a look of intimidation had spread across her face.

Justyn motioned them into the queen's room.

"We've heard some of what happened in Verlyn," Justyn said. "I suppose my apprentice is not coming back."

Shaeleen shook her head. She had taken a strange pleasure in killing Erwin. He had never done anything but treat her badly. "We'll find a new one for you."

"Hope it's soon. You young ones seem to be running the world now. I need to rest."

Tess laughed, and Cole and Shaeleen joined in.

Justyn opened the door to the queen's chambers and excused her servants. They walked to her bedroom and entered quietly. A single lamp was lit in the corner, giving a sickly dark feeling to the room. Justyn walked over to the queen and touched her shoulder.

"Your Highness," he said.

She opened her eyes, looked up at him, and smiled.

"We have guests."

The queen turned and saw Shaeleen and Cole.

"Queen Victoria," Cole said as he bowed low to her.

"TruthSeer and Wizard," the queen said. "We hear lots of rumors and stories these days."

Shaeleen smiled and nodded. "Let me set things right." And she told them all of what had happened.

"What news of Calix?" Cole asked after Shaeleen finished.

The queen looked at Justyn and Tess with wide eyes, then back at Shaeleen and Cole. "You mean you don't know?"

"Know what?" Shaeleen asked. "We've been on a ship for the last two weeks."

"King Calix and Commander Kerr went to North Bay to

secure things there," Tess began. Justyn let her continue with a wave of his hand. "From all accounts, they got into an argument on what to do in Gabor and Galena. They both blamed each other and got into a fight. Commander Kerr is much stronger than King Calix, and he slew him."

Shaeleen gasped and looked at Cole. There was no sorrow there, but a small light returned to his eyes that she hadn't seen since the battle in Verlyn.

"Your commander killed the king of Galena?" Cole said, his nostrils flaring.

"Cole!" Shaeleen said. "Let it be. Now Basil can become king. This is what we wanted."

Cole turned to her. "But he was still a king. Commander Kerr should be tried and punished."

Justyn cleared his voice. "The people of North Bay thought the same, Wizard Cole. They immediately ganged up on Commander Kerr and the few men with him. Even with the commander's power of the StrengthStone, he was overcome and put to death by stones and clubs."

Shaeleen cringed at the thought. Not a good way to die for anyone. But he had brought it on himself by his own treachery. Somewhere deep inside her, she realized she had wanted the privilege of taking down Calix and Kerr herself. Both had been condescending to her personally and had caused a lot of trouble in her kingdom, but at least the deed was done.

"TruthSeer," the queen called to her, and Shaeleen moved closer.

"Diamonique is pregnant," she said.

Shaeleen nodded. "We've heard that."

"Prince Basil will not be king," Queen Victoria said.

The implications of what the queen said sunk in deep to Shaeleen's heart, and she sat down on the edge of the bed. *Poor Basil.*

She felt Cole's hand on her shoulder and turned to see what he wanted. Sympathy filled his face. "I'm sorry, Shaeleen. Prince Basil would have made a good king, but Diamonique and Calix's child will be the next ruler of Galena. That is the law."

Shaeleen felt like all the air had been sucked out of her lungs. Since her first meeting with Prince Basil, she had seen him as a great man, compassionate and loyal. He loved his people. She had denied the feelings of the TruthStone time and time again when she thought about him being the king. No matter what she had done, she couldn't make it happen. No matter how powerful she was, she couldn't fix everything.

"It's not fair," she said quietly. She reached into her bag and pulled out the next pouch and handed it to the queen.

The queen gave it to Justyn to open. When he did, he gasped and showed it to the queen and Tess. The queen reached her hand out to hold the newly formed Red Jasper StrengthStone.

"It's beautiful," the queen said. "So bright and big."

Shaeleen didn't have much more insight to give and just smiled. She was glad she could help someone, at least.

"We can rebuild our kingdom, Justyn. My daughter will be queen here soon."

"Don't say that," Justyn said.

But he, as well as Shaeleen, knew it was true. The queen

had only weeks, or maybe even days, to live.

Cole and Shaeleen gave their leave and headed back to the ship. It had been a long day, and Shaeleen just wanted to lie down and rest. The next two stops would be more emotional.

They headed south, and the rocking of the ship soon put Shaeleen to sleep.

CHAPTER FORTY

"Shae! Shae, wake up." Cole nudged Shaeleen awake. Sitting up in bed, she rubbed her eyes and pushed her hair out of her face. Cole stood fully dressed, sword on hip, looking down at her.

"I'm going off at Stronghaven while you go on to Mistport first," Cole said with a firm voice.

Shaeleen thought about it for a moment. "All right."

Cole seemed surprised that she had relented so quickly.

"I do have a heart, Cole," Shaeleen said. "I know you want to see Diamonique."

"I . . . uh . . . That's not the entire reason," Cole stuttered.

Shaeleen tilted her head at him.

"Don't look at me like that. I know you can tell I'm telling the truth," Cole said, his eyebrows furrowed. "That's a big reason, yes—maybe the biggest, I'll admit." He blushed, and Shaeleen smiled back at him. "But I want to help also. With King Calix gone, I'm sure the city and kingdom is in an uproar. I'll find Prince Basil in Freetown and help get things under control here in Stronghaven. Then when you arrive, they will be ready for you."

"You're rambling." Shaeleen laughed and stood up. She reached over and gave her big brother a hug. "You are a good brother. I know you speak the truth. Go. Go and comfort

Diamonique and find Basil. Tell him . . ." Shaeleen paused as she pulled back from the embrace.

"Tell him what, Shae?" Cole said, a small grin tugging at his lips.

Shaeleen punched him in the shoulder. "Stop it. Tell him he better be in the city when I return. I need to speak with him and Diamonique, as well as Erlinda and Faegon, if they are still there."

Cole smiled more. "Is that all?"

Shaeleen stomped her foot. *Insufferable brother!* "Tell him it isn't a request; it's a command."

Cole laughed now. "Why don't you just admit that you care for him? He needs to know. He's lost a lot."

Shaeleen glared at her brother, then her lips turned up. "What am I to do? I don't know what my role is in the world anymore."

"Neither does he."

Cole had a good point. "I'll think about it." The boat came to a stop, so she and Cole went up on deck. The harbor was still in disrepair. Burned up docks and shops littered the ground around them. A temporary dock had been put together and, from the looks of it, quite hastily.

The captain lowered a plank and motioned for Cole to leave. He turned once and waved goodbye to Shae. She looked at the city that she thought once would be Basil's to rule, and her heart lurched for him.

"Cole," she yelled to her brother. Standing on the dock, he turned back around. He put a hand up to block the morning sun.

"Tell Basil that I missed him." There, she had said it. She missed him. Her face burned with the thought of it, but she didn't care. She was a woman and deserved to care for someone, didn't she? TruthSeer or not.

Cole smiled and waved once more.

Soon, the ship was on its way again.

* * *

At some point since they had left Verlyn over two weeks ago, someone on the ship had fashioned a flag in Shaeleen's honor. It held a green Moldavite TruthStone in its center, the five stones of power in a circle around it, all kept together with what looked like silver jewelry. Now as they coasted into the port at Mistport, Antioch, the flag blew in the breeze at the top of the mast.

The docks were lined with people—the largest reception so far. Shaeleen stood on the deck and scanned the crowd, but she was really only looking for one person. When she saw him, a grin filled her face. Standing behind the crowd, in front of a fancy carriage, stood Orin. He was dressed in a fine uniform of blue with an orange sash across the front. He appeared much older than his thirteen years.

He didn't smile, but he did hold up his hand toward her. Shaeleen's smile fell somewhat. This was going to be more difficult than she thought. She grabbed her bag and headed down the plank, two sailors escorting her. As she reached the docks, six soldiers escorted her through the crowd. Children, men, and women cheered for her.

"Hail the TruthSeer."

Shaeleen smiled. These people were genuinely happy, and it lifted her spirits. She had done something good on Verlyn, and now these people could live in peace without the threat of the shadow keepers.

Shaeleen waved at the crowd and let tendrils of colors swirl off her hands and over the group. They cheered and clapped their hands in excitement, and Shaeleen laughed with glee, truly happy for the first time in a long time. Maybe being a TruthSeer wasn't all hard.

She reached the carriage, where Orin and two other guards stood. He appeared better than when they had left, but did he still have the shadow inside him? She moved to give him a hug, but he turned aside and motioned her inside the carriage instead. Her heart fell. He still hadn't forgiven her.

"Orin," was all Shaeleen could bring herself to say.

He gave her a nod, and they both sat down in the carriage. It was quiet for a moment as they started off through the city. The crowd still cheered from outside.

"You look nice," she said to him.

He glanced down at his clothes and grimaced. When he looked up at her, he spoke for the first time. "My grandfather, the king, passed away a few days ago."

"Oh, Orin." Shaeleen covered her mouth, and tears came to her eyes. "I'm so sorry. I don't know what to say." It was surely a time of change. All the kingdoms but Shema would have a new leader, and even there, King Haelen would be a new man.

"Hence the clothes," Orin said with his hands spread wide.

Shaeleen's eyes went wide with the implications. "Your father will be the king, and you will be the prince."

A small laugh escaped Orin's lips. "Next in line for the throne—can you believe that?"

Thoughts of her recent escapades with Orin flashed through her mind—catching him stealing on the ship, helping her escape in Mistport, being taken captive at the compound, being cleansed. A small giggle escaped her lips. She knew it wasn't appropriate, but she couldn't help it. Orin's lips went up also, and he laughed. Soon, they were both laughing so hard that tears streamed down their faces.

"It really is quite funny, isn't it?" Orin said, mirth returning to his visage.

Shaeleen shook her head. "No, I mean, well . . ."

"Don't lie, Shae," Orin teased. "It'll hurt you." His eyes held compassion for her.

"I just can't believe it."

"Me either." Orin looked down at his clothes. "And I'm not sure I like it either." His eyes turned a shade darker at that.

He's still tainted by the shadow!

Shaeleen grew quiet for a moment, thinking about what to do. She moved next to him. He scooted over to make room for her, but his jaw was tight. She saw his face twitch slightly at the thought of her being so close.

"Orin, I can heal you now," Shaeleen offered.

Orin's eyes went wide, and he threw his hands up in front of him. "What if I don't want to be healed?"

Shaeleen groaned inside. "I have to, Orin." She wiped tears from her eyes. "I can't bear to see you like this. I have to destroy the shadow."

"Will you force me?" Orin asked.

Shaeleen readied a spell to protect herself if he lashed out at her. "No, Orin, I won't force it out of you." She sighed. "But . . ."

"But if not, you'll have to kill me?" Orin said, his dark eyes searching hers for confirmation.

"I don't know if I can do that either, Orin. I really don't. Please don't make me choose. Just let me help you."

Shaeleen could see the battle in Orin's mind, then he spoke so softly she hardly heard him. "Will it hurt?"

Shaeleen shrugged. "I really don't know." She pulled upon the stones of power and felt the light grow within her. "It may hurt me more than you." She reached over before anything else could be said and grabbed his hands. "I will ask permission this time, Orin. Can I enter your mind?"

Orin struggled for a moment, then finally nodded, though trepidation still filled his face. Shaeleen pushed the powers of the HealingStone deep inside of Orin, then pulled at the shadow that was still there, hiding in a corner. She called it to her. She felt the brunt of the power of the shadow and whimpered a bit. Orin tried to pull his hands away, but she kept firm. "It needs balance," she said.

She felt the power of the shadow mix with the power of the light. They pushed and pulled for a moment as Shaeleen drew it all back into herself, then she pushed the shadow power out of her hand. It flew through a window and dissipated out in the air—once again a part of the balance of nature and the stones of power.

Orin sat back and closed his eyes for a moment, then they popped open. "It's gone, Shae. That horrible taint is gone."

The carriage came to a stop at the castle gates. Looking out the window, Shaeleen saw Orin's father, Marcus, standing at the steps to the castle. His face was stern and serious.

"Orin!" Shaeleen nudged him. "Before we go inside, I have a gift for you."

Orin lifted his head, and his eyes went wide. "A gift?"

Shaeleen drew out a small pouch and placed it in Orin's hands. Carefully, he opened it and poured its contents out. A walnut-sized Red Jasper SpeedStone tumbled out. His eyes went back and forth between the stone and Shaeleen, not knowing what to say. He ran his fingers over it and took a deep breath. Then he smiled.

"I know I can never repay you for the harm I caused you," Shaeleen said as she wiped tears from her eyes. "Will you forgive me?"

Orin reached over and wrapped his arms around her. "There is nothing to forgive, Shae. It was that horrible shadow keeper, the Guardian Georrod, who took my power from me. "

"He is gone now, with the rest of them," Shaeleen said. "I thought it was the least I could do to return a SpeedStone to you."

"My kingdom will be blessed with this." Orin turned to open the door, but Shaeleen put a hand out to stop him.

"Orin, you misunderstand me. This stone is not for the kingdom—this stone is for you only," Shaeleen said. "Without you, I would've never been able to restore the stones of power to Wayland. Thank you."

Orin's grin grew bigger. He grabbed her hand, and together, they sped out of the carriage, across the grounds of the castle, and up the steps, appearing unexpectedly in front of his father.

Marcus jumped back, surprised by the sudden appearance of Orin and Shaeleen. "Orin, did you . . .?"

"Yes, Father." Orin laughed. "I just used the power of the SpeedStone again."

A big grin covered Marcus's face as he realized his son had been healed.

"Good to see you, TruthSeer," Marcus said, nodding his head to Shaeleen.

"Likewise, Your Majesty." Shaeleen bowed. For once, she thought it merited her decorum. Her brother would be proud of her. Marcus led them inside and into a private room. Shaeleen was still awed each time she went into one of the ancient castles. "I'm sorry to hear about your father," Shaeleen offered her condolences.

Marcus nodded his thanks.

"And what of the compound?" Shaeleen asked.

Orin and Marcus looked at one another, then Marcus spoke.

"We have come to an agreement. Once you destroyed the shadow keepers, the power over the compound disappeared. It is now just a normal village inside a large wall. The people there are free to live there without magic if that is their desire. As long as they uphold the laws, they will be left alone."

"And your wife?" Shaeleen asked, knowing it would be a sore subject.

"She has also elected to stay there for the time being," Marcus said, his lips tight.

The door opened, and TruthSeer Lana came in. She gave a low bow to Shaeleen. "TruthSeer Shaeleen. I hear you have saved Wayland and put an end to the shadow keepers."

Shaeleen smiled and rehearsed to them all of what had happened. Their eyes grew bigger and bigger as the story unfolded. Silence filled the room as she finished telling them about the new stones of power that had been created. She pulled out another pouch and gave it to Marcus.

"This is a new SpeedStone for the kingdom of Antioch," Shaeleen said.

Marcus held it in his hand—a little larger than an egg and dark red. "It's beautiful!" He bowed low to Shaeleen. "You will always be welcomed and honored in Antioch, TruthSeer. We will have a suite of rooms set aside for your use always."

"Thank you," Shaeleen said. "Also, an embassy from Verlyn will arrive shortly." She turned to Lana. "And in time, a new apprentice when you are ready. A new era is beginning in Wayland—an opportunity for all of us to work together. I will be forming a council of leaders, Verlynians, and TruthSeers that will meet periodically. When we are working together, we will be at our strongest."

The king had refreshments brought in, and they continued to discuss the powers of the stone, trade, the compound, and the upcoming council for the next few hours. Then Shaeleen excused herself to go back to the ship. She needed to return to Stronghaven. Orin offered to escort her.

They sat in a comfortable silence as they left the castle, but soon Shaeleen noticed they were going in another direction. She looked at Orin for confirmation.

"We have one quick stop," he said with a smile.

"But . . ." She had to get back.

Orin hushed her, and a few minutes later, they came to a stop. The door of the carriage opened, and Orin helped Shaeleen out. She glanced up and laughed, her eyes growing wide.

"Oh, Orin!"

Orin put his hand out, and Shaeleen walked ahead of him, her nose already twitching, smelling all the wonderful scents from the bakery in front of them. They opened the door and rang a bell. A man came forward.

"Hello, Tam," Orin said. "Brought back a repeat customer for you."

Tam laughed and gave Shaeleen a big hug. "Nice to see you again, missy." He waved his hand around his shop. "What's your choice of sweets today?"

"I want one of those sweet rolls you made me before with chocolate on it," Shaeleen blurted out before Tam had finished asking the question.

"Coming right up!"

Shaeleen immensely enjoyed the next few minutes. She let herself relax and tried not to think of anything but the delicious pastry. Then Orin escorted her to the docks. After a tearful farewell, she went back to the ship. The captain walked up to her with a twinkle in his eye.

"Where to now?"

"Home, Captain. Home," Shaeleen said. Then she

frowned. "By the way, sir, what exactly is your name?"

The captain laughed. "Most people just call me Captain." Abby came up next to him just then, and he gave her a hug.

A twinkle filled Abby's eyes. "My mother calls him Sugar." She giggled.

"Abby!" The captain swatted her bottom lovingly.

Shaeleen laughed. "I do like sugar."

The captain actually blushed. "My mother called me Remington."

Shaeleen raised her eyebrows. "Not bad, but I think Captain will do."

"Aye," the captain said and turned to order his men out of the port and on to Stronghaven.

CHAPTER FORTY-ONE

Two days later, in the early afternoon, Shaeleen stood on the deck of the captain's ship as they pulled alongside the temporary docks in Stronghaven. It had been almost five days since she'd left Cole there. There had been a thick fog earlier that day, and a slight mist filled the air. A mix of nobles, soldiers, and common people lined the shore as far as Shaeleen could see.

"Quite a reception for you," the captain said from behind her. Abby stood next to him and smiled at Shaeleen.

Shaeleen shook her head. "I had no idea."

"You're famous, Shaeleen," the captain said. "I reckon more famous than just about anyone in Wayland now."

"And Verlyn," added Abby.

The people cheered as men prepared for her to leave the ship. The sound was almost deafening. There were thousands of people there. She scanned the crowds for someone she knew, but it was hard with all the parasols and umbrellas. The crowd parted, and a parade of people walked down its middle. Shaeleen wiped the mist from her forehead and squinted to see who it was.

"Give them a show, dear," the captain said, looking at her fondly. "Give them hope."

Yes! Shaeleen thought. The people in her own city of

Stronghaven had been some of the hardest hit. Between Calix and the influence of the shadow keepers, the people had suffered much, so she gave them a show.

Gathering her hands in the air, she called the power forth—the power of not just any TruthSeer, but *the* TruthSeer. She brought forth waves of red from the StrengthStone, shot flashes of white high up in the air from the HearingStone, sent out ribbons of orange from the SpeedStone, then pink flowers of light floated around them from the HealingStone. Above their heads circled streams of blue—the sign of their own IntelligenceStone—and the crowd went wild, clapping, yelling, laughing, and dancing. With a loud clap of her hands, thunder sounded, and green light shot up as a pillar from the TruthStone. It parted the clouds of mist and pushed them away. Bright sunlight filled the sky and warmed the crowd.

She turned and hugged Abby and the captain. "Thank you," she whispered. "If you ever need anything, let me know. I owe you much." She kissed him on the cheek. "Take care, Remington." She pulled away, and the captain blushed and wiped a tear from his eye.

"Take care, yourself, TruthSeer."

Shaeleen turned back to the crowd and gathered all the colors together to form a walkway of light from the ship to the delegation on the ground. With a flourish, Shaeleen rose up in the air and walked along the rainbow of light until she touched down on the docks. Yells of amazement flew through the crowd, and people began chanting, "TruthSeer. TruthSeer. TruthSeer."

The light spread out in front of her in a pathway that she

now walked on. She heard a gasp and turned her head. *Lady Judith!* Ooh, how she hated that woman. She remembered the woman's rudeness and temperament the first time they had met.

Lady Judith's eyes opened wide as Shaeleen stopped in front of her. To Judith's credit, she didn't move. The nearby crowd quieted down to see what was happening. Shaeleen stood and peered up at Judith for hopefully the last time in her life. Pushing her palms toward the ground, she rose in the air until she stood a few inches taller than the lady and glared down at the cruel woman.

"Lady Judith, you are a traitor to Galena," Shaeleen said. "You will go immediately to the ship I just came from. You will tell the captain where you want to go. I really don't care. But you are now banned from the kingdom of Galena for the rest of your life."

Lady Judith stepped back. Her face went red from the public embarrassment. She stuttered for a moment, then looked around at her supposed friends, who quietly and quickly backed away from her. They obviously didn't want her punishment for themselves.

"You have no authority," Lady Judith said, trying to find her words.

Shaeleen turned to her left and saw the delegation stop. Queen Diamonique stood in front, dressed in all her regal splendor, not a hair out of place. Cole stood inches behind her, next to Basil. Lord Gregory and ex-regent Warin took up the rear.

Shaeleen, still standing in the air, turned back to Lady

Judith. "I have all authority, Judith. I am the authority of Wayland and Verlyn. I bow to no one. By the authority of the TruthSeer of all, I banish you from Galena and with compassion, I offer you safe passage to wherever you would go—as long as I never see you again."

The crowd was quiet after Shaeleen's words, then it erupted in applause. Lady Judith glanced around for her friends, but they were gone. She looked at her husband, Lord Gregory, but he kept his gaze ahead on Shaeleen. With a huff, Judith turned and headed toward the ship. Shaeleen looked up and nodded at the captain, who gave her a sour look. She hated to saddle him with such a passenger, but it was the only thing she could think of.

Once Judith was on her way, Shaeleen lowered herself back to the ground and turned to the delegation in front of her. Diamonique came up and gave her a hug. "Good to see you again, TruthSeer."

Cole hugged her next. "Quite the display." He smiled as he said it. "But it was good for the people. You've given them hope again."

Next, she found Basil's eyes. She didn't know what to say. He stood in green leather pants and a matching cloak. His mouth lifted into a grin, and his dimple showed. His dark blue eyes searched hers, and she felt a connection. He reached out to shake her hand, but she grabbed him and gave him a big hug. She couldn't stop the tears from coming and stood there, letting the cheers of the crowd fade from her mind.

"I've missed you, TruthSeer." Basil said, his voice smooth and full of feeling. She could feel his breath on her neck.

"Maybe not what I would have done to Lady Judith, but a fitting punishment nonetheless."

She pulled away with a laugh. "A little dramatic?"

Basil put his thumb and forefinger a small space apart. "Just a bit, maybe."

She took a moment to compose herself, then extended greetings to Lord Gregory and Warin. Lord Gregory slapped her on the back. "Not bad." He grinned. "No longer the girl I met at my house not many months ago, are you?"

She shook her head. "A lot has happened since then."

"Shaeleen!" She heard a voice and turned. It was her mother running toward her. Her father and sister, Alva, close on her heels. They all crowded around together, Cole joining them. A lot of hugging and kissing ensued.

The crowd began to thin as they sensed the show was over. Shaeleen looked at Diamonique, who nodded to her.

"Let's go to the castle," Shaeleen said. "There is much to discuss."

* * *

A half an hour later, a small group sat around tables in a room in the castle. A light meal had been prepared, and they ate for a moment as they gathered together. Shaeleen's family had been invited to join Queen Diamonique, Prince Basil, Lord Gregory, and Warin. Shaeleen noticed the absence of TruthSeer Erlinda and Wizard Faegon.

"Faegon was killed in the battle between Calix and Commander Kerr." said Cole. "We haven't been able to find

TruthSeer Erlinda or Basil and Calix's mother, Raisa."

Shaeleen caught Basil's eye from across the room, and she felt her face redden as she turned back to the conversation with Cole. "How is Diamonique?" Shaeleen asked.

"The Queen is a remarkable woman," Cole said, glancing her direction. She returned his gaze with a loving look.

"Cole?" Shaeleen said. "What's going on?"

Cole smiled. "Ahhh, so the famous TruthSeer doesn't know all?"

She glared at him, then laughed. "All right. Have your fun, but we have important things to discuss here." With that, Shaeleen walked to the front of the room and called for everyone's attention. Diamonique appeared a bit put out by not being the one in charge there.

Shaeleen rehearsed to them, like she had in the other kingdoms, all that had happened on Verlyn, much of which they knew from Cole. She also informed them of her travels to all the other kingdoms and what she knew from them.

"Wayland is at a turning point now," she said. All listened to her. Her mind went back briefly to when Melindra had first given her the stone and had told her that kings and queens would clamor for her attention and lords and ladies would want to be her friends. She looked around the room and eyed each person one by one. "Two hundred years ago, King Wayland received a precious gift from the keepers on Verlyn. We squandered that through the years by giving pieces away. The kingdoms grew apart by not working together. We will work together better in the future, and I will lead a council to do so."

Everyone in the room took in what Shaeleen was saying

and nodded their heads. Shaeleen paused a moment and drew out one last pouch and walked toward where Queen Diamonique, Basil, and Cole stood. "I'm not sure who gets this now." Shaeleen glanced back and forth between Diamonique and Basil, but Diamonique took it first. She opened it and held it out for all to see.

"It's the most beautiful thing I have ever seen," Basil said, his soft voice holding awe.

"It's been polished for years by the waters of Verlyn," Shaeleen said. "The Labradorite IntelligenceStone now belongs once again to Galena, but I do not know who rules Galena."

Diamonique rolled it around in her hands for a moment, and Shaeleen noticed a brightening to her already lively brown eyes and a flushing of her dusty brown skin. She moved the other hand to her belly. Then she moved that hand and took Cole's in it instead.

Shaeleen opened her mouth to say something, but Diamonique jumped in first. "As you know, my mother doesn't have long to live. When she passes away, I will become the queen of Gabor—a task that will be difficult in the months and years to come as we rebuild a kingdom torn apart by the treachery of its general and TruthSeer apprentice. I cannot rule both kingdoms. That would not be fair to either people."

Cole turned and looked at her with pride in his eyes. Shaeleen held her breath—a brief glimpse of foresight came to her again.

"My child, by law, will be the next ruler of Galena," Diamonique continued. "But that will be a long time from now." She paused for a moment and took the IntelligenceStone in her hand. She reached that hand out toward Basil. "Prince Basil, I give you this stone and ask that you rule as Regent in Galena until my child comes of age at seventeen."

An audible gasp filled the room, tears came to Shaeleen's eyes, and Prince Basil staggered a moment on his feet. He took the stone reverently in his hand, then kneeled down in front of Queen Diamonique.

"My Queen, you are as gracious and kind as you are beautiful and strong." Basil's voice was thick with emotion. "I accept the Regency of Galena and will do all I can to be the kind of leader you would wish me to be."

"Rise, Prince Basil," Diamonique said. "You have no need to bow to me. For but a few minutes of age, you would have been the rightful heir of Galena. I will not speak unkindly of Calix, for with all his faults he did treat me well and his child I will bear, but I do expect you will be a great ruler for all of Galena." She smiled brightly at him.

Shaeleen beamed and caught Basil's eyes. She bowed her head to him and mouthed her congratulations. Diamonique grew quiet and looked at Cole, who glanced back at Shaeleen nervously.

"Cole?" Shaeleen asked, feeling a prompting. "Is there something you would like to add here?"

Cole's face grew red, and he took a step away from Diamonique, turned around to face her, and knelt down on one knee. "Queen Diamonique, from the first time I laid eyes on you, I have not been able to get you out of my mind. Your graciousness and beauty captivated me, but your sense of duty and honor have astounded me beyond anything imaginable.

You have served the people of Gabor and Galena without any thought for yourself. I am only a humble man and hardly worthy of being by your side, but I would ask for your hand in marriage."

Shaeleen heard her mother gasp and smiled over at her in the back of the room. She held her father's hand tightly.

Diamonique looked down fondly at Cole and wiped a tear from her eyes. "Oh, Cole, you don't give yourself enough credit, but you are humble and I love that in you. You have become one of the greatest wizards in the land, brother and protector to our great TruthSeer, and yet your first thought among all the kingdoms was always of me and my well-being and that of your fellow men. With all my heart I gladly accept your proposal of marriage and welcome you to rule with me by my side as equals in the kingdom of Gabor." She reached her hand out and Cole kissed it, then arose.

"I love you, Cole." Diamonique said with a husky voice and pulled him tightly giving him a long hug.

Soon, everyone was around them, congratulating the new couple. Shaeleen's mother was already talking to Diamonique about wedding plans.

Shaeleen stepped back and found herself next to Basil.

"Shaeleen," he said. "You have honored us all by what you have done for us. We can never repay you."

"I always knew you would be ruler of Galena," Shaeleen said.

"But not king," Basil said with a raise of his eyebrows. "Thoughts of me always made you sick."

Shaeleen laughed and dried her eyes. "It wasn't thoughts

of you that made me sick, Basil. I just had to learn what the truth was, that's all."

"And what do thoughts of me make you feel now?" Shaeleen was surprised at his forwardness but smiled anyway. "Hmm . . . let me think." She put her finger to her head.

"Not what you think, Shae," he said with fire in his eyes. "What you *feel*. What is the truth of things between us?"

Shaeleen blushed and stammered. "Basil, I . . .." For a rare moment, Shaeleen was at a loss for words. What did she feel between them? She was still a few months away from sixteen; he was seventeen. They really hadn't spent much time together, but he was such a kind and compassionate man . . . and not bad to look at either.

"Yes, Shaeleen?" Basil prompted with a grin on his face, his dimple catching Shaeleen's eyes.

"Basil, you have a kingdom to run," Shaeleen said. "And I don't know where Erlinda is or if she will ever return, so there might be an opening for a TruthSeer. This person would have to work very closely with you, and you would have to confide in them and trust them. You would end up spending lots of time together. Know of anyone that would fit?"

Basil laughed, a deep joyous, enthusiastic laugh. "Yes, I do." With a flourishing bow, he continued, "TruthSeer Shaeleen, would you like to be *my* TruthSeer?"

"Just yours, Basil?" Shaeleen teased. "My, that's mighty presumptuous of you. But I think I could work it into my schedule." She looked around the room, then back at him. "I really would like to stay around here for a while."

Basil wrapped his arms around her and gave her a hug.

"Welcome home, Shaeleen," he whispered. "I really missed you."

Just then, someone opened a door. Shaeleen jumped out of the hug with Basil and quickly turned around. Basil straightened and visually examined the room, his hand going to the hilt of his sword.

Cole caught her eye, and everyone went quiet. "Is something wrong, Shaeleen?

"Oh no," she purred. "I just smelled the most wonderful thing. I think the servants brought in something sweet to eat."

The entire room laughed, and Basil ushered Shaeleen forward. The small group parted and let Shaeleen choose the first sweet roll. It was covered in cinnamon and melted sugar and was the most delicious thing she had ever smelled.

Cole turned to Shaeleen. "It's the least we can do for you, TruthSeer Shaeleen. May you lead us all wisely and always in the way of truth."

Everyone cheered while Shaeleen took the first bite, then the others joined in with treats of their own. Thoughts of war, death, fear, and the shadow were forgotten.

And for a time, light and truth ruled the continent of Wayland.

This concludes the TruthSeer Archives.

Other Series By Mike Shelton
The Alaris Chronicles

For 100 years it protected them…

…and now the magical barrier is about to fail.

What waits on the other side?

Bakari is nerdy and awkward. At 15, he's lived at the Wizard Citadel for most of his life. Everything seems to be working out like he'd hoped. He just got promoted to Level 1 and despite being painfully shy, he has a friend.

Kharlia knows medicine. And he really likes her.

When Bakari finds an ancient map that marks a source of power, he must check it out. With Kharlia by his side, they wander through the Kingdom toward the spot on the map. The trip isn't what they expect.

Magical creatures have made it through the barrier. Should they fight or flee?

Bakari knows they are in trouble. He isn't a battle wizard. As they struggle against the beasts, the worst thing Bakari can imagine happens.

Will they survive?

You'll love this first book in *The Alaris Chronicles,* because of the beautifully woven story with diverse characters, great adventure, and political intrigue.

Sign up on Mike's website at **www.MichaelSheltonBooks.com** and get a copy of the prequel novella e-book to The Alaris Chronicles, Prophecy of the Dragon.

Protect the youngest heir of the Dragon King. That is the mission given to Imari in this prequel novella to The Alaris Chronicles.

The Cremelino Prophecy

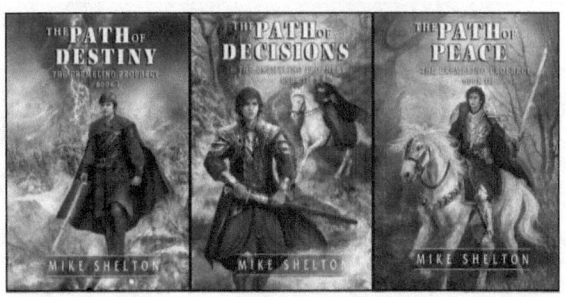

A Prophecy.

A Powerful Sword.

A Reluctant Wizard.

Wizards and magic have long been looked down upon in the Realm. So what happens when you find out you're a wizard?

Darius San Williams, son of one of King Edward's councilors, cares little for his father's politics and vows to leave the city of Anikari to protect and bring glory to the Realm.

But when a new-found and ancient magic emerges within him, he and his friends Christine and Kelln are faced with decisions that could shatter or fulfill the prophecy and the lives of all those they know.

Trying to escape fate, Darius learns that no matter where he goes, prophecy and destiny are waiting to find him.

If you love magic, sword & Sorcery, wizards, and epic fantasy don't miss this first book in The Cremelino Prophecy-- and discover what remarkable destiny awaits Darius.

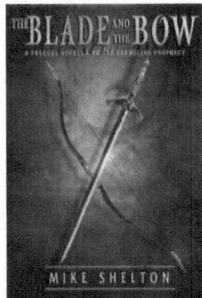

Sign up on Mike's website at www.MichaelSheltonBooks.com and get a copy of the prequel novella e-book to The Cremelino Prophecy, The Blade and The Bow.
Follow Darius and Kelln in one of their more fantastic adventures prior to The Path Of Destiny.

The Wizard Academies

He lost his family...

...He's got voices in his head.

And he's more powerful than they ever imagined.

Fifteen-year-old apprentice Kyril is sick of being bullied. And after a tragic fire leaves him orphaned with out-of-control thoughts and powers, he can't wait to escape constant taunting at the wizard academy. So when a dicey faction entices him with companionship, he ignores the grim warning signs.

Even as Kyril's power grows within the group, he's left out of the crew's dangerous plans to derail the authorities. And when being accepted comes at the expense of making questionable choices, he fears his newfound friendships aren't worth the deadly price.

Can Kyril master his new magic before his shady companions send him to his doom?

Mark of the Medallion is the spellbinding first novel in The Wizard Academies YA fantasy series. If you like sword and sorcery, enchanted adventures, and suspenseful coming-of-age stories, then you'll love Mike Shelton's action-packed tale.

About the Author

Mike was born in California and has lived in multiple states from the west coast to the east coast. He cannot remember a time when he wasn't reading a book. At school, home, on vacation, at work at lunch time, and yes even a few pages in the car (at times when he just couldn't put that great book down). Though he has read all sorts of genres he has always been drawn to fantasy. It is his way of escaping to a simpler time filled with magic, wonders and heroics of young men and women.

Other than reading, Mike has always enjoyed the outdoors. From the beaches in Southern California to the warm waters of North Carolina. From the waterfalls in the Northwest to the Rocky Mountains in Utah. Mike has appreciated the beauty that God provides for us. He also enjoys hiking, discovering nature, playing a little basketball or volleyball, and most recently disc golf. He has a lovely wife who has always supported him, and three beautiful children who have been the center of his life.

Mike began writing stories in elementary school and moved on to larger novels in his early adult years. He has worked in corporate finance for most of his career. That, along with spending time with his wonderful family and obligations at church has made it difficult to find the time to truly dedicate to writing. In the last few years as his children have become older he has returned to doing what he truly enjoys – writing!

mikesheltonbooks@gmail.com
www.MichaelSheltonBooks.com
https://www.facebook.com/groups/MikeSheltonAuthor/
https://www.facebook.com/mikesheltonbooks/
http://www.Twitter.com/msheltonbooks
http://www.Instagram.com/mikesheltonbooks
https://www.pinterest.com/mikesheltonbooks/